TURF WARS

Also by Olivier Norek in English translation

The Lost and the Damned

OLIVIER NOREK

TURF WARS

Translated from the French by
Nick Caistor

MACLEHOSE PRESS
QUERCUS · LONDON

First published in the French language as *Territoires*
by Editions Michel Lafon, Paris, 2014
First published in Great Britain by

MacLehose Press
An imprint of Quercus Editions Ltd
Carmelite House
50 Victoria Embankment
London EC4Y 0DZ

An Hachette UK company

A CIP catalogue record for this book is available
from the British Library.

ISBN (HB) 978 0 85705 966 6
ISBN (TPB) 978 0 85705 965 9
ISBN (Ebook) 978 0 85705 967 3

10 9 8 7 6 5 4 3 2

Designed and typeset in Garamond by Libanus Press Ltd
Printed and bound in Great Britain by Clays Ltd, St Ives plc

To Lulu, wherever you've gone

CONTENTS

PROLOGUE IN TWO SUMMARY EXECUTIONS

11 a.m., Monday, June 24, 2013
Malceny, Seine-Saint-Denis (93)

A face appears in the centre of the viewfinder.

"Target in position."

The man holds his breath. He squeezes his trigger finger more tightly.

"Are you sure?"

"Target confirmed."

Behind the half-open window in the empty flat, the fine net curtain is raised for a moment and the sun glints on the lens. Ten metres below, the target is sitting on the pavement in an old armchair, as if it were his living room.

"Go on, shoot."

Click. The first photograph.

This is the last day of Groupe Stups's surveillance operation. A requisitioned flat, three policemen, three camp beds and a week taking turns behind their telephoto lens to capture each transaction for posterity.

The arrest is set for six the next morning, at the home of someone they call "Target", the gang ringleader. But before taking him in, they have to gather evidence. Photograph after photograph, client after client.

Four floors down, one of the dealer's accomplices is waiting patiently in the shadow of a decrepit tower block, a few metres from the armchair. Hidden in a doorway, awaiting his orders.

Behind his lens, a police officer announces:

"Supplier in position."

Lookouts at both ends of the street, necks craned as they watch for any glimpse of patrol cars. The officer continues:

"Meerkat 1 and Meerkat 2 in position! The gang's all here. Their day's beginning."

Local residents step round these delinquents as though all this were normal. They know them and they're used to it.

They don't really have a choice.

11.05. First client. Stick of hash twenty euros, gram of coke eighty. No heroin – that only attracts wrecked addicts and problems. The first handshake between Target and his client is to pass the money discreetly. Another photograph. Without even getting up from his chair, the dealer makes a quick check of his meerkats. No predators in sight. Target indicates the required amount to the runner.

The runner disappears into the abandoned building and quickly reappears. Another handshake to say goodbye, and the hash is passed into the client's hand. Another photograph.

The police know this well-oiled routine will be repeated as many as fifty times throughout the day. The first of fifty clients: you need patience to build up a solid dossier.

"Second client approaching."

Black helmet on black moped. The bike slows, drawing level with the dealer seated like a king on his throne. Then, with a flick of the wrist, the rider revs up again, without stopping. Time only for a souvenir snapshot.

"Client aborted."

Behind his computer linked to the camera, Capitaine Sylvan asks his colleague:

"Do we know him?"

"Impossible to identify. Crash helmet and gloves."

The capitaine frowns.

"Ping me the shot."

The high-definition image appears on his screen. Sylvan analyses it. Rider wearing a helmet. Respect for the Highway Code is unusual around here. And at the height of summer, forty-two degrees, gloves and visor lowered, a black moped with no number plate . . . it doesn't add up.

In a corner of the room, stretched out on one of the camp beds, the third man gets up and rubs his eyes. He comes over to the screen.

"What's bugging you, capitaine? No number plate?"

"That among other things. The helmet and gloves as well. In this heat, that's a bit . . ."

Behind the lens, the photographer interrupts them.

"The moped's back. And he has a passenger!"

Sylvan leaps out of his chair.

"That's not a good sign! Switch to video!"

By now, all three men are on their feet. One is glued to the camera, the two others to the computer screen. Sylvan rages:

"Oh fuck, no, you can't do this to us . . ."

The moped slows again. The passenger plunges his hand inside his jacket. As they pass, he sprays the area with bullets from the gun in his hand.

The first slug splinters the window of a nearby café. The second shatters it. The explosion of glass sends all the customers to the floor. Panic, and the first confused shouts. The third buries itself in the wall a few centimetres from the face of the runner, paralysed with fear. Almost by chance, the fourth hits the ankle of Target, who was trying to escape but now plummets to the ground, screaming. Meerkats 1 and 2 sprint away and vanish round the corner. Target crawls to his armchair, trying to get to his feet. The scooter passenger has already dismounted. In two strides he is next to Target and levels his gun at his forehead. Detonation. A red mist spurts from behind the dealer's head, then evaporates. Unplugged, he slumps to the ground. The shooter lowers the weapon to his side. Looks defiantly around him, as if to say: "Anybody else?" Then climbs back onto the moped and taps the driver on the helmet. The bike speeds away.

Inside the apartment, the three cops are rooted to the spot. The photographer turns to the others.

"Now what do we do? Get down there?"

Frustrated, Capitaine Sylvan snaps his laptop shut as though slamming a door.

"From the fourth floor? By the time we arrive . . . All we'd do is blow our cover. Holy shit! Fuck . . . three weeks' work and now we have to start from scratch. Shit!"

On the pavement, curious onlookers form a circle around the body. Just to see. Feasting their eyes on this image of death they have just escaped from. Fascinated by the scarlet pool of warm blood spooling out from the shattered head.

A gang leader has been knocked off his throne. A 24-year-old thug whose realm consisted of no more than a few wretched streets.

* * *

7.30 a.m., Wednesday, June 26, 2013
Malceny, Seine-Saint-Denis (93)

In the underground car park of his apartment block, Sasha Dimov is struggling with his son's seat belt, his body twisted round into the back of the car.

"I can do it on my own, you know. I'm six now. I'm a big boy . . ."

So soon . . . like all fathers who only see their child one weekend every fortnight, Sasha tells himself his son has grown up too fast. Or that he himself hasn't paid enough attention.

"You know that from tonight you're sleeping at Mémé's?'

"Yeah . . . that's a rubbish way to start my holidays. How long for?"

"For as long as it takes Papa to sort out a few things and then we're off to the sun."

"Will there be a swimming pool?"

"Yes."

"And a jet ski?"

"That too."

"Will Maman be coming?"

"You ask too many questions. You'll scramble your brain."

The car sets off up the spiral ramp. A few seconds later, the headlights of a grey saloon car with tinted windows go on. It starts to follow them. The second basement, then the first. Once round the final curve, Sasha narrows his eyes to adjust to the daylight. Two metres ahead of him, a black 4×4 hurtles out from the side then brakes violently, darkening the exit and blocking the way. Sasha stamps on the brake. His son's body is thrown forward: the seat belt almost chokes him.

"What's wrong, Papa?"

Gripping the wheel with one hand, Sasha reaches for the gearstick with the other. Before slamming the car into reverse, he glances in his rear-view mirror. A grey saloon is up against his rear bumper. There's no escape.

The scene freezes. The engines of the three vehicles turn over. Time at a standstill in the eye of the hurricane. Sasha turns calmly towards his son, but his voice is quavering.

"Listen carefully . . . You're to do what I say without asking any questions, right? Do you know why?"

The kid has never heard his father speak in this tone of voice before. Fear flits from one heart to the other.

"Because you're a secret agent?"

"That's right, because I'm a secret agent. Now, undo your seat belt."

The kid does as he's told.

"O.K., that's good. Now lie flat on the floor, and whatever happens, don't lift up your head. Got it?"

"Got it."

"I love you, my boy."

Their eyes meet one last time. Sasha turns round in his seat. Two men in black balaclavas, the barrels of their guns pointing straight at him. As Sasha closes his eyes, a hail of metal smashes the windscreen, rips through his body, perforates the seats, and spatters the interior of the car with blood.

Like a giant echo chamber, the underground car park amplifies the sound waves from the gunshots. As they climb back into the 4×4, one of the gunmen feels the right side of his face through the balaclava.

"Fuck it, I've cut my ear."

PART ONE
REVOLUTION

I

10 a.m., Friday, June 28, 2013
Cité des Poètes, Malceny, Seine-Saint-Denis (93)

The two kids were dragging the heavy motorbike along the asphalt. The back wheel was immobilised by a chain their wire cutters hadn't even scratched. Their efforts in the heat had left them bathed in sweat. Panting, they finally reached the row of garages at the foot of the Verlaine tower. The two thieves stopped at the first one, exhausted.

"Fuck it, that's enough. I can't go any further, we can stick it in this one."

"There's a padlock."

"There are no padlocks here, this is our turf."

"Well, there's one on this one."

"So what? You've got cutters, haven't you? Get to it!"

The padlock gave way. While the first youngster held the bike upright, the other grabbed hold of the bottom of the iron shutter, which screeched as he pulled it up.

Unfortunately for them, the garage was already occupied.

As their eyes grew accustomed to the darkness and they realised what they were seeing in front of them, they ran for their lives, without giving their booty a second thought.

From the window of his lodge, the caretaker of the tower block had seen everything. As usual, he'd let them get on with it. And yet it was the first time they had behaved like that. Running off without finishing the job. Calm had returned to the concrete walkway, but he was still puzzled, staring at the motorbike on its side and the open garage. After a few moments, he decided to go and have a look. Just a quick look.

Peering under the raised shutter, he swore, took a step backwards, got his feet caught up in the bike, and fell.

He knew he ought to have gone in. To check whether the man was still alive, to put his fingers somewhere on his neck to search for a pulse, the way he'd seen it done on T.V. But he stayed where he was, unable to move, too scared to go inside the garage and have the shutter clang down behind him.

* * *

Extract from call to police emergency number on June 28, 2013. Communication begins 10.10.

"Police emergency service."

"Good morning. I'm the caretaker at the Verlaine tower block, on the Cité des Poètes estate . . . There's a guy in one of the garages. I think he's dead."

"Are you sure, sir?"

"No, I'm not . . . he's tied to a chair and there's tape round his mouth with blood on it . . . at least I think it's blood, but there's no way I'm going in there."

"Sir? Have you tried talking to him? He may be alive."

"Yeah, get a move on then."

Call terminated by caller at 10.11.

2

Control Room at Seine-Saint-Denis police headquarters

A buzzing hive where all the calls to the police emergency number are received, the room is lit by giant screens retransmitting live all the images from the region's C.C.T.V. cameras. The information about a possible dead body was passed from caretaker to call handler, and from him to Commandant Auclair, the Control Room chief. In his sixties, with a paunch typical of those who have done their stint on the beat, Auclair waddled across the huge room. He asked the operator who had taken the call to replay the brief conversation for him.

"Have you sent a patrol car?"

"Affirmative. It should arrive in a few minutes. I've also sent firemen, just in case . . ."

"Very good. I'll inform the Police Judiciaire. Who's on duty there?"

The handler opened the duty roster and flicked through a few pages.

"Capitaine Coste's group."

3

Emboldened by the presence of so many uniforms, the caretaker summoned up his courage. He even allowed himself to indulge his curiosity. Craning his neck above the police cordon like a periscope, he was now trying to see what only a few moments earlier he had fled from. His attention was distracted by the arrival of a car with a flashing blue light that slammed to a halt half on the road, half on the pavement. The two plainclothes officers who got out pushed their way under the yellow police tape in front of the garage. They took a quick look inside, then talked to a uniform, who jerked his chin in the caretaker's direction.

He saw them coming towards him. The first one, a man wearing jeans and a white T-shirt with a police lanyard round his neck, seemed quite amenable, despite his thuggish appearance. The other, a woman with a crew-cut and an exaggeratedly masculine build, had nothing appealing about her at all. As he had hoped, it was the man who spoke to him.

"Morning. Police Judiciaire, crime investigation unit. Are you the one who called the police?"

"Yes, that's me."

"Was it the person renting the garage who told you?"

"Renting the garage? Oh, nobody's done that for ages. I mean yes, but no-one leaves their car or anything valuable in them. They're all full of stolen goods."

"O.K., let's hear your story."

The male officer turned to his colleague.

"Johanna, call the forensics team. Tell them to bring a floor lamp. A powerful one. You can't see a thing in there."

The caretaker risked a comment:

"It's not worth it. You only need to switch the light on: the electricity is connected."

"Are you taking the piss? You tell me it's a thieves' warehouse, and you leave the electricity on? You could cut it, couldn't you? That would be a start."

"Tried that. Next day they set fire to my car."

"Did you report it?"

"No, I switched the electricity back on."

"Yeah, that makes sense. So what exactly do you do in your job?"

Piqued, the caretaker said drily:

"I look after a tower block on an estate where your colleagues won't even set foot anymore. I clean the staircase and the lobby when there's no-one squatting there, and the rest of the time, I close my eyes to everything. I try not to antagonise anyone so as not to get my face smashed in, and I tell the residents that I'm doing what I can."

"In other words, you don't do a whole lot."

"I do what I can. All on my own, and without that gun of yours."

The caretaker realised he had made a mistake and that, despite looking like a tank, the woman officer would probably have been more pleasant to deal with. Sure enough, she was the one who helped get her colleague off his back.

"What's wrong with you? Give him a break," she said, tugging at the man's arm.

The officer ran a hand over the damp nape of his neck.

"Sorry, it's this heat. It gets on my nerves."

Around them, at the foot of the neighbouring tower blocks, small groups were congregating, their hoods up despite the sun. Insults shouted at the forces of law and order, but nothing to worry about. It wasn't long before they were joined by more local kids, together with their older brothers, keen to stir things up a bit. Just as honey attracts wasps, so the police would doubtless be one of the highlights of their day. No way they were going to miss out on a bit of friction.

4

On instructions from the Police Judiciaire, the entrance to the garage was cordoned off. Only the doctor who had confirmed the death and the forensic team had been allowed inside. Now it was up to the two members of the crime squad to process their new investigation. The woman was taking notes while the man dictated.

"Male aged around thirty. Hands tied behind back. Feet fastened to a chair. Several layers of insulating tape wound round his mouth, partially covering nostrils. Traces of what could be dried, blackened blood visible on the tape, with a trickle running down from chin to neck."

The male officer bent down.

"Considerable amount of blood on the floor around his feet, most likely due to the two perforations to each knee. Possible use of an electric drill or an auger. No other sign of external injuries . . . No idea what he did, but the punishment was extreme."

By the time he straightened up, his female colleague had finished writing. She leaned over the victim's face until she was close enough to brush against it.

"Hey, Johanna! What on earth are you doing? Giving him a cuddle?"

"Don't be stupid. I'm sniffing him."

"Obviously. Why didn't I think of that?"

He let her carry on, waiting for her conclusion.

"It's chocolate."

"What?"

"It's not blood on the tape, it's chocolate."

"Are you off your head?"

"I've got two kids at home who stuff themselves like baby dinosaurs, and prefer fingers to forks, so I'll be the judge on this, if you don't mind."

A uniform came over, holding out a mobile.

"Capitaine Coste? I've got the investigating magistrate on the line for you."

The plain-clothes detective took the phone from him. At the other end of the line, the voice already sounded annoyed.

"Capitaine Coste?"

"No, he's not here this morning. This is Lieutenant Scaglia, his deputy."

"Fleur Saint-Croix, duty magistrate. I've been trying to get in touch all morning."

"Sorry. We were gathering information. So we have something to tell you."

"Understood, but in that case, get on with it."

The lieutenant walked back into the daylight outside the garage. He raised his hand to protect his eyes from the sun and began his report. The lock-ups that had become Ali Baba's caves. The tied and gagged victim. The holes in his knees. The insulating tape. The chocolate.

He had never dealt with this magistrate before. So, from the start, he was inclined to see her as a ball-breaker. He also decided she was new to Seine-Saint-Denis, and that if she had been sent there, it had to be her first posting. A recent graduate from the National Magistrates College, where no doubt she had learned by heart the maxim: *The public prosecutor and his associates direct the activities of the officers and men of the Police Judiciaire.* A maxim she had adopted too zealously.

"I'll authorise an autopsy. In the meantime, you're to carry out house-to-house enquiries in the whole neighbourhood. Seal the lock-up and bag up the ropes, the tape, the chair, the motorbike and the deceased's clothing. Interview the caller. And I want a fuller report by mid-afternoon. By then, I hope you'll have identified our victim. Did you say that these single-owner garages are being used to store stolen goods?"

"Not in so many words, but yeah, that's what the caretaker says."

"Perfect. Let's get a move on then. Tell the police at Malceny what I want them to do: get permission from each of the owners and have all the garages opened. I need an inventory of what's in every one of them."

Bullseye. A wet-behind-the-ears magistrate convinced she was going to bring justice to Seine-Saint-Denis with an iron fist. He tried politely to object to her instructions.

"Excuse me, madame, but we've been here less than an hour and I can already count about forty curious onlookers. Mostly youngsters in hoodies. For the moment, we're not touching their lock-ups, so they're calm, but as soon as they see the police van arrive, the temperature's going to rise. It's guaranteed to set the estate ablaze, the same estate where you're asking us to go door to door . . . with all due respect."

Fleur Saint-Croix was indeed very young, and this was her first posting. But despite her lack of experience, she had a rare quality that often prevented her from letting misplaced pride cause her to come a cropper, and allowed her to see when another opinion was more valid than hers. All of which did not prevent her from clearing her throat irritably as she responded:

"Yes . . . Fine . . . Right . . . Suspend those instructions, I'll think it over."

Then, without so much as a goodbye, a thank you or an apology, she hung up.

Lieutenant Scaglia went over to the squad of local police. He handed the mobile back to its owner, who was busy studying the scattered groups of youngsters, waiting for a spark.

"Things kicking off?"

"Slowly for now, lieutenant, slowly. What does the prosecutor's office say?"

"We remove the body, seal the lock-up, and you can beat it out of here. You're in luck – the magistrate wanted all the other garages opened at first."

"With a surprise behind every door, like an Advent calendar. We owe you one."

"Yeah, well, keep that in mind: it looks as if we'll be on the case in your area for a good few days."

"Well then, welcome to Malceny, lieutenant. You're going to love it."

* * *

At the foot of the nearby Rimbaud tower block, a young man was watching closely how events were developing. He was far enough away from the crime scene not to be conspicuous. Earbud in one ear, a dazed look on his face from his breakfast joint, he was almost blindly typing a text on his mobile:

Lock-up busted. Hnouch on scene.*

A young black kid in a T-shirt, tracksuit bottoms and black trainers came over and squatted beside him on a car seat that had no car around it. As he sat down, he said:

* Arabic word meaning "snake".

"Have you warned the Boss?"

"I can't believe that bastard in there's dead. I never saw it coming. We were feeding him, weren't we?"

"Whatever, we were going to finish him off anyway. Well, have you warned him?"

"I just sent him a text. What about you? Did you take the pictures?"

"Not the uniforms, they won't be doing the investigation, but I've got the two plain-clothes ones."

"Did you keep your head down?"

"Don't worry, Driss, nobody noticed me. Nobody ever does."

"Yeah, right, dude. Enjoy it, you're only twelve."

The youngster rummaged in his pocket and forwarded the pictures to Driss.

"Here, send him the photos, they'll interest him."

"Thirty seconds, while I finish a sext."

This was one of his favourite pastimes. Moroccan in origin, Driss had well-defined features and a smile for the camera that brought him a lot of success and filled his contacts with conquests.

Despite his tender years and a companion twice his size, the little black kid's voice turned harsher.

"Hey, Driss! You can fuck later. Send the photos now, for God's sake."

"O.K., Bibz, stay cool."

5

The couple embracing under the huge glass roof of Gare de Lyon in Paris were seemingly unaware of the crowd milling around them. The man, nearing forty, had hair sprinkled with a few grey strands. Nestling on his shoulder was the head of a slightly younger woman, her green eyes moist. They clasped each other's hands, then released them, only to reach for them again, as though either of them could have flown away. Under the triple archway of the station entrance, a young girl was playing on the Steinway piano put there for travellers to use. Just like in the movies, farewells and reunions could now enjoy their own soundtrack.

For her holidays, Léa had rented a small cottage deep in the countryside. Three weeks far away from it all in the south of France. And yet she seemed reluctant to pick up her suitcase and head for her train, searching for any excuse to miss it. Victor tried to reassure her.

"I'll come and join you in a couple of weeks. That'll give you time to get some rest and visit your parents. But you know, maybe having me around 24/7 isn't such a brilliant idea."

"I realise that, but there's nothing I can do about it, it's a chemical thing . . . We're at the start of our relationship, and that stimulates the same areas of the brain as drugs do. Loss of appetite, stress, sleepless nights. I'm swimming in dopamine, and when you're not around I miss it."

"Is that a declaration?"

"It's the best you're going to get on a station platform, you little shit."

So much for having a forensic pathologist as a girlfriend! Victor burst out laughing at the idea of a possible future with a scientist who could talk dirty. The black sheep of a bourgeois family, she couldn't have chosen a better slap in the face than to fall in love with a policeman. Whenever she made the mistake of mentioning it, her father, the director of a private clinic in Paris, merely responded with a shrug.

The fact that the first meeting of the police capitaine and the pathologist had been across a blood-spattered stainless-steel table, over a body opened like a book, and that their relationship had developed as the number of murders they investigated had grown, did nothing to lessen the magic of their story. It made it unique.

Their relative intimacy was disturbed by a buzzing that Léa recognised at once.

"It's your work mobile."

Without bothering to check who the caller was, the man answered.

"Capitaine Coste, what can I do for you?"

"Ronan here. Sorry to interrupt your lovey-dovey moment."

"Tell me."

"Malceny. An as-yet-unidentified victim, found dead tied to a chair, tape round his mouth, in one of the lock-ups at the Cité des Poètes estate. Holes drilled in his kneecaps. Johanna and I aren't sure whether death was from loss of blood or a surfeit of chocolate, but she can explain that better than me."

Coste decided not to even try to understand what the last part of this report meant.

"Is there going to be an autopsy?"

"Yes, boss. You've got an hour to dry your tears and hotfoot it over to the I.M.L."*

"Who've we got as investigating magistrate?"

"Fleur something or other. A new one, with a double-barrelled name as usual."

"A new one? She's going to want to make her mark, and that's never a good thing. Don't mention the other lock-ups – she'll get you to open them all. If every stolen article has to be investigated, you'll send the Malceny stats through the roof. They're going to hate you."

Slightly put out, Ronan pretended to be offended.

"I'm not a complete idiot."

"I'm almost convinced. Is Sam with you?"

"Sam at a crime scene? That I would love to see. But no, he stayed in the office."

"Send him a photo of our client. He can ping it around to see if anyone can put a name to him. It's worth a try. Then tape everything up and start the door-to-door with Johanna. If the atmosphere's too hot already, leave it until tomorrow."

Ronan, who was receiving the same instructions for a second time, really was offended this time.

"Thanks, none of that had occurred to me."

Back next to the tied-up corpse, he gave full vent to his exasperation.

"Do this, do that . . . why do I feel like I'm on work experience today?"

Léa had caught a few snatches of the conversation between the two men, enough to arouse her interest.

* Institut Médico-Légal. The Medico-Legal Institute in the centre of Paris.

"A new case? With a dead body?"

"Yes, but you're boarding the train. The I.M.L. can just about manage for three weeks without Dr Léa Marquant."

"Have it your own way. You'll get to meet my nice pathologist colleague and his magnificent moustache. You won't find your work as sexy, that's for sure."

She kissed the crook of his neck and inhaled his smell.

"You'll see, you're going to miss me too much."

He studied her in her skimpy summer dress, her chestnut hair loose around her bare shoulders. It was quite possible he would miss her. Even a great deal. And a holiday "to get away from it all in a cottage in the middle of nowhere" would have delighted him, were it not for the fact that said cottage in the middle of nowhere was less than thirty kilometres from the Marquant family home. The whole scenario reeked of being an underhand way of introducing him to her family.

As jumpy as a cat getting wet, Victor Coste considered this far too rushed. Newly discovered emotions. *Her* hairbrush in *his* bathroom. His desire to be with Léa grated against his need for solitude, which got in the way of being a couple. Simply put, his inability to live with someone else. So many contradictory notions trapping him in a net of confusion. Although his profession brought him into daily contact with the worst mankind had to offer and he never lost his composure, he found himself on the verge of a panic attack over an affair of the heart. This bachelor fortnight would do him the world of good.

A dulcet voice filled the station, heralding the imminent departure of the train for Nice, and the end of their prolonged goodbye.

6

1 p.m., June 28, 2013
Institut Médico-Légal, twelfth arrondissement, Paris

Despite the siren and the whirling blue light, Paris set him back by fifteen minutes. Once he arrived, he parked in one of the reserved spaces, lowered the sun shield with its police logo, and hurried on. He took the alleyway leading to the old Victorian building that housed the I.M.L., which was crammed between a modest park and the banks of the Seine. Once inside the two old wooden gates, he skirted the interior garden with its sprinkling of bushes and broken fountain, and headed for the reception desk.

"Good morning. Capitaine Coste. I'm here for an autopsy with Dr Léa Mar . . . Oh, sorry . . ."

Behind the desk, the secretary smiled knowingly.

"Force of habit, perhaps?"

Coste fished a crumpled piece of paper out of his jacket and corrected himself with an embarrassed smile.

"You're right. I have an appointment with Dr . . . Serge Atlan."

"That'll make a change for you."

"So I've been told."

Unless you work at the I.M.L., there's only one reason to go there, and that's to identify a loved one. Or, more unfortunately, to be that loved one. With an average of three hundred and fifty autopsies a year, it's highly likely you will bump into a grieving family, which is why the reverent silence of a cemetery reigns inside the building. Coste allowed himself to be led through this atmosphere of respectful calm to the autopsy room. The receptionist swiped her card on the magnetic pad and wished him luck.

The room was white tiled throughout, and dominated by a central operating table. On it was laid a corpse that was occupying the pathologist's full attention. Wearing a pair of protective plastic glasses and an as-yet-pristine white coat, and sporting an impressive moustache, he was leaning over the body, inserting a metal rod into one of the holes drilled into its kneecaps. The unusual sight of a small toolkit placed directly on the dead man's thorax caught Coste's eye.

"Dr Atlan?"

The other man didn't even raise his head.

"Capitaine Coste, I presume? You're late. That might not bother Dr Marquant, but it annoys me. It implies that, just because my clients are dead, there's no need for you to hurry."

Coste did not react to this frosty reception, and the pathologist continued in a similar tone.

"I began without you. Hand me a four-millimetre bit – my gloves are covered in blood."

Doing his best to cooperate, Victor went over to the table, rummaged in the toolkit for a moment, then gave up.

"I'm sorry, but I can't tell the difference between one bit and another. May I ask what you're doing?"

The pathologist interrupted his procedure and studied him for the first time.

"Perforated flesh with slight burns to the edges. Your victim was tortured with a drill. I'm trying to discover what diameter bit was used. It definitely wasn't three millimetres."

As he spoke, he gently withdrew the metal rod with a moist sucking sound, then searched in his toolkit himself until he found another one. He held it up to the capitaine.

"Four-millimetre bit. It's written on it. I've been told you're a good investigator, but I must say I'm rather disappointed."

"I've been told you are downright unpleasant. No reason to quarrel with that description so far."

The introductions over, the doctor stared Coste in the eye and offered him the ghost of a smile. Then he pushed the metal bit into the left kneecap: a perfect fit.

"I can't tell you whether it was a wood or metal bit, but it was a size four, that's for sure."

Placing the bloody implement back in his box, he added almost impatiently, like someone who has just been given a gift:

"So, shall we open him up?"

The casual observer would have regarded what followed as a series of barbaric, unspeakable acts. But it was routine for a certain breed of policeman, to which Coste belonged. He had often told himself that families should never find out the details of an autopsy. A performance lasting less than an hour that not even the most violent horror movie could begin to match. To safeguard his mental health, Coste no longer viewed the corpse as human: it was just another part of the investigation.

To avoid thinking they had loved.

To avoid thinking they had been happy.

At least for the duration of the autopsy.

Wielding his scalpel confidently, Dr Atlan made deep incisions behind the biceps, wrists and thighs, and the muscles flopped out onto the table. In a clinical, neutral voice, the pathologist began to outline the ordeal this nameless victim had been put through.

"Numerous subcutaneous bruises to arms and legs. He was obviously beaten. Or he struggled. With several people, to judge by the number of blows. Help me turn him over."

Coste pulled on a pair of gloves, followed Atlan's instructions, then took two steps back. Before the pathologist cut open the body and the smell of death wafted through the room, he took a small tube of ointment from his pocket and spread some under his nose.

"What do you use?" asked Atlan.

"Tiger balm."

"I prefer Vicks. It blocks out the smell, it's just as minty, but it stings a lot less. You should try it."

After this manly exchange, the doctor resumed his task. Placing the tip of his scalpel just under the Adam's apple, he penetrated the skin, then drew the blade down as far as the pubis. He inserted the scalpel under the flesh on both sides until the skin was detached, and then sliced delicately until the entire chest cavity was exposed, like a strongbox revealing its treasure.

He picked up a pair of clippers and cut the ribs one after another with the sound of dry branches snapping. That done, he took hold of the sternum and lifted it as if it were an ordinary lid, so that the interior organs appeared beneath the harsh ceiling light. A stench of putrefaction filled the room.

Lungs, spleen, liver, intestines, bladder, stomach. Dr Atlan removed them all with his scalpel so that a sample could be taken for analysis, but he already had a hypothesis.

"O.K. It looks like a textbook case to me. Discoloured face, congested mucus membranes, purplish lungs. Congestive lesions on liver and kidneys. Blood dark but still fluid. No excoriation from fingernails or hand-shaped bruises. That means I'm discounting strangulation and instead going for asphyxia from suffocation."

"That's quite likely. His mouth was taped up."

"You could have told me."

"Certainly I could, but that would mean I was influencing your conclusions. I prefer you to make up your own mind."

This remark amused the pathologist. As he readjusted his protective glasses, he unwittingly smeared them with blood.

"Influencing my conclusions? We're talking about science here, not psychology or astrology. I only take into account the evidence, not suppositions. Besides, the tape is only one element. The full picture is more complicated."

Opening the dead man's mouth with a dry click, he pushed his fingers inside, then inserted a cotton bud.

"See this sticky stuff? There's more of it in his nostrils and airways. However, I'm not at all sure what it could be . . ."

Coste on the other hand had a theory, however outlandish it might seem – one that had been suggested by Ronan. Death by . . .

"Could it possibly be chocolate?"

Intrigued, the pathologist went to the end of the table where he had left the internal organs, and picked up the stomach.

"It could indeed. Let's see what he ate that day, shall we?"

He made a horizontal cut in the organ and emptied the contents into a cylindrical plastic bowl with the biohazard label symbol: a circle surrounded by three crescents on a yellow background.

"He doesn't seem to have had a lot to eat, but I'll get the alimentary bolus analysed. You'll have your answer within forty-eight hours."

"Is there any way of speeding things up?"

The doctor held out the stinking pot.

"Yes, capitaine. Taste it yourself if you wish."

Coste changed his mind.

"Two days isn't so long . . ."

The autopsy was almost finished; there was only one thing left to do. But it was the hardest to watch. And, above all, to hear. The scalpel traced a line all around the skull, from behind the ears to the back of the neck, and then across the forehead. The scalp was peeled away from the bone as roughly as one might rip up an old carpet. Then it was folded down over the face, as if the pathologist were trying to spare the deceased the sight of this final outrage. With the loud whirr of a dentist's drill, the circular saw cut round the brain pan, spraying a jet of white powder onto the pathologist's protective glasses and mask. Moist and pink, the brain was laid bare. It was weighed and inspected, just like the other organs.

"O.K. To confirm: several softened areas, entirely compatible with suffocation. I think the gag produced an oxygen deficiency. Dizziness, nausea and vomiting, which points directly to suffocation by choking. In view of the congestion in other organs, I calculate that death took place only a few hours ago. Almost certainly last night."

If Léa Marquant had been conducting the autopsy, her conclusions would have been identical, but more graphic:

"Your client choked on his own chocolate vomit. And if you'd shown up a bit earlier, you'd have been able to save him."

It had been two hours since he had left her on the platform at Gare de Lyon, and Coste still couldn't make up his mind if he missed her or if he felt liberated. The pathologist brought him back to reality.

"I'll put his things in a bag for your investigation. If you examine the crotch of his jeans, you might find urine stains. It's common in this kind of death. Now it's your turn."

"Meaning?"

"You wanted to find out if I knew what I was doing. Now it's my turn to see if you justify your reputation, Capitaine Coste."

Coste was amused by the challenge. Léa was in the habit of doing the same. Could it be a tic all pathologists shared? He took his time to sift through all the information and arrange it in some kind of order.

"If the victim was fed, that means he was in the lock-up for quite a while. At least forty-eight hours. Long enough for him to need food."

"So was this a kidnapping that went wrong?"

"Not necessarily. The handiwork with the drill suggests the opposite. You don't make holes in a hostage. At most you cut off a finger or an ear to show you mean business, but even so, that's very Hollywood."

Coste turned away from the corpse and spoke directly to the pathologist.

"What kind of secret could it be that a four-millimetre drill bit wouldn't make you reveal?"

"None, I should think. The pain would be too intense."

"And yet they had to do it twice."

"Maybe your guy was very brave."

"That's possible. Or he had a secret he absolutely could not betray. Now at least we know what we're looking for."

"A secret?"

"One that would provide a motive for the killing. But the worst of it is, this is only the first act. He was tortured to get information, so we can expect a follow-up. This murder is nothing more than a prelude. There's a more important objective behind it."

The pathologist had not expected to be impressed by Coste.

Not to this extent anyway. He had looked askance at the relationship between Léa Marquant, his student protégée, and this police capitaine from Seine-Saint-Denis. Now he had to admit that, in addition to a not unpleasing physique, Coste was quite stimulating intellectually. He could understand why she had been attracted to him. In spite of their unpromising start, the two men ended up shaking hands.

Once alone, Dr Atlan took a reinforced plastic bag and poured all the now useless internal organs into it. Carefully sealing the bag, he laid it in the thoracic cavity, then replaced the sternum, a piece of the puzzle that fitted perfectly. Then he sewed up the skin all the way to the stomach. When the dead man's relatives came for the formal identification, they would never imagine what their loved one had been subjected to. A bit like sweeping dust under the carpet and then swearing you've cleaned properly.

Outside, Coste breathed in deeply to refresh the air in his lungs. You can put up with the smell of death, but you never get used to it. Even the exhaust fumes from the vehicles already nose to tail on the Paris streets early that afternoon were preferable.

His mobile began to vibrate in his pocket, putting a stop to his timid breathing exercises.

"Victor Coste. Who's speaking?"

"Hi there, it's Sam."

"So you played hookey this morning, did you?"

"Go easy . . . I leave the legwork, the haemoglobin and stiffs to Ronan and Johanna. They're very good at it. I save myself for the technical stuff. Besides, if I go to a crime scene, I vomit, so . . ."

"It seems vomiting is all the rage today. Do you have anything on our client?"

"We don't have the fingerprint results yet. Neither Groupe Crime 2 nor the organised crime people had anything on him. But luckily Capitaine Sylvan's unit found a match."

"Groupe Stups? And?"

"And it's mayhem here. I haven't been told anything more, but there's a lot going on. An emergency meeting. Get back as quick as you can, you're already late."

As he had suspected, this was only the first act of the drama. Coste liked being right, even if most of the time it meant his day was shot to hell.

7

A heat fierce enough to melt metal had descended on the three-storey glass headquarters of the Seine-Saint-Denis Police Judiciaire, the S.D.P.J. 93. As though already admitting defeat, the building was surrounded by the stifling estates of Bobigny, their dilapidated tower blocks reaching up to the sky.

Carrying a cup of coffee in one hand and a cumbersome plastic bag in the other, Coste pushed open the door to Groupe Crime 1 with his foot. His team were already inside: as usual Ronan was engaged in his favourite pastime of persecuting Sam. They were both sitting on the comfortable three-seater sofa which occasionally served as a bed when investigations stretched on into the night. Holding up a tablet, Ronan was trying to show his long-suffering stooge the video Groupe Stups had made a few days earlier.

"It's evidence. You're going to have to see it sometime."

"Fine, I know what it is. An execution shown live. Nothing more than a snuff movie. I can understand watching it once, but you've got it on a loop. You don't just revolt me, you worry me."

Sam, or, more formally, officer Samuel Dorfrey. A long thin streak of a young man, built like a computer technician, with a sweet face that wasn't really an advantage in their line of work. When he was standing next to his partner Ronan, with his athletic frame and tough demeanour, the casting error was even more blatant. Sam was no doubt the only police officer in France who couldn't stand the sight of blood, still less that of a corpse. Drafting him into the crime group might have seemed absurd, but Coste was well aware of his qualities. He came to his rescue in a fatherly manner.

"Ronan, leave our pet geek alone. Each to their own."

He threw the bag he'd been carrying straight at Sam, who caught it with both hands, and only then wondered what was in it.

"What's this?"

"A present from the lab. Our victim's bloodstained things. Careful, they're still wet."

Disgusted, Sam leaped up from the sofa, and dropped the package as if it could contaminate him. "Fuck! You're as bad as each other! Do you rehearse your lines before you come in?"

Ronan burst out laughing. Coste sat down at his desk and relayed the pathologist's initial findings.

"We're leaning towards manslaughter. The gag partly covered his nostrils. The lack of oxygen brought on nausea, and he choked on his own vomit. Johanna was right about the chocolate, though I'm guessing that didn't make his death any sweeter."

"Is that what they mean by a 'Nutella moment'?" suggested Ronan.

Then, taking pity on Sam, he picked up the bag with the stained clothes.

"It's alright, little man, I'll deal with it. I'll lay them out in the drying room before bagging them up. Jo, could you type out a request for the lab?"

Busy behind her computer, Johanna De Ritter, the group's

latest recruit, waved a sheet of paper that had just emerged from her printer and dropped it on his desk.

"Done. Always one step ahead. Maybe because I don't spend my day squabbling with my colleagues, I've got more time."

Coste enjoyed watching this well-oiled machine at work. The banter among his team was a positive sign.

"Good, so things are moving. You almost don't need me. Maybe I should have taken that train this morning . . ."

"And I wouldn't have hesitated in sending a R.A.I.D. task force* to smoke you out, capitaine!"

Everyone turned towards the person who had just joined their conversation. Standing in the doorway was Commandant Marie-Charlotte Damiani, overall head of the two crime units: Groupe Crime 1, under Coste, and Groupe Crime 2, led by Capitaine Lara Jevric.

"We've all been asked to join the big boss in the meeting room, so I have the length of the corridor to brief you. The situation is a bit complicated."

"Let's walk slowly then."

As they crossed the frosted glass walkway linking the north and south wings of their headquarters, Commandant Damiani leafed through a police report. She skimmed the few pages before passing it to Coste.

"Your corpse goes by the name of Karim Souki. He was identified by Groupe Stups."

"That's what I was led to believe."

"They were on his tail for months, so it's quite possible the boss will ask you to work together."

"A joint investigation? But they're on another planet."

* Research, Assistance, Intervention and Dissuasion. R.A.I.D. units saw action during the 2005 and 2006 riots.

"Victor, I'm retiring in two months and I've no stomach for a fight. I've got white hair, persistent sciatica, and memories of forty-six years' worth of delinquents. I know you can't stand the Groupe Stups lot. So don't worry, I'm going to hand the investigation over to Groupe Crime 2 and Capitaine Jevric."

"She'll be perfect."

"You don't believe a word of it, but it's kind of you to say so."

When they reached their destination, Ronan opened the door to allow the rest through. Commissaire Stévenin was already waiting for them in the meeting room. Forced to wear a suit even at the height of summer, he envied his officers their jeans and T-shirts. In one corner, Capitaine Sylvan was talking to two of his men. Ronan and Sam went over and shook hands.

When Johanna approached, towering head and shoulders above them, the Groupe Stups men had to raise their heads six inches to look her in the eye before they could shake her hand. She took her seat between Sam and Ronan and complained in an undertone:

"Why does nobody ever give me a peck on the cheek?"

Neither of them dared offer an explanation, preferring to bury their heads in the folders in front of them.

Sylvan was now standing by the briefing wall, on which were stuck three photographs of dead bodies, surrounded by arrows and scrawled hypotheses and questions. When everyone was seated, he pointed his pen at the photograph furthest to the left. They all waited for him to speak.

"This is Sayid Laouari, alias 'Mr Do-it-All'. Well known in Malceny. He kept an eye on the entire drugs chain, from purchase to distribution, and sold his own junk. Hence the nickname. Born in 1990, he departed this world on Monday, dispatched by a bullet to the head in the middle of the street while we were watching and filming, as you've been able to appreciate. A good old-fashioned contract, carried out according to the rules of the game. A moped, a rider, a shooter and goodnight, ladies and gentlemen. The killer didn't even bother to recover the bag of shit in the tower block behind him."

Damiani judged it was the moment to add a few words of explanation for the benefit of Coste and his team.

"Plainly a drugs-related murder. That's why I've accepted the boss's request for Groupe Crime 2 and Groupe Stups to work together."

At this point, Commissaire Stévenin realised someone was missing from the meeting.

"Where, by the way, *is* Capitaine Jevric?"

Embarrassed, Damiani replied at once:

"She'll be here very soon, sir. Sylvan, have forensics come up with anything?"

The head of Groupe Stups continued with his presentation.

"One of the bullet casings was found, still partially intact. Even so, ballistics can't link it to any known weapon. The same goes for the moped. No number plate. Far too common a model. In short, we don't have even a hint of a lead. But just between us, if it had only been Laouari who was shot, I wouldn't have lost any sleep . . ."

He pointed his pen at the second photo. A car with smashed windows; all that could be seen inside the blood-spattered interior was the upper half of a body slumped over the steering wheel.

"Unfortunately, two days later, as he was leaving an underground car park, Sasha Dimov was murdered in his car. His kid was on the back seat. The boy is alright, but he's seriously freaked out. He's in a catatonic state at the children's psychopathology unit at Robert-Debré Hospital. For the moment, we can't get anything from him. Two firearms were used for this contract. This time, ballistics can tell us that one of them is the same as in the first execution. To go from there to saying it was the same shooter is reasonable, but it's not a sure thing."

The door opened and Capitaine Lara Jevric's head appeared in the frame. As always when she was late, she was quick to put the blame on her team.

"Sorry, one of my guys messed up a procedure. I had to sort it out."

Scanning the room, she added:

"Were we supposed to bring our teams? I thought it was just for the group capitaines."

A word and a rank she was particularly fond of.

Used to her games, half of those present put on a wry half-smile, while the commissaire pretended not to have heard. Sylvan invited her to find a seat. Since all the chairs were taken, she tried to balance on the arm of one of the armchairs, but her generous frame did not allow that kind of acrobatic manoeuvre, so she chose to remain standing.

"Don't worry, Lara," Sylvan continued, "we began without you, but you already know our first two victims. You've arrived just in time to hear about the third."

He turned back to the whiteboard and went on:

"So, victim number three: Karim Souki. Found dead this morning in a lock-up at the Cité des Poètes estate. Forensics are doing what they can to recover fingerprints and D.N.A. samples, but it could take time."

Sylvan turned towards Coste, who for a while had seemed to be distracted, no doubt wondering about the next act of the drama.

"Victor, you're just back from the post-mortem. Did they come up with anything?"

"An all-inclusive stay. Fed, housed, tortured. Sorry, nothing else. I'm not sure whether they were going to take him out anyway, but the fact is he didn't give them the chance. He died alone like a hero, choking to death. Damiani tells me you were on his case?"

"Yes, on all three of them, in fact. That's our problem: Malceny is the hub for drugs in the Île-de-France region. Laouari, Dimov and Souki were the head honchos. They've controlled three-quarters of the trade for four years now, with no competition."

Lara Jevric wanted to make her presence felt.

"So, champagne all round! You've had seventy-five per cent of your dealers taken out in four days. That means you can go on holiday just in time for July."

"Thanks, that's an interesting analysis, but in fact the opposite is true," Sylvan said. "Three executions in less than a week is no coincidence. It's a revolution. A revolution that leaves us up shit creek. It's a game changer. We've no idea who's replacing them, we don't know their names, their mobile numbers, or where they live. We're in the dark about their new turfs, where they're going to deal from, how they're going to operate, what gear they're offering. Their teams and suppliers are going to change as well. It's like starting a family tree all over again. To conclude, as from today we have no idea what's going on in Malceny."

The response left Jevric feeling stupid, but since that was an emotion she often experienced, she wasn't giving up yet.

"Wait a second. The first murder was on Monday. The second Thursday, and the last one this Friday morning, is that right?"

Without holding out much hope, the others nevertheless waited for her hypothesis. She went on:

"Groupe Crime 2's shift finishes on Thursday, so Friday's stiff is Coste's, isn't it?"

Irritated rather than disappointed, Commissaire Stévenin decided to retake the reins.

"Lara, the three cases are linked, we're not going to split them into three investigations. But if that seems too complicated a strategy to you, we can talk about it in my office."

Which meant "Shut your trap", as Jevric immediately understood. Damiani smoothed things over.

"To be fair to Jevric, I propose that Coste's team stay on duty for the next fortnight. Assuming you agree, Victor, of course."

"It's a bargain that suits me fine," Coste said. "And anyway, just between us—"

His whole team tried to interrupt him, as though what he was about to say would bring down a curse on their heads:

"Don't finish your sentence, Victor!"

"You'll put the evil eye on us!"

He was amused by their superstition, a smile playing on his lips.

"What? Come on, children . . . what could possibly happen in a fortnight?"

8

Sylvan had insisted Coste stay in the meeting room after the others left. When they were alone, he came straight to the point.

"I asked Damiani if I could work with your team, and instead I get fobbed off with Jevric. I guess you've got something against Groupe Stups. What's your problem?"

Coste cleared up the misunderstanding.

"I don't have one. It's just that the way you deal with things doesn't interest me. I need the human factor. It's what gets me going. You only deal with junkies, and you spend the rest of your time with dealers and pushers. And when you manage to put one behind bars, somebody new replaces them in less than forty-eight hours. Honestly, I don't know how you keep going."

"And you prefer a fortnight on duty to investigating the murder of a dealer?"

"Yes, no question. Besides, it's manslaughter, not murder."

"So it's not worthy of Groupes Crime?"

"You got it."

"May I at least have your opinion on the case?"

"If you insist . . ."

Coste opened one of the folders and swapped the photos round.

"I think you've got the chronology of the deaths wrong, and

the third victim is in fact the first. Maybe not the first to die, but definitely at the root of things. Souki had both his kneecaps drilled because someone was trying to get him to tell them something, and it was only afterwards that the other two were taken out."

Sylvan did not look convinced.

"Tortured to get the name of the two other ringleaders? That's info that every delinquent in Malceny has. Every eight-year-old, in fact."

"O.K., so let's say Souki knew other, less public, info. On your video you showed us that the shooter killed the dealer and lit out without taking the bag of drugs. That's odd, isn't it? Unless he had no interest in wasting his time over such a small quantity."

Sylvan had a light bulb moment.

"Because he already knew where the main gear was stashed! Do you think that's why they did their handiwork on Souki? To get him to tell them where they hide their stuff?"

"If this really is a revolution, it's one thing to use violence to take over the territory, but you also have to have something to sell."

"Hang on, so that means Souki knew where the other two stashed their drugs?"

"Why does that bother you?"

"That implies they trusted one another. That they worked together. That's uncommon. They were much better organised than I thought."

"And that meant it was necessary to take them out together. Almost simultaneously."

"But if the first one, Laouari, was bumped off on the 24th, why was Souki still in the lock-up four days later?"

"Once you've got info, you have to go and verify it. They

must have wanted to keep him alive until they'd visited all the stashes and checked them. Besides, it could be that his gaolers don't even know he's snuffed it."

"Seriously, Victor, why don't you work with me on this one? Jevric's team is decent enough, but she hasn't the faintest idea how to lead: she never lets them take any initiative. If only she wasn't so useless. I can't understand why the big bosses let her stay on as head of the group."

"Because she's up for promotion to commissaire. And they look after their own. If it seems as though she's joining their ranks, they'll treat her with kid gloves. They think as much about their careers as we do about our investigations. Which explains a lot of the decisions they make."

Sylvan wasn't convinced for a second.

"That doesn't change a thing. Whenever she opens her mouth, I feel like slapping her."

"That's a healthy reaction."

* * *

Ensconced in the office sofa, Sam was trying to make up his mind. Even though they had been taken off the case, the vendetta was playing out in Seine-Saint-Denis, on their patch. Since the flapping of a butterfly's wings could cause a hell of a mess on the other side of the world, it was likely that the three murders would have repercussions in the near future.

He took several deep breaths and pressed play on the video he had downloaded to his tablet. At the far end of the sofa, Ronan had not missed the struggle going on in his partner's mind.

"Atta boy."

Sam answered with a "Fuck you" that sounded like a friendly "Thanks".

9

For half a century, Monsieur Jacques had been a witness to the complete failure of the concept of a happy suburb. Initially he had been won over by the promise of individual gardens and pleasant flats. So he'd moved to Malceny and the Beaux-Enfants estate when his wife was pregnant with their first child.

After the events of May '68, the dream of getting away to the country seemed to be within reach just beyond the gates of the capital. Proud inhabitants of secure H.L.M. social housing settled far from the already congested inner city that everybody wanted to escape.

Monsieur Jacques had loved his wife to the end and was loved in return, but he was proud above all of having a daughter who lived in the United States, something he considered a success in itself. A plastic Statue of Liberty and other "Made in U.S.A." trinkets were on display in a cabinet in his living room. Lost among countless pieces of junk kept religiously as proof that he had really lived.

In the final stages of her illness, his wife had been confined to bed. That made things a lot easier for Monsieur Jacques: he could continue to lie extravagantly about life beyond the drawn curtains.

He never told her about the burnt-out vehicles, how the area was deteriorating, the kids who insulted him when he went out shopping, or the time when he was mugged and had his wallet stolen. The one where he kept the photograph of their kiss on Île du Vert-Galant beside the Seine. That, in fact, was what helped him withstand all the blows . . . And of course he had never mentioned the man who had one day approached him at the foot of the tower block and with whom he had struck a deal.

And then one morning she had passed away, without suffering, like someone falling asleep, and he had nobody to tell lies to anymore.

The accumulation of burglaries, harassment, increasing dilapidation and gratuitous violence had led his neighbours to leave the tower block one by one. Monsieur Jacques would have liked to follow them, but Paris had become impossibly expensive, and in his eyes (as though he were a child again) far too big. And despite everything, this was his home. He had his memories, at a point in his life when they were all that was left to him. And so, to inoculate himself against solitude, he had adopted a cat. A big black tom with a white belly, left on his front doormat by his last remaining neighbours. He had called him Monsieur Chat. For six years now, the animal had purred quietly as the old man poured out his secrets to him.

All the other flats around him fell empty, leaving the already shabby tower block virtually abandoned, with graffiti all the way up to the second floor, mailboxes stripped of addresses, and dark corridors that bordered on a health risk. So, before pulling it down, the Malceny town council housed immigrants there. This wasn't difficult, with ninety-five different nationalities to cater for. And Monsieur Jacques felt even more lost: the different skin colours, customs, religions, even languages. Twenty years earlier, he would have been curious to learn about all these differences, but at his age it was enough for him occasionally to listen to arguments in an array of languages, his ear pressed against his front door.

Every Saturday at around three o'clock in the afternoon he was in the habit of meeting Madame Rose for a game of bridge and a few glasses of port at the Malceny Old People's Association. Both of them were widowed, and Rose and he allowed themselves to flirt with their eyes. Sometimes even with their fingertips. Without admitting it to themselves, and because their age didn't permit a great deal more.

At the end of each month, Monsieur Jacques turned up at Malceny police station, where a charming policewoman took him by the arm to accompany him to the cash machine and make sure he could withdraw his pension without any unfortunate encounters. On the way they chatted about the weather and about life, or what was left of it. She told him of her son who was having problems at school, and her partner, who didn't like her being a cop. Would she have been so friendly if she had known the old man's secret? If she had known what he kept in his bedroom wardrobe, in a hard shell suitcase hidden behind a box of books?

Not the revolver and box of cartridges. The rest of it.

10

In the lift, dressed in black from head to foot, the young kid known as Bibz was waiting patiently, hands stuffed in his pockets. Beside him, Driss was finishing rolling a joint, blocking the lift door with his foot as it tried to close every four seconds. Colin, the third member of the group, finally showed up. His jeans hung off him, showing his underpants, and his sweatshirt was several sizes too big. His blond hair stiff with gel, he looked like a scarecrow dressed in rags far too big for it.

"It's on the fourteenth floor," he told them.

The lift juddered before it began to rise.

"Where do you get your nickname, Bibz?" Driss wanted to know.

"It's because of my ma. She called me and my brothers almost the same thing: Hadidou, Habibou and Amidou. We didn't know who she was shouting at when she was drunk, so we gave each other nicknames."

The scarecrow sniggered. "Yeah, she didn't exactly bust a gut when it came to naming you all, did she? Don't you reckon she was just takin' the piss?"

Drawing himself up to his full twelve-year-old height, Bibz stared him up and down.

"First, when you've got a name like Colin you best keep

your trap shut. Second, if you carry on talking like that about my mother, you won't get out of this lift alive."

He sounded utterly serious, so the last few floors went by in silence. When they reached the fourteenth, they inspected all the front doors. One of them alerted the others.

"Jacques Landernes, it's here."

"Check it out, he's got a Welcome mat."

Sitting at his living-room table with its plastic tablecloth, with the radio on in the background and a cup of instant coffee, Monsieur Jacques was finishing a letter to his daughter, full of the same white lies he used to tell his wife. On his lap the cat, better than a rug in such damp, oppressive weather, pricked up its ears when it heard the doorbell. Actually shifting its fat arse would have required something more urgent, and it was only because its elderly master got up that the cat grudgingly accepted the need to transfer itself to the adjoining bedroom. The bell rang a second time to remind Monsieur Jacques to get a move on, and moments later he finally opened the door.

Three shadowy silhouettes pushed him back inside. One of them forced him up against the wall, clapping a hand over his mouth; the last one slammed the door shut. He was almost lifted into the living room and forced to sit at the end of the table. Against all expectations, it was the youngest of the three who took control.

"No worries, pops. Stay cool."

"What do you want?"

He wished his voice was under control, but as it was it simply confirmed to them that he was terrified, caught in the trap that his own flat had become.

"We're not going to search, right? You're going to show us."

"O.K. . . . O.K. . . .wait a second."

Monsieur Jacques stood up, a little surprised that his legs could still carry him. He went to the chest of drawers by the front door, where his wallet lay. He took out the 1,100 euros of his pension, and laid it on the table. The three intruders glanced at each other in astonishment. Driss, the joint smoker, decided to wake up.

"Hey, asshole, what kind of tip is this?"

Bibz thought he had done all he could, and now his very limited patience was exhausted. Leaning over the old man, he stared straight at him. Two black marbles devoid of all emotion. Then he punched him right below the eye, fracturing his cheekbone. Given Bibz's size and age, the other two were amazed at how violent the blow was: in less than twenty seconds, the left side of Monsieur Jacques's face had swelled up and turned purple.

"Jeez, old folk bruise easily!"

"You've coloured him in!"

Bibz addressed Jacques again.

"Listen, we know what you keep here. We want to see it, that's all."

The pensioner cottoned on immediately.

"But you're not the right people. You're not the right people," he protested, his voice quavering.

"You're going to have to get used to our mugs. We're the ones you have to listen to now."

Monsieur Jacques led them into his bedroom. A dog would have defended him, but the cat, lying on its side on the bed, simply observed them with no great interest. Cats are useless. The old man opened the wardrobe doors and pointed out what they had come for, behind a box full of books. Colin, the one whose clothes were three sizes too big for him, pulled out the suitcase and laid it on the bed. Bibz opened it and checked the contents. Loaded revolver, two boxes of cartridges, and a bag with two bundles of banknotes. Then he checked the rest of the inventory. Two 500-gram blocks of cocaine. Another filled with one-gram wraps of the same. Eight 500-gram blocks of cannabis resin, and two filled with four-gram lumps ready for sale. Leaving aside the cash, there was about fifty thousand euros' worth in there, which meant a hundred and fifty thousand at street prices. When you know that in Seine-Saint-Denis people can get killed for a misjudged look, Monsieur Jacques had a hundred and fifty thousand reasons to be worried.

"Take a picture," Bibz instructed one of the others. "That will reassure the Boss. Then put everything back where it was."

The old man looked surprised.

"I don't understand. You aren't going to steal anything?"

"Why do you want us to steal it? It's all ours now. And you don't change jobs, you're still the minder. From now on you're working for us, and this is our place too. Do you have a spare set of keys?"

"I'm sorry, I don't."

"Get one made quick if you don't want us to knock the door down if you don't happen to be in."

While he was talking, Bibz rummaged in his pocket and took out a wad of twenty-euro notes.

"Here, five hundred euros."

"Normally it's only three hundred a month . . ."

"You're getting a raise. Boss's orders. To keep you on side, apparently."

The old man muttered anxiously:

"Alright. But what if the others come back? They weren't exactly polite either."

"Don't you worry about that. We've sent them on holiday."

Reassured by the surprisingly businesslike tone of the conversation, Monsieur Jacques plucked up his courage to ask:

"And . . . what if I want to stop?"

Enraged, Bibz grabbed him by the collar and threw him down onto the bed. The cat leaped up and tried to escape the room through the forest of legs rising in front of it. One of the intruders gave him a kick that flung him against the wall. He let out a painful meow. The old man was almost begging:

"No! Please, don't hurt Monsieur Chat."

Driss, the joint lit and dangling from the corner of his mouth, guffawed.

"Have you seen the size of that thing? It's not a cat, it's a fuckin' pony. And *la hchouma*:* he's gone and called it Monsieur Chat."

Colin added mercilessly:

"Nooo! Did Bibz's mother give him the nickname?"

For little Habibou, several red lines had been crossed. The old man didn't want to be their minder anymore, and now these two pricks were dissing him. He seized the revolver from the suitcase, grabbed Monsieur Jacques's shirt, ripping off a few buttons, and forced him to his feet. Then he pointed the gun at the other two.

"Into the living room, you bunch of losers."

None of them said a word. When they reached the table, he shouted at them, gun in hand:

"Sit down!"

Bibz went into the kitchen. There was the sound of plates smashing, then he came back carrying the microwave. Placing it on the table in front of them like a television set, he unplugged the radio and connected it. He went back into the bedroom

* "The shame" in Arabic, especially in Morocco.

and reappeared carrying the cat by the scruff of the neck. Opening the microwave door, he threw the cat in and switched the oven on full.

"I don't think any of you have got it into your thick skulls who's in charge here. I'm the one who talks to the Boss on the phone. I'm the one he gives orders to."

The cat was revolving slowly, like a ballerina on a musical box. Its fur began to crackle and give off smoke. A long, uninterrupted howl escaped the illuminated oven. The metal buckle on Monsieur Chat's collar began to give off sparks and then small flashes.

"You, pops, are going to work for us just like you did for the others."

The water molecules inside the cat had reached boiling point. So had its blood and brain. Its meowing became louder and louder, like the howls of a breastfeeding baby.

"As for you two smartarses, if either of you mentions my mother again, I'll put a bullet in your mouth."

The cat's fur began to ripple as though it was shape-shifting. For several seconds, a sustained jet of blood spurted from its eyes, until the animal literally exploded against the glass front of the microwave. Monsieur Jacques was choking with rage and sorrow. The other two had lowered their eyes a few seconds earlier to spare themselves the sight of this agonising death.

Bibz's voice was calm once more.

"Has everyone got it now?"

11

Bibz did not think he had gone too far. "Too" was an idea he had trouble defining. He had always lived with "too"s. Too poor, too violent, too solitary. Unknown father, alcoholic mother. Eldest brother in prison for having avenged the next one down in an affair whose origins nobody could remember. Educated with blows or a belt depending on the teacher. Bibz had quickly learned the need to be respected at all costs, never to lower his eyes (even when faced with a good thrashing), and the certainty that for every blow received you had to reply with a hundred. Bibz was too young, too small. Easy prey. He had been forced to make himself too hard.

By the age of eight he was already fending for himself. By ten, he had to look after his mother when her family allowance was cut off. No school, no education, unable to read or write, and his future didn't figure on any existing pathway. He was a street kid, and if he reached adulthood, he would be a pariah.

Too little would ever be offered to him or even made accessible. He had to take things by force, snatch them, thieve, purloin, steal, cheat, threaten, and hit hard when cornered.

Bibz knew how to load a gun and use it. How to hot-wire

a car. How to threaten and follow through. He knew all the shortcuts and underground passageways in several estates. The ABC of his daily life. Simple strategies for survival.

Ethno-psychiatrists are fond of trying to understand patterns of thought and their link to evil in terms of context, place and culture. So an individual born in a country at war will have a different attitude towards violence from that of a kid in Paris's posh sixteenth arrondissement. If anyone had studied Bibz's case, they would have considered him a child soldier. One of those handed a Kalashnikov and sent to the front.

In the alley alongside the tower block, Bibz stood a few metres ahead of his two colleagues, who were still shocked into silence by the microwave incident. At past eight in the evening, the summer sun cast lengthy shadows, dusting the towers and rare greenery with a golden haze, like a deceptive advert. As the Boss had instructed, he called and gave his report.

"Bibz here."

"Habibou, good to hear from you."

The Boss had met him one evening almost a year earlier at the foot of his building. Bibz's face was bloody from yet again refusing to lower his eyes when faced with someone too big and too strong for him.

"It's fine with the old guy. He'll do it."

"Did everything go smoothly? No problems?"

"Apart from the two assholes you've foisted on me. They don't know how to keep their traps shut."

"No-one listens to vulgar people, Habibou. No-one."

"Sorry, but I nearly took one of them out."

The Boss had looked after Bibz like a big brother, and regularly involved him in jobs that allowed him to earn some money. He had never hit or insulted him. He hadn't even put him down.

"If you lose your authority, you lose everything. How did you deal with the situation?"

The young boy recited:

"Violence creates fear, and fear makes people submit."

"You've done a really good job, Habibou. I'm proud of you. Call me back after you hit the second address."

The trust the youngster had in this man bordered on adoration. If he had put him on a cliff edge and told him to jump, Bibz wouldn't even have let him finish the sentence.

When the Boss ended the call, the reproving eyes of his neighbour were still on him. He apologised politely and focused once more on the voice of the professor in the Sorbonne lecture theatre. He was reaching the conclusion of an evening class on economics and business management, a module in research, strategy and organisation.

Up on the fourteenth floor, Monsieur Jacques had put on a pair of marigolds and approached the microwave, carrying a refuse bag. As he opened the oven door, the smell of boiled flesh and charred fur overwhelmed him. Was it the stench, the sight of the cat, or the realisation that he wouldn't ever be able to use the oven again? He closed the door immediately, unplugged the oven, wrapped the lead round it, then stowed it in the bag.

His eyes came to rest on the unfinished letter to his daughter. "Nothing changes here. Life is fine and set fair like the weather. Apart from the courage to come and visit you and undertake such a long journey, there's nothing more I could ask of Our Lord."

How tired he was of lying . . .

It was only at that moment, as though the fear and violence had befuddled his brain, that he remembered Rose, his Saturday flirt, his bridge companion. His heart began thumping against his chest, and his fingers were shaking so much it took him two attempts to dial her number correctly.

12

Seated on the carpet in a pastel-coloured bedroom, her back against the bedside table separating the two children's beds, Johanna was finishing reading them a story under a shaded violet lamp. The one about a boy and girl abandoned by their parents in the middle of a forest, who discover a gingerbread house that a greedy witch uses to trap children. Enough to induce nightmares, but as good a way as any to prepare them for the outside world. Once the witch had been dispatched into the oven, Johanna closed the book.

From the left-hand bed, her daughter asked a question.

"Can a child really kill a witch?"

"A witch, an ogre or a dragon: everything's possible when a brother and sister look after each other."

On the other side, her brother, not much older than her, was puzzled. Lost in thought. Johanna gave them both a good-night hug, and switched off the light. In the silent room lit only by the night-light, the boy whispered:

"I love you, but if there's a witch, I'd leave you to it."

From under the other duvet, a faint, querulous voice replied:

"Don't say that . . ."

Johanna went downstairs to the living room. All the windows were open, in an attempt to catch the slightest breeze. She rejoined Victor, Sam and Ronan round the coffee table. Her husband, Karl De Ritter, brought them a jug full of crushed ice cubes, chopped mint, rum and slices of lime. She sat on the sofa and, addressing nobody in particular, commented:

"Children's stories are really violent, aren't they? I wonder if I wouldn't be better off just telling them what we get up to?"

Sam, who was probably about as fragile as the two children, said sarcastically:

"That's right, you should wake them up and tell them about the guy with the holes drilled in his knees. Then they could smoke a fag and knock back a mojito with us. O.K. with you, Karl?"

Accustomed by now to the harmless taunts of his wife's colleagues, Karl smiled and filled their glasses. Once he had overcome his natural mistrust, he had come to appreciate each of the members of Coste's team. Coste himself, the protector. Sam, the vulnerable one. Ronan the impetuous. They complemented one another, trusted each other. It had taken time, but now that he knew them better he felt reassured.

"Sorry to play the party-pooper, but we're on duty tonight, so only one glass . . . Alright, children?" Coste said.

"Are you joking, Victor?" Ronan objected. "You said it yourself: what can possibly happen to us in a fortnight? We've got all the time in the world. For a start, Karl could tell us how he and Johanna first met . . ."

On the defensive, Johanna flashed her husband a warning look.

"I forbid you to tell them, Karl! Ronan turns everything into a dirty joke, even the most beautiful love story."

Before her husband could defy her and tell everybody how one rainy evening she had changed his flat tyre in less than six minutes, Coste's mobile rang. They all recognised the ring tone. His work phone. A sound they had come to detest. They put their glasses down, awaiting the verdict.

"Capitaine Coste here."

"Good evening, Victor, this is Commandant Auclair from the Control Room. You have a new client in Malceny."

"Give me the details."

He jotted down the facts in a notebook. By the time he ended the call, Sam, Ronan and Johanna had already picked up their things, ready to go. Before leaving the house, they recovered their guns from the hall wardrobe and slipped them into the holsters on their waistbands. That was something Karl would never get used to. Why did certain people risk their lives to protect others, and above all, why did his wife? He loved her all the more for it, but worry gnawed at his stomach.

"Take care, Johanna."

She squeezed his backside.

"Keep the mojitos in the fridge. And you're the one who'll need to take care when I get back."

13

On the ninth floor of the tower block, Sam was happy to wait at the end of the corridor, outside the security cordon.

"You know the tape isn't for you, don't you? You're allowed through it," Johanna teased him.

"Is it disgusting in there?"

"No, it's bearable. You can come in."

The uniforms stood aside, and Sam entered the flat. Coste was kneeling beside the body of an elderly woman stretched out on the floor. Her eyes were still wide open, a painful grimace on her face. In the background, the police radios crackled with news of what was going on in the region.

"Sam, go and get the info from the first responders. Name of the caller, time and what they saw. Johanna, call forensics; until they arrive, we keep our hands to ourselves."

Ronan appeared on the threshold.

"I talked to the medic with the fire crew. Death from natural causes, probably a heart attack. She's called Rose. Rose Carpentier, born 1945. Natural deaths are for the local station, aren't they?"

"Yes, usually. If it wasn't for one particular detail," Coste said.

Ronan took a closer look around.

"Yeah, well, it's true that's not so common."

Scattered on Rose Carpentier's body and all around her were dozens of crumpled twenty-euro notes. Sam meanwhile had got the information requested of him and conveyed it to his colleagues, carefully avoiding looking at the floor.

"She was found like this by her Pakistani neighbour. Given how nervous he was, I'm willing to bet he has no papers, and we won't get much more out of him. He called the emergency services at 9 p.m."

Coste raised his eyebrows, and so did the others.

"He discovered her like this . . . You mean the front door was wide open? And the money's still here?"

This second detail threw a spanner in the works. They were interrupted by one of the uniformed officers.

"My colleague has warned me that a magistrate is coming up in the lift. Fleur Saint-Croix. Do you know her?"

Ronan blew out his cheeks.

"Shit, it's the same ball-breaker as this morning. Doesn't she have a life, for God's sake?"

When the lift doors opened at the end of the corridor, a young blonde with a page-boy haircut and a leather briefcase under her arm made a stunning entrance. First because she was undeniably pretty, and second because her small pumps, her slightly too short skirt and her tight-fitting blouse clashed with her surroundings. Sam voiced what the others didn't dare say.

"Don't you think the magistrate looks a bit tarty?"

Ever the expert, Ronan corrected him.

"I'd say she was pretty sexy, but you're right, she isn't exactly dressed for the occasion."

His voice trailed off as she approached them. She studied them one by one, before instinctively addressing the man standing behind the others. Broad shoulders, three days' stubble and a piercing gaze, he wasn't particularly big or tough-looking, and yet without her being able to explain why, it seemed obvious he was in charge.

"Capitaine Coste? Fleur Saint-Croix. You've wasted no time."

"Good evening, madame. The same goes for you."

"An elderly individual found dead on a mattress of money seemed to me interesting enough to merit a visit. Which of you is Lieutenant Scaglia?"

Ronan stepped forward.

"I thought I had asked you for a report by this afternoon on the lock-up at the Cité des Poètes. Did you forget, or do you enjoy confrontational relationships?"

"My apologies, madame, but I'm no longer the person you need to speak to about that. The investigation has been transferred to Groupe Crime 2 under Capitaine Jevric. She's the one who should have sent you the report."

This reply appeared to satisfy Fleur Saint-Croix, and she resumed her conversation with Coste.

"Capitaine, what are your initial impressions?"

"Well, I'd say . . . Graduated from magistrates' college less than a year ago. High opinion of herself. Father no doubt a policeman. A desire to go one better than him by becoming a magistrate. Not yet familiar with the protocol which states that if you have something to say to a member of my team, you need to go through me first."

Not only did Fleur Saint-Croix take this without a murmur, but her unexpected smile defused any hostility in the atmosphere.

"And the investigation, capitaine? What are your first impressions about that?"

Coste considered his barb had struck home and closed the parenthesis.

"As you can see. A little old lady covered in banknotes. What's surprising is that her neighbour found her with the front door wide open. All that money up for grabs and yet nobody touches it, as though it were poisoned . . . It's as if everybody knew you didn't mess with Rose Carpentier."

Ronan raised the police tape, and Fleur Saint-Croix stepped into the room. She glanced down at the corpse without any obvious emotion, then stood to one side to avoid getting in the way. Coste pursued his train of thought out loud.

"We're losing focus. Let's set aside the fact that she was a pensioner, apparently with no police record. When we come across someone with five hundred euros in crumpled twenty-euro notes, what's our first thought?"

"We think of a small-time dealer," Ronan said. "But I have serious doubts that at her age, Rose . . ."

He stopped, finally understanding what Coste was implying.

"Shit, it's not her savings, it's her wages! And the dealer is her employer. Rose is a minder."

"And if it weren't for her heart attack, we would never have got wind of it. A lucky break. For us rather than for her, I mean," Sam said.

Silent until now, Johanna joined in.

"If – as Groupe Stups seems to think – there's been a putsch against the gang leaders in Malceny, maybe the new bosses came to say hello. They take the opportunity to show they're serious about it. The old woman flips, her heart can't take it, and she has a heart attack in a shower of cash. Capitaine Sylvan is looking for sophisticated safe houses for the drugs, but they're in the safekeeping of an old granny above all suspicion. Almost undetectable."

Sam, who as the whole team knew had his little vices, took the risk of sharing his experience.

"O.K., as far as coke or heroin goes, but if there had been a large amount of cannabis in here, I would have . . . well, I mean there should have been at least some sort of smell."

"Not necessarily."

"So there's only one solution."

"The Dog Unit."

14

Sitting on a mattress on the floor of his room, Bibz was finishing a takeaway kebab. For a long time now, he'd been accustomed to his mother not cooking for him. The one brother of his not in jail only came by occasionally for a change of clothes or to hide from the police, and they rarely bumped into one another. The usual decor: a poster from the film "Mesrine"; another with Tony Montana, guns at the ready; a third with Brando in "The Godfather". Given the grisly end of each of his heroes, nobody could have accused Habibou of being overly optimistic. He had chosen a certain way of life, and he knew how likely it was to end badly. His mobile rang, and he wiped his mouth on his sleeve. It was a short conversation that immediately led to another one.

"Boss, Bibz here."

"I'm listening, Habibou."

"The cops are swarming round the old woman's place."

"No, they can't know what's going on. Unless that is . . . how did your interview with her go?"

"Don't worry. Well, at first she freaked. I think she was more scared of Souki's gang than of us, so we had to explain we were the new bosses, but she was alright when we left. She was trembling, but it was O.K."

The man on the other end took his time to think things over.

"For now, nobody moves. Make a few calls, get people together, but we don't try anything so long as the cops don't react. They could be there for loads of reasons."

15

Emy arrived, more than a little overexcited. She was pulling so hard on her leash that her breath rasped in her throat. Her handler was struggling to control her.

"You're going to be the death of her! She was already beside herself down in the lobby. Is this place built of hash or what?"

Like the witch's house in Hansel and Gretel would have been if an addict had built it, thought Johanna with a grin.

The trained Belgian Malinois burst into the apartment, yelping with frustration, almost snapping her lead, skidding on the lino and sticking her snout everywhere. She paused for a moment in the kitchen, then barked out loud. From behind the fake backboard of the cupboard under the sink, Sam pulled out six plastic packets filled with white powder. Emy was rewarded, and directed towards the other rooms. In the bedroom, the side of the mattress had been cut open, so a hand could be pushed in. Sam took out six brown oily slabs. More rewards. In the bathroom, the wooden side to the bathtub was removed, revealing another four identical packets. Further in, they found a linen bag containing a tight wad of banknotes. This time, only high denominations.

Fleur Saint-Croix, Coste and his team stood around the living-room table, where the packets had been stacked, lost in thought. Though Johanna anticipated the answer, she asked the question anyway.

"This is obviously another case for Groupe Stups. Are you going to pass it on to Sylvan and Jevric?"

"No way. They can have the gear, but Rose is ours."

Sam, meanwhile, was looking puzzled. He still couldn't understand how such a large amount of cannabis had evaded his sense of smell.

"There's at least twelve kilos of uncut shit here! We should have smelled it from the corridor!" he burst out.

Picking up one of the packets, the dog handler said:

"These are smell-proof bags. Two zips, reinforced plastic, completely watertight. No chance of detecting them if you don't have a nose like Emy's."

Saint-Croix stepped carefully around the still very excited dog and approached Ronan.

"How much do you think all this adds up to?"

"If those are 250-gram packets, and those others are a kilo, I'd say at a rough guess . . . Two hundred thousand euros at street prices. Then there's the wad of notes."

"That's a lot."

Far too much, Coste thought.

He glanced out of the bedroom window. Their unmarked car. Two vehicles with the police emblem on their sides, one of them guaranteed to stir up the estate with its whirling blue light. Added to those, the Dog Unit van and the firefighters' truck – they were waiting for the forensic team to arrive so they could remove the body. Coste, who had come expecting a murder, hadn't thought to be discreet, and was regretting it now. News of their presence must already have spread, and when two hundred thousand euros are involved, news like that travels very fast indeed. Thanks to the light from the few surviving street lamps, he could make out groups of silhouettes gathering nine floors down, still well away from the tower block. This is going to get out of hand, he told himself. He looked across at Ronan, who had also come to the window and had reached the same conclusion. They conferred in low voices.

"This is going to turn nasty, Victor. They'll never let us get out of here. Not with the stash."

"I know. This block has become a coffin. I'll radio the Control Room for reinforcements. Go and brief the magistrate."

Ronan asked the young magistrate to go with him into the bedroom and sit on the bed. He crouched down in front of her, but, already anxious, hands clasped round her knees, she didn't give him time to begin.

"You weren't expecting to find so much – is that it?"

"Yes, madame. It's not good news. If we'd known, we'd have taken precautions. But we'll get out of here, as we always do. Capitaine Coste is in touch with Control. A Rapid Response team will soon be here as backup. You know who they are: the giants in body armour you see in all the news reports. They look as if they're indestructible. Everything will be alright, and tomorrow you'll have a nice story to tell."

In the living room, Coste ended his call and brought everyone together to reassure them.

'I've just spoken to Commandant Auclair. I've cancelled the forensic team for security reasons. The Rapid Response team should be here within three minutes to help with our evacuation. Sam, take photos of the flat and the crime scene, so that we at least have some record of the layout. Then find me a suitcase to put all these packets in. Johanna, when the time comes, make sure you shield Sam on the way to the car. Ronan, stay as close as you can to the magistrate. Dog handler, you stay with the uniformed men."

"What about Rose?" Sam asked. "We can't just leave her here."

"I'll take care of Rose."

As he spoke, a black shadow flashed past the living-room window. A sixty-kilo manhole cover dropped from above plunged down and smashed into the roof of one of the police vehicles. The one with the flashing light, which it crushed before it punched through the roof and almost cut the car in two. The sound of crunching metal could be heard even nine floors up.

"It's kicking off . . ."

A hundred metres away, their sirens howling, two black vans hurtled into the estate. One of them headed up the forecourt; the other sped on to what was left of the children's play area. The driver of the first van performed a handbrake turn, bringing it to a halt directly in front of the tower block entrance. The other one parked several metres ahead of it. The side doors burst open. The first squad of five men wearing helmets and exoskeletons* ran into the lobby, shields raised. The second group encircled the other vehicles and prepared to repel any attacks. They were confronted by a shapeless mass of unidentifiable silhouettes. Amid whistles and shouted insults, a hail of stones and then a pétanque ball crashed into one of the shields, followed by twenty or more other projectiles of various sizes. Two of the officers got out their Flash-Balls, the other three their tear-gas launchers.

On the tower block staircase, a race against the clock began. Coste was carrying Rose as if she were his bride, followed by Johanna, Sam and the suitcase. Ahead of them, Fleur de Saint-Croix was clinging to Ronan's arm. Emy had stopped barking,

* Reinforced plastic armour used in riot situations. It protects ankles, tibias, knees, genitals, arms, elbows, shoulders. Weight: 7 kilos.

perhaps more aware than any of them how dangerous the situation was. They emerged into the lobby, where the Rapid Response team was waiting for them. When he saw Coste, their commanding officer looked worried.

"Is there a casualty?"

"She was already dead. We're the ones you have to get out of here alive."

Outside, the landscape had been transformed in less than thirty seconds. The police in body armour were confronted by clusters of hooded youths waving their arms wildly to attract the police's attention, but also to show they weren't armed. Paving the way for those hidden behind them to launch their attacks. A scaffolding clamp the size of a fist flew through the air and splintered a policeman's visor. He fell to the ground, and was immediately helped up by his partner. Behind them, a moped came speeding towards them. The passenger threw a flaming bottle under the police car already damaged by the manhole cover. The car caught fire with the sound of exploding glass.

Inside the lobby a few metres from these skirmishes, the Rapid Response commander opted for a more robust exit than he had at first thought necessary. He yelled his orders:

"Forget reading the riot act! Fire two rounds of sting-ball grenades before we go out! And then three stun grenades once we're outside! We escort them to the vehicles, jump in, and get the hell out of here!"

Shields were raised, the glass entrance door was opened, and the grenades were launched over the heads of the police cordon. After two seconds they exploded, fragmenting into thousands of tiny plastic projectiles that struck the angry mob knee-high, momentarily dispersing them.

When Ronan checked to see if the magistrate was ready to run for her life, he found only a terrified little girl sitting on the ground, staring blankly, arms wrapped round her knees. He took her by the shoulders and shook her roughly. To no avail.

Taking advantage of the first salvo, the evacuation process began. A first stun grenade was launched. The violent bang assaulted eardrums on both sides of the front line; the blinding white light seared their retinas. Taking advantage of the confusion, Sam and Johanna were able to reach their car without a problem. The uniforms and Emy, tail between her legs, ears flattened, were also escorted to safety. Two tear gas grenades were fired into the crowd together with a second stun grenade. Protected by a shield, Coste carried the old woman's body to the waiting fire truck, its back doors wide open. He climbed in and laid Rose on the stretcher inside, then turned to leave. One of the firemen shouted at him:

"Stay here! We'll take you with us!"

Deaf to the suggestion, Coste jumped down, grabbed a shield from the Rapid Response van and sprinted back towards the tower block. The only member of his team left in the lobby was Ronan: the young magistrate's temporary paralysis meant he had missed the mass exit.

Ronan shook her again, even more violently, and she finally came out of her funk.

"Listen to me!"

Grasping her by the back of the neck, he forced her to look him in the eye.

"Look at me! We're getting out of here, O.K.? It's chaos outside, so only listen to my voice, and don't pay any attention to what's going on around you. Shut your eyes and let yourself be led. Tell me you've understood, for God's sake!"

"I understand."

At that moment she would have followed him anywhere. Seconds later, Coste appeared with the shield.

"Would you like a coffee, or are we getting out of here?"

Ronan put his arm round the magistrate and seized her firmly by the waist. Coste raised the shield, kicked the door open, and they ran faster than they had ever run in their lives. At first, Fleur Saint-Croix was choked by the tear gas burning her throat, nostrils and eyes. A stun grenade launched as a diversion made her jump, and at the same moment she felt the heat from the burning police car. She was bundled into a vehicle, heard the doors slam, the tyres squeal, the shouts die away in the distance. When a few seconds later she risked opening her eyes there was no more estate, no more explosions. Only their ragged breathing, a city at night, and an eerie silence.

"Everybody in one piece?" Coste said.

"Shit, that got hot."

"Scorching hot, I'd say."

In the back seat, Fleur was still clutching Ronan's arm. After a few kilometres, Coste calmed things down by reverting to routine.

"We're going back to headquarters. Johanna, you put the drugs in the safe. Sam, call the Rapid Response people, the Dog Unit, the firefighters and the local Malceny police. I want to make sure nobody was injured. Then we'll have a drink. One or fifteen."

He looked in the rear-view mirror.

"Ronan, can you take the little one home?"

"I'll see to it."

16

Rue Mademoiselle in the fifteenth arrondissement. After a silent journey from the outskirts back to the capital, Ronan parked outside a nineteenth century Haussmann apartment building and switched off the engine.

"Are you going to be alright, madame?"

"No, not at all."

Though the car was stationary, she didn't budge.

"Why so formal all of a sudden, lieutenant?" she asked, with the hint of a smile.

"I'm sorry, in certain situations I forget to be polite."

Fleur Saint-Croix turned towards him.

"It seems to me you saved my life. That's bound to change our relationship."

"You're exaggerating. I got you out of a spot of bother, that's all. If they'd really wanted to do us harm, they'd have chosen other weapons – not just a scaffolding clamp and a Molotov cocktail. Dealers know nothing good comes of attracting our attention. It was a bunch of kids trying to intimidate us."

"Who exactly are 'kids' in your eyes?"

"I dunno, youngsters between ten and twenty-five."

She turned away from him and folded her arms.

"I'm twenty-five."

Ronan wrinkled his nose and muttered "shit" under his breath. He tried to rescue the situation.

"Well, in any case, you were very brave."

"Yes, flat out and trembling, I was a real warrior! My heart is still racing. I'm afraid I won't be able to close my eyes tonight."

Silence. Long enough for a decision to be made.

"Would you like me to come up with you?"

If he hadn't suggested it, she would have.

"Now that really will change our relationship."

Fortunately for their privacy there were no cameras in the entrance to her building. Nor in the lift or the corridors.

PART TWO

THE QUEEN

17

For ten years now, the Malceny Boxing Club had occupied a former goods depot on the outskirts of town. In the deserted changing rooms, Markus was waiting patiently between two rows of lockers. The sounds of the ceremony reached him only faintly. Seated on a bench, fists clenched, Markus was no longer there. He was already in the ring.

In the main hall, chairs had been arranged in a circle around the ring. The first guests were taking their places, amid an atmosphere of palpable excitement. A long banner hanging from the roof beams proclaimed the club's initials in gold letters: M.B.C. Red and white posters on the walls proudly announced the afternoon's event:

JUNE 29 AT 2 P.M.
LAUNCH OF THE EDUCATIONAL
BOXING PROJECT
In the presence of the Mayor of Malceny
Exhibition Bout – Sparring Match
MARKUS vs. G.H. GORDAH

Born in Benin twenty-one years earlier, Markus was a giant, weighing ninety-nine kilos and 195 c.m. tall. Gokay Hasib Gordah, ninety-seven kilos and 185 c.m. tall, was a

26-year-old Turk. Both were experienced. And both were motivated by the same ambition: to punch their way out of this dump of a town.

Seated in the front row, Monsieur Bastide, the club president, wearing a M.B.C. jogging outfit that couldn't have been used since its owner passed the hundred-kilo mark, leaned over to the mayor.

"Educational boxing is usually reserved for kids between eight and thirteen. It's a discipline that teaches respect for the rules. Just shadow boxing, no real punches. Technique, nothing more than technique."

"Your athletes look a bit older than thirteen to me," the mayor said ironically.

"Markus and Gordah? They're the club's two great hopes. They're not used to exhibition bouts, but they'll put on a show for us today. It'll get the enrolments going."

Not only did she feel she was wasting her time here, Andrea Vesperini, the mayor, had no real desire to sit through a pointless session of pat-a-cake between two hulking brutes. Summoned by the town hall, the photographer from the local rag, *Bonjour Malceny*, was busy immortalising a personal appearance designed to make Vesperini seem more approachable. Wearing a silk tabard, but over a pair of jeans to show she was in touch with ordinary folk, she had submitted to the round of handshakes, closely watched by Maud, her press officer.

The club president itemised the work carried out thanks to a grant from the town hall. His saccharine tone belied the months of negotiations it had taken to get this far. An exhausting arm wrestle that had resulted in the refurbishment of the municipal swimming pool being cancelled in favour of the boxing club. Six months before elections, this Educational

Boxing Project had exhausted the Sport and Community Action budget.

The referee was in the ring, microphone in hand. Gordah was dancing on the spot, launching a rapid succession of jabs in the air. The hall was full; any latecomers would have to stand. Then the changing-room door opened, and Markus strode out. He slipped between the ropes without looking at the crowd. He was so focused that the sounds and images around him were blurred. His universe was now confined to these thirty-six square metres.

The club president repeated yet again:

"Madame le maire, it's an honour to have you here."

She didn't believe it for a second, but smiled all the same.

"Monsieur Bastide, I've fought hard for your club, so there was no way I was going to miss the grand opening."

She turned towards the person sitting on her right. A man in his forties, with black hair, a pock-marked face and a serious demeanour.

"I'm sure you know Monsieur Salah, my deputy in charge of community services. He's been following your project with great interest."

Bastide's tone was even more syrupy.

"My dear Monsieur Salah, and you also, of course, madame le maire: I'm sure that many people here wish to thank you."

Vesperini looked around to make sure all her team were there. Maud, sticking to her like chewing gum, her town hall secretary, and her chief of staff. She fixed her attention on Maud.

"You look tremendous with your hair down. They only have eyes for you!"

Her press officer gave the ghost of a smile at this barbed compliment. In the ring, the referee was imparting his final instructions.

"Gentlemen, this is an exhibition match. You know the rules. Shake hands, and when the bell goes, come out fighting."

The two bodies in the ring soon settled into a combat rhythm to the sound of imaginary music. Gordah began to dance rapidly round his opponent. Markus watched him, simply shifting his stance in response. Then the punches began. The Turk threw a jab-jab-counter combination. Straight left, straight left, then straight right, followed by a hook that bounced off his adversary's extended arm. From the first punch, Markus had realised what the pattern would be, and soaked up the blows. An exhibition bout, he'd been told.

Maud's mobile began to vibrate. Glancing at the message, she opened the attachment and found, hours before it was due to come out, the front page of *Le Parisien*: "Wild West in Malceny – Bloody Settlings of Accounts". She showed her phone to the mayor seated in the row in front of her.

The mayor sighed. "Oh shit, we've hit the headlines again."

In the ring, Markus threw a straight right, then kept Gordah at bay with two long-distance jabs. If he had followed through with the punches, he would have done damage, but his fists stopped just short, like a dog on a leash snarling a few inches from your nose.

Clutching the mobile, Vesperini was no longer following the bout. Her eyes went from the screen to her press officer, then the two of them exchanged concerned whispers. Three murders already. At the height of summer, with no other news to occupy them, the media were bound to go to town on it. Just before her re-election campaign? No way.

End of the first round. At the bell, the president got up and went to talk to the referee. Since the guest of honour seemed more interested in her mobile than in the fight, Bastide decided on a change to the rules. He and the referee exchanged a few words. At the start of the next round, the two boxers received fresh whispered instructions.

"Gentlemen, forget the exhibition. Make your punches count. Wake the audience up for me."

The bell rang. Gordah renewed his little dance and tried the same combination again: jab-jab-counter. Markus saw the punches coming and easily dodged them. Then he feinted to the left and threw a hook that smashed into the Turk's head. Gordah bounced against the ropes, which buckled under his weight, and almost fell into Vesperini's lap. She looked up and peered into the boxer's blank gaze. Maud leaned forward to continue their conversation, but Vesperini waved for her to be silent. The fight was becoming interesting. Bastide regained his smile.

Gordah came round and lowered his guard in defiance, to show it would take more than that to subdue him. And more than that duly arrived.

There are several combination punches in boxing; each of them has its own distinct rhythm. The quick-quick-hard, the feint-hard-hard, the hard-quick-hard. Markus chose the simplest and most destructive: hard-hard-hard.

Facing the now fully conscious Turk, Markus avoided a first straight left, then a second, as quickly as if he were being fast-forwarded. As the second blow ended in mid-air, he covered up behind his guard and unleashed two hooks to his opponent's head, blinding him. He crouched down, twisting his body, then straightened up. Concealed by his torso, his right fist only became visible at the last moment, as it crashed into Gordah's jaw. The uppercut was so vicious the Turk's two feet left the floor, and his head jerked back. He spat out a stream of spittle and blood. Seemingly weightless for a moment, his body hit the canvas with a dull thud. The crowd held its breath. Markus moved to the centre of the ring. Without waiting for the count, he raised his two arms high in the air in victory. The whole audience rose to its feet. After a few seconds' stunned silence, shouts and applause filled the room.

While the hubbub continued, Vesperini stared at Markus. He had demolished his opponent with incredible violence, and she had enjoyed it. She could feel an excited warmth in the pit of her stomach.

"He's the one I want."

18

Once in the back seat of her official saloon, Vesperini was finally able to let her smile drop. This was one of the few places where she could relax, protected by the tinted windows. Exasperated, she shouted at the driver:

"What the fuck is Salah up to?"

Naturally, the driver made no reply.

Inside the boxing club, her deputy, Azzedine Salah, was finishing a conversation with Bastide, while Maud was carefully deleting all the unflattering photographs from the journalist's camera. Her work as a censor done, she hurried towards the line of official cars, making sure on the way that she tied her hair back in order to avoid another "compliment". As she got in, she warned the other two passengers:

"Just so you know, we've been crucified by the press again. The Queen is really not amused."

"Thank God we're not in the same car," Vesperini's chief of staff, Baptiste Cardel, said. "Poor Azzedine is going to get it in the neck."

Azzedine Salah had in fact just climbed into the leading vehicle, alongside Vesperini. When he saw her stern face, he was glad he had some good news.

"Don't worry, I managed to persuade Bastide to lend us

Markus. With the shit storm that's about to hit us, we're going to need him."

Vesperini corrected him.

"That shit storm is going to hit me, Azzedine, not you. Only me. Weren't you supposed to keep them under control, those little runts? Tell me why they've been on all the front pages for the past week?"

"We have to see how hot the atmosphere is on the estates. I'll go and find out. I know those 'little runts', as you call them, very well."

Vesperini raised her voice indignantly.

"That's why I recruited you, isn't it? But enough is enough: social housing for their parents, home help for their grand-parents, town hall jobs for their brothers and sisters, jobs they don't even have to turn up for. And that's not all! Throw in the cars, the endless petrol coupons . . . It costs me at least fifty thousand euros a month to keep them under control. And now they start shooting one another. Is that how they thank me?"

"Well, it's not such bad news after all. This way there's less to pay out."

The mayor looked at her colleague with a mixture of pity and scorn.

"What do you know about tarantulas, Azzedine?"

Her deputy said nothing. He knew it was a rhetorical question.

"The tarantula is a sedentary spider. It hides in a corner of your house and doesn't move. If you disturb it, it'll come back. Except that this time you won't know where. That's when it becomes dangerous. I didn't train those three spiders just for them to be trodden on. Where will the next three be hiding?"

Since he had no idea, Salah waited for the storm to pass.

After a glance down at his watch and at the print copy of the day's agenda, he leaned forward towards the driver.

"Can you make Malceny-Bobigny in ten minutes?"

The man behind the wheel didn't even bother to turn round.

"No sweat."

Vesperini's friendly smile was back.

"You know I couldn't manage without you, don't you?"

"You often tell me so, madame."

"Good. So what's next on the agenda?"

"The photo op at Police Judiciaire headquarters."

19

Ronan arrived a good two hours late. In the corridor he ran into two members of the Section Financière; as he passed, they held their noses and rubbed their eyes. When he reached the Police Judiciaire office, he scarcely had time to sit down in his chair before Sam turned the fan in his direction.

"You're wearing the same clothes as yesterday."

"See how you're obsessed with me?"

"No way . . . you still reek of tear gas. So I'm guessing you didn't sleep at your place?"

Ronan tipped his chair back and closed his eyes.

"She has an apartment you can walk around in. I mean, she has corridors . . . I've never had a place with a corridor. Mine has an entrance hall, living room, kitchen, bedroom, all in one."

Sam raised his snout from his computer.

"You're from different worlds. She must find you exotic."

"That doesn't sound like a compliment."

"It isn't."

At that same moment, Coste and Johanna were briefing Capitaine Sylvan's team in the Groupe Stups offices. Five men and one woman who looked like junkies and dressed as though they slept rough, they fitted in well with the decor. Pinned to the right-hand wall, a poster illustrating the different ecstasy tablets and L.S.D. blotters available on the market. In one corner, a glass case stuffed with sealed packages of samples of all known drugs. Grass, coke, crack, heroin, ketamine, opium, different pills that had a variety of effects, G.H.B., magic mushrooms. Behind Sylvan's desk, there was a Jamaican flag below the French one, and photographs of their biggest hauls. His favourite? The one on the tarmac of a runway at Roissy, showing him standing beside a pallet loaded with three hundred and fifty kilos of pure cocaine. On the back wall, a covered-up briefing board. Following several unfortunate or deliberate leaks, Groupe Stups no longer trusted anyone, so all their investigations remained secret.

"It's weird," Sylvan said. "We're investigating murders, and you, Victor, make a big drugs bust. Do you think we're sitting in the wrong seats? We're working together, after all."

One of Sylvan's men put two cups of coffee in front of their guests. When he offered sugar, his clear, level voice was in sharp contrast to his old bag lady appearance.

"Don't get carried away. I'm only dealing with Rose," Coste told the Groupe Stups chief.

"Who?"

"Rose, the little old lady we found surrounded by drugs."

"Ah yes, your famous mantra. No victim, no motivation."

Johanna joined in:

"Well, anyway, you've got at least one other stash to uncover. Dealers don't put all their shit in one basket."

"That's right. We'll send someone later this afternoon to the estates in Malceny. If there's gear on offer, that means they're still getting it from somewhere."

Sylvan turned to the only woman on his team, a youngster with long hair under a black baseball cap.

"Chloe, can you play the hooker desperate for her fix?"
"Oh no, not this evening. My parents are coming round."

* * *

The meeting room had been cleared for the occasion. With the chairs stacked elsewhere, all that remained was the main table on which the packets of cocaine and cannabis resin had been laid out next to the twenty-five thousand euros. Prominent on the back wall, a huge framed poster showing the Police Judiciaire's logo: a view of 36, Quai des Orfèvres cut out in the shape of the Seine-Saint-Denis département. Not a thing of beauty, to be honest.

And to be even more honest, this wasn't the drugs haul of the century, nor even of the year, but the mayor of Malceny had let it be known she would be passing by the Police Judiciaire's offices to thank them. Commissaire Stévenin, who knew a good piece of publicity for his service when he saw one, had put himself in charge of the event. Vesperini had a similar talent, but as her car was being parked in its reserved space, guarded by two police officers, she was concerned by how few people were waiting for her. This wasn't going to make much of a splash in the media. Salah tried to reassure her.

"I've got hold of *Le Parisien.* They've promised me a photo plus caption. We'll probably get regional T.V. as well."

"There's always regional T.V."

A few moments later, in front of two microphones and a T.V. camera, Vesperini chose the appropriate tone of voice from her varied repertoire. Determined and uncompromising. With a hint of vibrato.

"In other towns, I hear of other mayors suggesting the army step in. In other towns, I hear of other mayors suggesting legalisation. But what I mostly hear are people trying to avoid their responsibilities. Army officers do not run towns. It's not by tolerating today what was illegal yesterday that we will solve the problem of our rundown estates and our alienated young people. That comes down to daily efforts by the state, the municipal authorities, the police and the justice system. Efforts which have already borne impressive fruit."

Her press officer quickly put a stop to a stream of awkward questions. The journalists were interested less in the drugs haul than in the murders. That was why they were there. Only Maud and the town hall's official photographer had accompanied Vesperini in the lift up to the press conference.

"Who's responsible for this speech?"

Fearing another outburst, Maud had hesitated.

"I wrote it this morning. It was passed by your chief of staff."

"It's perfect."

Before the lift doors opened, the Queen added:

"You know I couldn't do without you, don't you, Maud?"

20

"Would you like a dog to replace him?"

Monsieur Jacques did not even raise his head. Slumped in his chair, he was waiting for them to leave.

He had gone with his black eye to the Malceny Old People's Centre, as he did every Saturday, hoping to see Rose there. He had waited. Refused to join a first round of bridge. Then a second, before leaving without any explanation. He'd never liked card games anyway.

"I've got a neighbour who has a litter of rottweilers in his garage. I can get one from him if you like. They defend you better than a cat."

After leaving the centre, Monsieur Jacques had gone home. For the fiftieth time he had dialled the number of his friend – his only real one – and Rose's phone had rung and rung in an empty flat. He had sat motionless at his living-room table, and if he'd been able to pass away there and then, it would have been a relief. Then the doorbell had rung. Those bastards who had roasted Monsieur Chat. And now this improbable discussion.

"Besides, rottweilers are affectionate. Well, do you want one or not?"

When Jacques politely refused, the youngster opposite him stubbed out his joint on the oilskin tablecloth.

"Alright, go screw yourself then. I was just trying to be friendly."

In the kitchen, Colin was ransacking the already empty fridge. Bibz came out of the old man's bedroom, carrying a heavy backpack filled with the gear to be sold that day.

"Hey, pops, shouldn't you have something for me?"

Jacques rummaged in the bowl of odds and ends that stood in front of him. In among the coins, used batteries and stray buttons, he found the spare keys to his flat. Bibz took them from him and turned to his colleagues.

"Alright. I've got the keys and the stuff. We're outta here."

The front door slammed. Jacques was alone again, in a flat that was silent save for the sound of his own breathing. A flat which three children who had lost all their innocence could now access at any time of the day or night.

* * *

Bibz laid the backpack at the Boss's feet and took his place alongside him. In all, around thirty people had been summoned. The meeting was taking place on the ground floor of a tower block. A community centre with bare walls and a worn carpet, and a sign on the door that read F.M.H.: Friends of Malceny-Haiti. Nobody there could have been more than twenty years old, apart from the Boss. He began to speak.

"Some of you worked with Souki, others with Dimov or Laouari. You're bound to have noticed you've been twiddling your thumbs for the past week. Now I'm offering you the chance to work for me. You're not obliged to, and there won't be any reprisals. If anybody wishes to leave, they should do so now."

Nobody moved. The concept of loyalty was not especially relevant to their line of work.

"Perfect. So, a shift lasts from ten in the morning to ten at night. Basic rate of a hundred euros a day for the lookout, two hundred for the runner, and two hundred and fifty for the dealer. If you sell more, you'll earn more. No cheating the clients, no violence. Zero tolerance on that point. We have merchandise to sell, and that merchandise is available in many other places, so we look after our clients and we win their loyalty. And no cutting the drugs. We supply top quality product, and we want that to be known. Accounts to be settled every weekend. This centre will be our 'hub', and all our meetings will be held here. Bibz will give you the amounts you need every day. To find out your turf, see Colin."

Still wearing clothes three sizes too big for him, Colin nodded energetically so that everyone could identify him, sending his unruly hair flying.

"Before you leave, Driss here will give you each a mobile. They're clean – only to be used for work. They have two numbers stored for you to contact us if there are any problems. Don't add any others."

Among the baseball caps and hoodies in the audience, one of the youngsters raised his hand as if he were at school.

"What if we're arrested?"

"That'll be paid for. Two hundred euros for each twenty-four-hour period in custody, provided you don't grass on anyone. If you're charged, that'll be another two hundred, and if you're given a prison sentence we'll pay for a lawyer and consider compensation on a case-by-case basis."

A high-pitched voice rang out.

"Do the youngest have to be lookouts?"

"Yes, the under-thirteens don't risk going to jail, so they stay as lookouts. No change there. You create a diversion if the police come, and, if possible, you recover the bag with the gear."

Another hand shot up.

"Can we carry weapons?"

"Negative. No guns, no knives, no tear gas. You're selling merchandise, that's all. If you run into problems, you raise them here, but you don't settle anything on your own. I'm in charge of security. Any other questions?"

The Boss had outlined everything in a way they could all grasp: an introduction explaining the laws of competition, how to minimise risk, employee protection, salaries, financial compensation. And legal guarantees.

Once the merchandise had been distributed, the "traders" left the room. The Boss had a new mission, and dismissed Driss and Colin, leaving just him and Bibz.

"I need you this evening. You're going to pay a visit to an old friend. Learn his address by heart: 23, Avenue Victor Hugo."

"23, Avenue Victor Hugo. No problem. What kind of visit?"

"That'll depend on him. Go with your usual team. I'll add someone extra, to take care of security."

"Do I know him?"

"Everybody knows him. It's Markus."

"Yeah, well, that's security enough for me. What's the guy's name?"

"Salah. Azzedine Salah."

"Never heard of him."

"You're much too young. He belongs to the old school."

21

In the Police Judiciaire meeting room, Vesperini had posed alongside Commissaire Stévenin behind a table piled with drugs and money. As journalists aren't usually welcome in police stations, it was the town hall's official photographer who took the souvenir portrait. Before leaving, the mayor told the commissaire she wanted to meet the officers who had seized the drugs.

In his office, Coste was discussing with his team a case that seemed to be going nowhere. Sam's summary wasn't exactly encouraging.

"Rose Carpentier. Widow. Children and grandchildren scattered all over France, but none of them live locally. No record and no leads."

"Even if we find the guys who called on her, we can't say for sure they caused her heart attack," Ronan said. "We're heading for a brick wall, aren't we?"

Johanna thought the same.

"We'll have to wait until Sylvan and Jevric get their hands on the little bastards who are setting Malceny alight. And our guys will probably be among them."

Coste groaned. "So that's your solution? To wait for Groupe Stups to step in and sort it out for us?"

None of the others spoke up. His team were all of the same view, and he could not convince himself they were wrong. Besides, the weather was fine and hot. Really hot. They all had better things to do than stay shut up in their office. He accepted the inevitable.

"O.K., scram! Take the afternoon off; I don't want to see you again until tomorrow. I'll call if there's any news."

Sam immediately thought of online poker. Ronan was already starting to plan his evening with a very young magistrate.

"Thank you, papa," they chorused.

Johanna liked nothing better than to spend an afternoon with her children. She leaned over to Coste and kissed him on the cheek.

"You're a sweetheart, boss."

The office emptied in less than a minute. Coste wasn't bothered by being on his own. He picked up the landline and dialled a number. He had no need to say who was calling.

"What's it like there?"

"Pretty, calm. There's a river. The water's icy, but you can dip your toes in. There's a garden as well. All in all, I'm bored stiff, and it's doing me a lot of good. What about you? Are you on a case?"

"A little old lady nobody gives a damn about."

"Except for you, I suppose."

"Unfortunately, in this instance I have very little idea what to do."

"I leave you for three days and you've already created another phantom?"

On the other end of the line he could hear a bird singing and the sound of a church bell. It was as though she had sent him a telephone postcard.

"It sounds idyllic."

"What? You mean those birdies and the bell? By the end of the day they drive you nuts, but apparently it's like the traffic in Paris: after a while, you get used to it. By the way, speaking of Paris, my father's gone back there. Problems at his clinic. Nothing serious, but he's convinced he's the only one who can deal with them."

"And your mother?"

"She's patiently awaiting his return. I've seen it ever since I was old enough to understand. I even promised myself I'd never be that sort of woman. And yet I go back and forth every day to spend time with her. Did I tell you their house isn't far away?"

"Yes, I think you mentioned it."

"Apart from that . . . do you miss me?"

It took Coste several seconds to come up with the right answer.

"It's possible."

It took Léa less time to come up with her reply.

"Prick."

As Coste was leaving his office, he bumped into a young woman with her hair tied back, wearing an immaculately tailored suit. She seemed to be lost.

"Can I help you?"

"Commissaire Stévenin told me I could find Capitaine Coste in the Groupe Crime 1 office. I'm Maud Jeansac, the mayor's press officer. She would like to congratulate him personally for the drugs haul in Malceny."

Public relations were not one of Coste's strong points. He put on his most innocent expression.

"You've just missed him, but I'll pass on the message."

22

As always, the queue was endless. Reporting an incident, a logbook entry, or simply looking for someone to talk to: the crush at the police station at Malceny only eased up at nightfall, and even then only marginally. The young woman on the front desk listened, gave information or directed the visitors as appropriate, hardly ever raising her head from her computer.

"Good afternoon, mademoiselle, I've come about . . ."

The policewoman rudely interrupted the man in a bored monotone.

"I.D. or residence permit, please."

A driving licence appeared under her nose and she recorded the surname, first name and time of arrival. Landernes, Jacques, 17.15.

"How can I help you?"

The old man began again.

"I can't get hold of a friend of mine. She doesn't answer her phone and she didn't turn up today to a meeting we'd arranged. I'm starting to worry."

"Listen, monsieur. We haven't had any vehicles free all morning. I'm sure she'll be in touch before too long. It's always the same. Come back in twenty-four hours if she hasn't shown up."

Then the young officer made the mistake of looking up and

saw a wizened old man in a suit that was too warm for the weather, smiling a faint sad smile that seemed adopted by force of habit so as not to disturb anyone and have them believe everything was fine. On the driving licence she was still holding, the young Jacques Landernes had long hair and a future full of promise. It seemed not much of it had been fulfilled. Forty years later he was standing in front of her, eyes moist with unshed tears.

"It's just that she's my friend . . ."

She regretted the brusque way she had received him, and almost immediately snapped out of her robotic state.

"Give me her name and address. I'll ask a patrol car to call round there."

Monsieur Jacques wrote them down in his sloping, cramped handwriting, and the woman took the piece of paper to the duty officer.

"We don't have any spare cars."

"I know, we never do. But do me a favour, would you? Slip it in between two calls, it'll only take five minutes. A little old lady on radio silence. No news of her for several days . . ."

The duty officer put down his coffee and took the piece of paper.

"Rose Carpentier? Hang on, that rings a bell."

He shuffled his chair over to his computer screen and tapped in her details.

"Well, that explains it. She died yesterday."

The young policewoman absorbed the news.

"Shit. So what should I tell him?"

"You tell him nothing. You confirm we're sending someone round and take down his details. I'll inform the Police Judiciaire."

23

Vesperini had devoted the rest of the afternoon to administrative business, and that was more than enough to put her in a bad mood. There were piles of documents on her desk awaiting her signature. Each of them concerned a project, a request, an event, expenditure, problems. On the conference table a few metres from where she was sitting, yet more files. On the dark wooden sideboard behind her, still more. She had no wish to deal with any of them.

Salah stuck his head round the door. He had three folders under his arm.

"You wanted to see me, madame?"

"Azzedine! Come in."

The room-temperature whisky made the ice cubes explode with the sound of splintering glass. Her deputy valued these private, intimate conversations, during which it seemed to him Vesperini allowed her mask to slip. After almost eight years of collaboration, bringing her towards the end of her second term as mayor, they knew far too much about one another for any conflict to arise.

Now they were sitting side by side in two armchairs.

"The elections are in less than a year, and I start my campaign in five months."

"Are you worried?"

"I'm worried about losing control of certain neighbourhoods. After all they've cost us! I've lost track of how much it's been."

"I've got their files from Delsart, your alchemist finance officer."

"After the kind of day I've had . . . Go on, I'm listening."

"Sayid Laouari. Social housing for him and his parents. A car. Holidays in Thailand for six. Three years in a row: he must have appreciated that. A job for his sister in the municipal library."

"I can't even remember what he looks like. Go on."

"Sasha Dimov. The usual expenditure on holidays and social housing, but he cost us a bit more because of his 'Friends of Malceny-Haiti' association. He would have been hard put to point out Haiti on a map, but it seemed like a good idea at the time. After the earthquake in 2010, Haiti was in the news, and nobody was going to question it. Twenty thousand euros a year for the past three years."

"Which we got from where, exactly?"

"From the budget for urban improvements for the disabled. Then again, nobody was going to argue or investigate."

"Why does his name ring a bell?"

"He's the smart one of the three. He stung you at the last elections. He managed to get more than six hundred proxy votes."

"Sasha Dimov! He waited until I was in the runoff vote and sold them to me for a fortune, just before the polling stations closed. We were well and truly had on that one. Smart indeed. Who else?"

"The last one is Karim Souki. All his little brothers work in the town's green spaces: at least, that's what it says on their employment contracts. Three of our municipal cars ended up with his cousins in Algeria. The slogan MALCENY: TOWN OF THE FUTURE on their sides must look great in the desert. Every year we send him and his family on winter sports holidays, and two of his grandparents are in care homes at our expense."

"It's not a town hall anymore, it's Santa's grotto!"

"Look on the bright side – you're going to be saving money."

This comment was poorly judged, and Vesperini looked at him condescendingly.

"Salah, do you really think I'm a philanthropist? If I pay out, it's because behind the scenes I get back more than I spend. I need them to keep the peace for me. I need them to get the votes of all those who can't even write their name or stuff a ballot paper in the box. I need them to help calm their friends when there's a riot brewing. I need them to discreetly sort out any misunderstandings with my opponents, and to sabotage their campaigns. I need them for so many things, I can't do without them. Absurd as it may seem, those thugs are part of my staff."

"There's nothing absurd about it . . . and anyway, it gives you the chance to quote Victor Hugo, and you love that."

"Sartre, Azzedine, it's Jean-Paul Sartre. 'My hands are plunged in shit and blood. Up to the elbows. So what? Do you really think one can govern innocently?'"

Vesperini glanced at her watch, and refreshed the two whiskies.

"I can't be late. It's my daughter's birthday this evening."

"She's twelve, isn't she?"

"Yes. Still a baby."

Whenever the subject of Estelle came up, she became vulnerable, almost tender. But never for very long. She soon recovered her composure.

"Has Maud given you tomorrow's schedule?"

Salah handed her a detailed agenda. She scanned it and wrinkled her nose.

"It's as I feared. Lunch with those little old folk in their care home."

Salah tried to reassure her. "It'll only take an hour of your time. Your chief of staff can take over after that. They're being driven in a coach for a chocolate tasting sixty kilometres from here."

"Poor Baptiste! But . . . isn't it a bit early for sweeteners like this? They'll have forgotten all about it in a few weeks."

"They're not all senile, so it's better to ramp things up gradually. We'll organise several similar trips. We need to get them used to the idea so they won't be surprised when we bus them to the polling station."

"And that'll win us fifty votes at most, when my three dealers brought me at least fifteen hundred!"

The message could not have been clearer, and Salah caught on at once.

"I'm waiting until nine this evening, when the sun starts to set and the estates wake up. Then I'll go and test the waters. As for you, you've got a little girl who must be getting impatient . . ."

He picked up the three folders and was about to leave the room when Vesperini said:

"Azzedine?"

"Madame . . ."

"Take care."

24

Standing in front of the full-length mirror in his bedroom, Azzedine took off his suit.

He had done well since leaving the neighbourhood.

During her first period as mayor, Vesperini had set great store by establishing a recruitment campaign for young people. The official literature included notions like "inclusion", "second chance", and "the fight against unemployment". Above all, it was a way of identifying those who could act as links between difficult neighbourhoods and the town hall.

Azzedine had therefore been one of the three hundred and fifty school-leavers without qualifications whose police records and contacts on the estates mattered more to her than their C.V.s. Most of them had been fired in less than two months, but Azzedine had hung on. Following a stint as an entertainment organiser to test his commitment and docility, he became "neighbourhood relations officer" before gaining full-time employment as youth services coordinator. Being part of Vesperini's team gave him status, but also kept him grateful. A good salary, with a hundred hours of fictitious overtime a month to sweeten the pot. When he found a partner, they were rewarded with social housing, and out of the blue she was found a job as a secretary in the town hall. Although she and

Azzedine had recently separated, he had insisted on her being kept on, and the mayor had agreed. In Vesperini's second term, he was elected a councillor and landed the position of deputy mayor responsible for community affairs, a job he'd held for almost four years now.

Yes, he had come a long way . . .

He hung up his suit, put on an old pair of jeans, trainers and a loose-fitting shirt. From the back of his wardrobe, hidden behind a pile of jerseys, he took a mace canister the size of a small fire extinguisher. A gift from the police. The municipal police – Vesperini's police. He hooked it onto his belt. Despite its size, it could be concealed by his shirt. He might have come from an estate, but he had embarked on a career that exposed him to charges of selling out. Returning to the neighbourhood might not be so simple. The estates were isolated, boasting of how different, how anti-authority they were, with their own codes of conduct and their own laws. The vast majority of their inhabitants no longer considered him one of their own. He was a *poucave,* an informer who'd gone over to the side of the rich. So a degree of caution was necessary.

He was looking out of the window watching the setting sun, when, just as he had decided it was the right moment to go in search of information, his doorbell rang. His daughter was with his ex-wife, and his ex-wife loathed him, so he wasn't expecting anybody. He quickly made sure that the mace canister was securely attached.

When he opened the door, it was as if he was confronted by a second, far more impressive one.

"Markus?"

Behind the boxer, Salah recognised two youths whose brothers he had once hung out with, years before.

"Colin? Driss? Shit, you've grown . . ."

He might not have noticed the little kid, who seemed almost too young to be out at this time of night, if the boy hadn't taken the initiative.

"Get in and shut up. This isn't a family reunion."

Bibz shoved him aside and strode into the apartment. Salah had taken part in several raids, so he knew the difference between a raid and a friendly visit. Unfortunately for him, the four individuals on his doorstep appeared to be set on the former. For one thing, they were wearing gloves, though it wasn't particularly cold. He tried to defuse the sudden tension.

"I was just going to see the community leaders on the estates. With everything that's going on, I'm concerned. I wanted to see if there was something I could do for you."

With the back of his hand, Bibz swept everything off the living-room table, then sat down on it, his feet up on a chair.

"That's good of you. As it happens, there *is* something you can do for us."

Salah knew he shouldn't come across as aggressive, but he also knew that to take things lying down wasn't a good idea either. He ignored the brat perched on his table and addressed the others, who were potentially more dangerous.

"Listen, lads, you look really pissed off, but I've no idea why. Markus, can you explain, please?"

The boxer remained in the corner of the room, saying nothing. Colin and Driss stared at the floor. Bibz had not moved: he was letting the anger seethe inside him.

"Hey . . . I'm talking to you, and you don't even look at me? I call that a lack of respect, you sonofabitch."

Salah couldn't get his head around it. This kid, no taller than a rubbish bin and weighing no more than forty kilos soaking wet, was the one in charge. He wasn't going to stoop so low as to be afraid of him. He ignored him a second time.

"Colin, Driss, my old lady looked after you when you were small. Shit, tell me what's going on!"

Bibz looked left and right, as though searching for something. He jumped down from the table, walked over to Azzedine, and squared up to him.

"Do you have a cat?"

"What? No, I don't have a cat."

The kid looked disappointed. He sighed.

"O.K. then, we'll have to do it the old-fashioned way. Markus, stick his head in the sink."

In the moment, Azzedine forgot about the mace at his waist. Markus dragged him into the kitchen. When they reached the sink, he took him by the shoulders and put his head under the tap.

"For fuck's sake, you guys! What's going on?"

Bibz turned the hot tap on full.

"Right, asshole, you've got twenty seconds before it starts to burn."

"O.K., O.K., what do you want?"

"Oh, so you can see me now, can you?"

The water in the tap went from cold to lukewarm. From there it quickly became boiling hot, and Salah began to shout, his face enveloped in a cloud of steam.

"Yes, I see you! Alright, I see you. I swear that . . ."

A thousand red-hot needles pricked his scalp, ears and cheeks as the water scalded his skin. His words ended in one long scream. He struggled; Markus had to hold him more tightly. Colin, who was probably the most sensitive of the three, tried to bring the torture session to an end.

"That's enough, isn't it? That should do it."

Bibz had judged it would take another ten seconds for him to be given the respect he felt he deserved, but before he could give the word, Azzedine pushed Markus aside with his hip, plunged his hand under his shirt, and sprayed all round him. The cloud of mace hit the three youngsters right in their faces. They staggered away from him, coughing and rubbing their eyes. Azzedine could still feel the burns on his own face and scalp, but this was no time to give in to the pain. He aimed the mace at Markus, but before he could spray it, the boxer's fist smashed into his nose.

A knockout blow.

When Salah came round, there was a moment of uncertainty. That moment when you tell yourself none of what had gone before had taken place. He was sitting on his sofa, with the mace canister at his feet. His four attackers stood facing him, still blurred. Given the pain he was feeling, he guessed his nose wasn't where it should be, and the blood on his shirt confirmed it. Reality caught up with him soon enough.

"Alright. You're a pretty brave guy," Bibz conceded.

The living-room windows had been flung open to let in some air. Driss had a handkerchief in his hand, and Colin was still coughing. Markus approached Salah and handed him a phone.

"Take it. There's a call for you."

Azzedine's right ear was still agony, but in spite of everything, he held the mobile to it. He didn't recognise the voice, but he listened no less carefully.

"Good evening, Monsieur Salah. I hope you're in good shape."

Azzedine had no difficulty working out the roles they all

played. The enforcers were in his apartment, and the man who gave the orders was on the other end of the line. And he was the victim. Not a role he would have chosen for himself.

"No. Your guys burned my face . . ."

"Perfect. That means I have your attention. If I'm to believe the newspapers, you lost three of your protégés this week. To tell you the truth, it wasn't news to me."

Salah was breathing heavily, more terrified than in pain.

"You've got it wrong. I'm nobody. Just the mayor's deputy. I don't have any power!"

"Don't sell yourself short. You're much more than that, Azzedine. You're the link between the two extremes of Malceny. Between those who work in the open, and those who remain hidden. You know how things work. And above all, you have Vesperini's ear."

Salah breathed a little more easily. If they saw him as a messenger, perhaps he had a chance to get out of this. His only option was to cooperate.

"And what should I say to her?"

"You already know what I want. We're going to be your new protégés."

"You want their territories?"

"Thanks to their recent deaths, I think the turf wars have already been settled."

"So do you want places where you can sell with no worries? I can provide them for you. Ones that won't be detected. In the town centre."

"The town centre? What would we do there? That's not where we feel at home. We're already outsiders less than a kilometre from our estates. You're mistaking our aims. A dealer is like a footballer: our careers are short, and we have to guarantee our futures. Do you really think we only want to spend our days sitting in the corner of some lobby selling our gear packet after packet, gram after gram? To end up either in prison or in a coffin? We want more than that, Monsieur Salah. We want everything. We sell drugs to control the neighbourhoods, and we control the neighbourhoods so that you can't do without us. That's the only way we can get your attention. The only way to survive. In reality, all this is your fault to some extent. If we didn't scare you, you'd just abandon us."

"Tell me what you want. I'll do what I can. I'll talk to Vesperini."

The answer was short, and Salah moved the mobile away from his ear to talk to the three intruders.

"Apparently you've got a list for me."

Driss fumbled in his pocket and took out a folded piece of paper. He handed it to the deputy mayor, who read it line by line, then brought the mobile back up to his ear. They weren't going to like his conclusion.

"It's impossible. What you're asking for is simply impossible. Not now. We're less than a year from the elections, and the coffers are empty. The housing, the cars, the permanent contracts and the rest are negotiable, but as for the two hundred thousand euros, even if you stick my face back in boiling water, it can't be done. We've already siphoned off funds from everywhere."

"And yet . . . you'll have to find a solution. After the last haul the cops seized, we can only keep going for another two weeks at most. We're going to have to make a trip to Spain for fresh supplies. And for that we need cash. Lots of cash."

"You don't understand. You just need to be patient. To wait for her re-election and our new budgets."

"Patient? Patience is weakness."

At this point in the conversation, the Boss already knew

he hadn't aimed high enough. He adopted a reassuring tone.

"Well, we've taken up enough of your time, Azzedine. It's getting late. My men will leave you in peace."

That appeared to be it for their conversation, but Salah knew that if he handed back the mobile that would be it for him as well. When he stayed silent, Bibz snatched the phone from his hands.

"Boss?"

"We'll get nothing from him. We'll have to move on to the next person."

"What about him?"

"He can be our message. Be creative."

The youngster finished the call and stuffed the mobile in his pocket. He thought it over for a few seconds, then turned to Salah.

"So you like mace, do you?"

Salah was pinned down on the sofa. Driss held his arms while Colin grasped his legs. Bibz sat on his chest but, with the energy of despair, Salah kicked and writhed to escape their grip. Knocked off balance, Bibz regained control of the situation by pressing his fist against Azzedine's windpipe, almost crushing it. A simple technique that prevented his victim from moving. Turning round, the kid called out to Markus. His childish voice became that of commanding boy soldier. It was enough to freeze the blood.

"Hey, are you going to lend a hand or what?"

The boxer had stayed in the background, refusing to believe what was going on.

"I was never told things would go this far," he protested.

"It'll go as far as the Boss has decided."

"Without me. You're all crazy. I'm outta here."

Markus gave them all one last horrified look and walked

out through the front door. Colin and Driss were delighted that for once someone had succeeded in shutting up this psychopath in short trousers. A psychopath who, as a result of this setback, was already in a rage. His two accomplices paid the price.

"The Boss will settle that with Markus: they know each other. But you'll have me to deal with if we don't get the job done."

Bibz picked up the mace and forced the nozzle into Azzedine's mouth. Colin and Driss redoubled their grip on him. Bibz held the deputy mayor's nose and sprayed the noxious gas without stopping. Salah tried in vain not to breathe in, but as the gas hit the mucous membrane in his throat, the pain became unbearable. He screamed, expelling the air from his lungs. After choking for a few seconds, he was forced to take a deep breath and fill them again, only this time mace replaced the oxygen. He convulsed briefly and in less than twenty seconds he was dead.

The cloud of gas spared none of them. The Boss's three envoys leaped off the body and ran to the window in a desperate attempt to get some air, spitting, coughing, saliva on their lips, snot running from their noses. Afterwards they washed their faces in cold water. When they had recovered, Bibz cast a dissatisfied look over the scene. In his eyes, the message wasn't clear enough.

"Colin, get me a saucepan."

Holding the handle in one hand, he used the other to force the gas canister deeper into the dead man's mouth, then aligned the throat vertically as if he was going to knock in a nail.

At the first blow from the pan, Assedine's jaw cracked in two. At the second, three quarters of the canister was buried,

25

So far that evening, Sam had lost round after round of online poker. He signed up for a new game, and prayed he would get better cards. To his astonishment, in the first deal he got a pair of aces. And a text message from Coste.

Karl De Ritter emerged from his shower. Wiping the steam off the bathroom mirror, he took a good look at himself. He flexed his muscles, and told himself Johanna had nothing to complain about. He was expecting to find her stretched out on the bed seductively, but when he went into the bedroom she was sitting there, in tracksuit bottoms and a fitted T-shirt, staring at her mobile. The distressed look she gave her husband put paid to their plans for the evening.

"You must be joking, Jo! Soon I'm going to have to make an appointment for a fuck!"

Karl put on a shirt and went downstairs to make her some coffee while she finished getting dressed. He was already regretting his reaction.

Before leaving, Johanna looked in on the children. She went up to their beds as quietly as she could and breathed in the smell from the crook of their necks.

*

Ronan and Fleur Saint-Croix arrived together at 23, Avenue Victor Hugo in Malceny. A fact which escaped no-one. Coste and the rest of the team were already there, but they had the decency to make no comment. At least, not then and there. Ronan glanced at the corpse and moved to a corner of the room. Fleur took up position in the opposite one, as though they were strangers. A young community policewoman was just completing her statement, notebook in hand.

"Anonymous call to police emergency number at 22.15 hours. Victim is Azzedine Salah. The deputy mayor of Malceny. The front door was open, and the lock had not been forced. The victim probably knew his attackers."

"Go gently with your Hollywood conclusions," Coste observed. "In fact, it simply means the victim opened the door. You can't be sure whether it was to strangers or to people he knew."

The officer shut her notebook, slightly put out. She had hoped to shine in front of the Police Judiciaire, but it seemed she had messed up already. Her two uniformed colleagues exchanged sly smiles. She was the youngest member of the municipal police, and was often obliged to sit behind the desk at the station. Thanks to this faux pas, she was no doubt going to be put back in her box for a good while. Coste, however, wasn't in the habit of doing people down, so he quickly gave her a second chance.

"O.K., so what would you do next?"

Ronan and Johanna leaned against the wall, curious to hear her ideas. The young policewoman recovered her composure. She took a good look at the crime scene. A kitchenette that opened onto the living room. A big table with six chairs round it. A long sofa. The lifeless corpse, mouth open wide, teeth smashed, throat distended, eyes staring. She took a deep breath.

"First, get forensics to check for traces and prints. There's still a smell of mace. If their eyes were streaming or they had to spit it out, that would leave a lot of D.N.A."

"Agreed," Coste said, "but I'm not as optimistic as you are. Can't you smell something else?"

Fleur Saint-Croix turned to the others in the team.

"What's he up to?"

Ronan smiled. He remembered how Coste had recruited him in the same way, eight years earlier, at a crime scene.

"He's finding out what she's made of."

The officer went from the kitchen to the living room, trying to put a name to the lingering smell. Her two uniformed colleagues were no longer looking so smug.

"It smells of . . . cleanliness, swimming pools, chemicals . . . Oh damn, it smells of bleach."

"That's right. They probably sprayed it everywhere they'd been. Your D.N.A. samples will have been compromised."

"So . . . so they're pros?"

"No, you're jumping the gun again. They could very well just have watched a few crime series on T.V., like everyone else. This profession of ours hasn't had any secrets for a long while now. But getting back to the here and now, isn't there something you've forgotten?"

"If you mean going door-to-door, you're the one who's being too hasty, capitaine. In Malceny, this block is known as the Citadel. You're in the most luxury social housing in the whole town. Thirty dwellings on six floors. Fifteen apartments occupied by people close to Mme Vesperini, our mayor. Friends, family or collaborators. Ten others where high-ups from the prefect's office live. The remaining five were obtained in the usual way."

"Meaning?"

"Paying fifteen thousand euros key money to the woman in

charge of social housing in Malceny. Well, formerly in charge, because right now she's suspended pending investigation. Here, subsidised housing benefits those with fat salaries. Believe me, if there's a problem in the Citadel, it has to be dealt with swiftly, considering the status of the people who rent here. So if you really want to go door-to-door at midnight, it's up to you."

At that moment, a menacing voice at the front door interrupted their discussion.

"Do you have any idea who I am?"

Access to the apartment was guarded by a uniform, who found himself in a tight spot because yes, he knew very well who she was. In the living room, the young policewoman whispered for the benefit of Coste and his team:

"That . . . that's Vesperini."

This time, Coste could not avoid her, so he stepped forward and did his best to calm things down.

"Madame le maire, a pleasure to meet you. Capitaine Victor Coste, Police Judiciaire. The forensic technicians should be arriving at any moment. Until then, I'm sure you'll understand that the crime scene shouldn't be contaminated. But if you have any questions . . ."

The mayor's attention was caught by his last few words.

"The . . . crime scene? But I thought it was an accident. What happened here?"

"From our initial findings, Monsieur Salah appears to have been suffocated, but we need more time, madame – we've only just arrived. By the way, how did you come to hear about the incident so quickly?"

A little further down the corridor, a young woman who until now had remained silent came to the apartment doorway. Coste recognised her at once.

"Good evening, Capitaine. Maud Jeansac. I'm the mayor's press officer."

She was introducing herself to Coste for the second time. He shook her hand, slightly embarrassed at having lied to her only a few hours earlier. They exchanged knowing looks.

"I live on the top floor. I saw the flashing lights and was worried. I also thought it was an accident. When I realised it was Monsieur Salah's apartment, I immediately informed Madame Vesperini."

Visibly distraught, the mayor took some time to absorb the news. Then she said:

"Capitaine, I know that you've been very busy in my town recently. In no way do I wish to minimise the importance of your other investigations, but I would like your assurance that this one will receive your full attention. Monsieur Salah was more than a colleague, he was a friend. You will have total cooperation from our people."

She turned to her press officer.

"Maud, make a list of everybody who works or has worked with Azzedine, and make sure the capitaine gets it."

"I imagine you yourself will be on that list," Coste said, addressing the mayor.

"And I'll be the first to be interviewed, if you so wish. I left Monsieur Salah this evening just after eight o'clock."

"Did he say he was meeting anyone in particular later on?"

Vesperini thought about this for a moment. The murder had occurred just after her deputy had volunteered to take the temperature on the estates . . . that might not be a coincidence.

"We talked about my daughter's birthday, the agenda for tomorrow, and that's all. No, I can't think of anything."

"We'll need to search his office. Written authorisation from you would facilitate that."

A series of images flashed through Vesperini's mind. Her work agenda. The dossiers. The computer files. It would be a good idea for her to get in before the police and make a preliminary sweep of her deputy's affairs. Her night was just beginning.

"There'll be no closed doors or obstructions. Maud, you're responsible for assisting the Police Judiciaire in their work. If there's the slightest problem, contact me."

She turned to Coste.

"Capitaine, we'll let you get on, but I remain entirely at your disposal. I know Monsieur Salah's family personally, so I'll inform them of his death, if you see no objection."

Coste could not, and so, after they had shaken hands, he was able to go back inside the apartment. Ronan was checking the living room, staying a sensible distance from the body. Johanna and Sam were in the study, opening drawers and going through files. At this point in the investigation, the slightest scrap of paper could be important. Fleur Saint-Croix went over to Coste.

"Well, capitaine, obviously I'll assign the case to you. You are to . . ."

She hesitated for a moment, then changed tack.

". . . to do as you see fit. But I'll expect a detailed report by nine tomorrow morning."

Before she left the apartment, she couldn't help casting a last glance in Ronan's direction. He responded with an indiscreet wink.

"I see you've softened up our young friend," Coste remarked once she had gone.

"Yeah, I told her a bit about you. She knows the investigation will go smoothly and she won't have to worry."

"I hope you're behaving yourself . . ."

"That's funny, Sam's already said the same thing. But just between the two of us, relationship advice from Victor Coste . . . forgive me if I don't take it entirely seriously?"

Coste was stung by this, but he didn't get a chance to respond, because the young policewoman was addressing him.

"Capitaine, if you can spare us, we've been called to give backup at a domestic that's turning nasty."

"No problem. Fax us your report as soon as possible, will you?"

She nodded, but as she was walking towards her two colleagues, she remembered something.

"Oh, one last thing, capitaine. Did the Malceny duty officer call you today?"

"Not that I remember."

He looked across at Ronan, who also shook his head.

"I was on the late-afternoon shift on reception. An old man came in. He was worried about not having had any news about a friend. Rose something. An elderly lady who apparently died yesterday. You're working on that case, aren't you?"

"Rose Carpentier?"

"Yes, Carpentier, that's the one. You look surprised. Apparently it slipped my boss's mind . . ."

"Someone Rose knew! We've been looking for them for twenty-four hours now!"

He snatched her notebook and wrote his mobile number on it.

"It's my personal phone. I want his details the minute you find them, even in the middle of the night. What's your name?"

"Emilie, capitaine."

"You can leave out the capitaine," Coste said with a smile.

*

When Emilie and her colleagues had left, Ronan raised his head from his notes. He could see his team leader was lost in his own thoughts, all of them about Rose.

"That's it, another euro in the slot, and off we go again. Victor, if I'm rubbed out one day, I want you on my case."

"Don't be stupid. If you're rubbed out one day, it'll probably be by Sam, and I won't be able to do a thing."

Ronan smirked.

"What about her? Are you taking out an option?"

"In a few years' time. She's still too young."

26

Sam arrived at headquarters at 8 a.m. He wasn't normally an early riser, but he knew that in an hour's time the summer weather would turn the city into a sauna. So he was hoping to enjoy the cool air while he could.

At his computer, he retraced Monsieur Salah's final steps thanks to the signals activated by his mobile. His movements confirmed the information provided by Vesperini. The phone had gone from the town hall to his home and that was that. Nothing conclusive there.

To be completely sure, and even though the deputy mayor had been a victim, Sam typed his details into the S.T.I.C.* database. Looking into any youthful misdemeanours could give them a better understanding of him. Sam wasn't disappointed. Flabbergasted, he read the long list of offences the deputy mayor had been charged with.

"It's a joke! It can't be the same person!"

He checked the spelling, the date of birth, and went over it twice, but the result was the same. He continued his search

* Système de traitement des infractions constatées. System for Treating Infractions and Crimes. A database containing, among other things, all the offences committed in France, together with the identity of the perpetrators, their accomplices and the victims.

by going through the deputy mayor's known accomplices. What came up on the screen had him leaping out of his chair.

"Oh fuck! It's Christmas!"

When Sam came bounding into Coste's office, the rest of the team were still on their first coffee of the morning, and to see so much energy so early on merely reminded them how tired they were. They had spent most of the night at the deputy mayor's apartment, and had gone home for only a few hours.

"Hey, all of you, I've got news! Listen up, it's complicated, you're going to have to concentrate. Especially you, Ronan."

Ronan gave him the finger. Sam said excitedly:

"Monsieur Salah hasn't always been a good boy. In fact, he's had quite a few brushes with the law."

"Isn't that essential for a career in politics?" Johanna asked sarcastically.

"But it's not just brushes," Sam insisted. "He's been in jail twice. Once for breaking and entering when he was twenty-one. A second time when he was twenty-six, for drug trafficking. Arrested during a car chase between Amsterdam and Paris. Sixteen kilos of grass in the boot. Two years in prison for him and his accomplice, one Karim Souki."

First came the impression that they knew the name, as though it was flitting about in their memory without any of them being able to pin it to a particular face or event. Then the image became clearer, and they all shouted in unison:

"Karim Souki! The guy with the drilled knees?"

"Death by chocolate!"

Coste seized Sam's findings and studied them closely.

"You really do get to know someone by the people they surround themselves with. I think now we've learned a little more about Madame Vesperini. Sam, call the town hall and summon the mayor for tomorrow morning. If she has a gap in her schedule, of course."

Still excited by his discovery, Sam could see no reason for the delay.

"Why not right away?"

"Because I'm expecting someone."

* * *

Coste placed the two scalding cups down on his desk. After his sleepless night, he was setting great store by the effects of caffeine. Monsieur Jacques picked one up and blew gently on it. He had been told to come at ten, but had appeared thirty minutes early. Time was something Jacques had in abundance. Tweed jacket, corduroy trousers and a stick propped against his leg: you could tell his age just from the way he dressed.

"Monsieur Landernes, thank you for taking the trouble to come in."

Jacques did not raise his eyes from his coffee. He asked, in what was barely more than a whisper:

"Did she suffer?"

"I beg your pardon?"

"I go to the police station on Saturday to say I'm worried about my friend, and the next day I'm called in by the Police Judiciaire. Without wishing to jump to any conclusions, I think I understand what's going on."

True to form, Coste didn't beat about the bush.

"She died of a heart attack at home on Friday. And no, she didn't suffer."

Monsieur Jacques was clearly relieved to hear this, and his gaze drifted towards the office windows and out into the distance.

"Would you like me to suspend the interview? I can leave you on your own for a while if you prefer," Coste said.

"No, let's get on with it."

Victor opened a file in front of him and pulled his computer keyboard closer.

"How did you meet Rose?"

"At the bridge club in Malceny. You call her Rose?"

Coste did not know how to reply.

"It's funny," Jacques continued. "People often call us old folk by our first names, as if we've become children again."

"Did she have any problems you knew of?"

"Yes, probably the same as mine."

"Just so we understand each other, I'm not talking about health problems. I'm afraid you might not know everything Madame Carpentier was mixed up in."

Monsieur Jacques put his cup down on the corner of the desk, and smoothed a crease in his trousers with the palm of his hand.

"I preferred it when you called her Rose, but if you mean the drugs she hid in her flat, don't worry, I've got the same amount in *my* wardrobe."

Coste stopped taking notes, and pushed the keyboard away from him. Without a word, he drank a mouthful of his coffee. Amazing how a single sentence can turn your day upside down. Fumbling in his pocket, he took out a packet of cigarettes.

"Does it bother you?"

"Not at all. I myself smoked for thirty years. And anyway . . . on a day like this . . ."

Victor held out the packet, one cigarette protruding. The old man took it with eager fingers, leaned in to the lighter flame, and inhaled deeply. He was confronting an old demon and taking immense pleasure in their reacquaintance. He inhaled another lungful before saying:

"I imagine you'll want to start again from the beginning?"

* * *

For the rest of his story, Monsieur Jacques had more of an audience. Sam and Ronan occupied the sofa, and Johanna stood in a corner, arms folded. Coste had taken his telephone off the hook so they wouldn't be disturbed. Though slightly hesitant at first, the old man gained in confidence as he spoke.

"My name is Jacques Landernes. I'm seventy-eight years old. I'm a widower, and I have a daughter who lives in the United States. She's the only family I have. I've lived in Malceny for almost forty years. I met Rose Carpentier at the bridge club, and we used to see each other there every Saturday. One day I was mugged outside my block of flats. The next day, a young man came up to me in the street and asked if I wanted some extra cash and protection. That was how I found myself with a suitcase full of drugs and a monthly wage of three hundred euros. I knew Rose had the same problems of feeling unsafe and finding it hard to make ends meet until the end of the month, so I mentioned the opportunity to her."

He stopped when he noticed the capitaine was no longer typing.

"Aren't you taking notes?"

"I'm not sure yet what to do with you. But don't stop, go on."

Jacques collected his thoughts.

"We only had to follow a few rules. To be at home on Wednesdays and Saturdays, and to warn them if there were any police in the building. There were never any changes to the agreement. Until last Friday, that is. Then three youngsters came and told me they were in charge now."

"Had you ever seen them before?"

"Never."

"And the black eye, is that their calling card?"

Monsieur Jacques didn't reply, but touched his left cheekbone, which was still agony.

"Could you describe them?"

"Two aged about sixteen. One Arab, the other a white kid wearing strange clothes that didn't fit him at all. But neither of them seemed to be the leader: that was the smallest one. A young black kid of only thirteen, if that. His friends said his name, or rather his nickname . . . but I can't remember it. And I can't explain it. I can't recall their faces, either."

"Don't worry, that's completely normal. Almost a quarter of our victims don't recognise their attacker. We call that the tunnel effect. Stress and fear make you concentrate on something else, and the details aren't recorded in your mind."

Survival. Monsieur Chat. Rose . . . the officer was right, he hadn't thought about anything else.

"Are you sure about the age of the leader? I know people grow up fast in Malceny, but even so, that's a bit young."

"Believe me, he was the one who hit me."

Coste had still not typed a word. Listening to the old man's confession was like watching a man dig his own grave. He looked round in turn at each member of his team, all of whom were unusually silent.

* * *

Jacques Landernes had been sitting patiently in the waiting room for almost half an hour. Without a guard or handcuffs. He had been expecting to be led straight to the cells, and he found the police's methods increasingly bizarre.

In view of the heat, Johanna had been given the task of going for some cold drinks. Arms loaded with icy cans, she took the stairs to the top floor. At the end of a corridor, she climbed a flight of narrower, steeper steps that led to a door. She pushed it open with her shoulder and found herself out on the headquarters' flat roof, which was often used during the day for private discussions. Matters were discussed frankly, details thrashed out or mistakes admitted, far from any indiscreet ears. From time to time, in the late afternoon, cans of beer would be cracked open to celebrate a good result.

Johanna rejoined the rest of the team. The sun beat down on their heads, so hot it was almost unpleasant. A stool, a wobbly three-legged armchair and three mismatched deckchairs stood on the asphalt-coloured gravel. The others were already seated, so she took the vacant armchair.

"So, do you think they were lovers?" Ronan joked.

Jacques and Rose, a couple united in misfortune. Johanna thought back to Jack and Rose, the two lovers in the film "Titanic". Together with "Mad Max" and "The Exorcist" it was her favourite film. She kept the thought to herself.

"If you're too squeamish to arrest him," Ronan proposed, "I'll do it for you. He's up to his neck in drug trafficking, isn't he?"

"I know," Coste conceded. "And it might be the best thing for him. But our bosses will never allow us simply to arrest him. They'll want to use him. At some point, the dealers will need to get their hands on fresh supplies. If we keep him in now and seize the drugs, they'll never come back to the flat. Groupe

Stups aren't going to want to pass up this chance. They'll use him as bait. Lie in wait for the dealers and catch them red-handed. They may only be small fry, but Sylvan will put pressure on them to find out who their boss is, and then charge him with the three murders."

"What about Jacques?" Johanna asked with concern.

"Once the dealers have been arrested at his place, Jacques will be fingered as a grass," Ronan said. "In a week, two at most, he'll wind up dead."

"That's what I need Sylvan to understand," Coste said with a sigh.

"He's smart enough to understand that you don't try to solve three murders by inviting a fourth. It would be like taking out a contract on the old boy."

"The truth is, it's not Sylvan who worries me," Victor said. "It's Jevric. She would sacrifice him without a qualm. To deprive her of an arrest with maximum media coverage would be like stealing her three breakfast pains au chocolat. Her claws would be well and truly out."

27

"Well, frankly, you can go fuck yourself, Coste!"

A predictable reaction. He would have liked to talk to Sylvan on his own first, but Lara Jevric, the head of Groupe Crime 2, must have had some kind of futuristic G.P.S. device because she always turned up precisely where she was least wanted. When Victor entered the Groupe Stups office, she was already sprawled on their sofa, taking advantage of the Ramadan honey cakes, a present from one of the team's *oumayma.**

After the lightning, thunder.

"And may I know why it was you who interviewed the little old minder? Was I dreaming when you turned your nose up at the drugs case in front of the boss? I'm sorry, but we have to send him home, stake out the place, and wait for the dealers to come for their gear. We can always ask for a witness protection order if things turn nasty."

"Stop right there, Jevric," Coste protested. "If things turn nasty, the only way we'll know will be when we trip over his dead body. If your arrest takes place in his flat, or even a few metres from it – if there's the slightest link to him, he's a dead man. As for your witness protection scheme, it's hard enough to get accepted for terrorist cases, so imagine what it would

* Affectionate term meaning "mother" in Arabic.

be like for an old age pensioner caught up in a sordid drug deal. Dream on."

The worst of it was that Jevric was well aware of this. She was quite happy to accept any collateral damage if it helped further her career. She was about to launch a second round of arguments when Sylvan cut her short, saying in a neutral voice:

"I agree with Victor."

Still sprawled on the sofa, the enormous Groupe Crime 2 capitaine almost choked on her cake. The icing sugar left her with a pencil moustache. The Groupe Stups chief took advantage of her efforts to get her breath back.

"Your strategy is a good one, Lara, but it puts our only asset in peril. Serious drugs offences and murder are involved here, and Victor is talking about the only surviving witness to all this. It would be good to keep him safe and sound, wouldn't it? We'll find some other way, at some other time."

Coste could hardly believe his luck at gaining this unexpected ally.

"You could use photo surveillance to identify the dealers. You could even put a video camera in the old man's flat."

But Jevric just couldn't let it go.

"You go on about surveillance and gathering info when this is the fourth murder on our plate in less than a week. Don't you reckon it's time to take action?"

"Then Landernes would be the fifth."

"And anyway, how were you hoping to get him out of there?"

"We could arrest him. Make a circus out of it. In broad daylight, with five patrol cars – flashing blue lights, make as much noise as possible. We seize the drugs and he'll be brought to trial. He'll be given a suspended sentence, and nobody will suspect that he blabbed. The courts see drug minders like him as victims, and never send them to prison. So Landernes won't be running any risk. Either from justice, or from the street."

Jevric, still not bothering to sit up, snorted derisively at Sylvan's plan, so Coste took it upon himself to speak to her more gently.

"Lara, there's what the Penal Code says you should do, and there's the right thing to do. You're surely not going to risk the life of a poor old man just to nab a couple of lowlifes who – when it comes down to it – are never going to tell you who the boss of the network is. They're more scared of reprisals than they are of us."

The two men's arguments held water. Jevric appeared, if not convinced, at least resigned. Against all expectations, she gave in.

"Do as you like. And since you seem to agree with one another, I'll leave it to you to explain everything to Damiani and the big chief. I'm not sure they'll back you up."

* * *

Damiani wasn't concerned with moral questions. She came to a conclusion that had more to do with sound accounting. A drugs case going belly up rather than the threat of another dead body: the decision was simple. All she had to do was convince the big chief.

Meanwhile, in the Police Judiciaire waiting room, Jacques Landernes was still sitting patiently, like a schoolboy called to see the headmaster, unaware that only a few metres away his fate was being decided. The Groupe Crime 1 team were also in the dark, hanging around waiting for their bosses' decision. Coste decided to take matters into his own hands.

"Johanna, type me out an arrest warrant. Then we'll go and recover the gear from his flat. Sam, warn the Dog Unit and the Rapid Response boys. This time we're not going there with flip-flops and beach towels. Ronan . . ."

At that moment, the name Fleur Saint-Croix came up on Ronan's mobile, and the personal won out over the professional.

"Sorry, Victor, can I have a couple of minutes?"

He didn't wait for a reply, edging towards the door to find more privacy.

"Hi there. Have you ever been on the Grand Palais's glass roof? I've got a friend who . . ."

He came to a halt in the middle of his sentence. His smile evaporated.

"Are you joking? That's completely ridiculous."

All the others stopped and stared.

"Really? You call me Lieutenant Scaglia now, do you?"

The rest of the conversation left him speechless, and he hung up without so much as a goodbye.

"Has she dropped you?" Sam said. "I did warn you."

"I'd have preferred that. Jevric has just short-circuited us."

The metaphor fitted the person, but Coste refused to believe it.

"That's impossible. She accepted our argument less than a quarter of an hour ago. How did she sell her story to the magistrate?"

"She promised her an arrest within the next few days. An arrest that would get them closer to the three murders. We're stuck in limbo, and she offered something concrete. It didn't take long for Saint-Croix to decide. There's a team going into Monsieur Jacques's flat tonight."

Johanna clenched her fists.

"Jesus, I thought I'd seen every kind of bitch, but she's something else."

The office door opened and Damiani poked her head in.

"I've just seen the big chief. You've been screwed by Jevric, haven't you?"

28

For the second time that day, Coste's team were braving the fierce sun up on the flat roof of their building.

"They say they'll put the old man up in a hotel room while they're carrying out the operation," Ronan began.

"That must be their idea of witness protection. So after staying a night in a crappy Formule 1 room, he goes back home and everyone's forgotten him? I know dealers aren't the sharpest tools in the box, but they're not goldfish either. They'll remember. It's ridiculous," Sam groaned.

Johanna was worried because their team leader didn't seem that concerned. As though he'd already turned the page on Jacques. She had been expecting him to clash directly with Jevric and set the whole building buzzing, but there he was, sitting on the roof, staring out over the city as if it could offer him a solution to the problem.

"Hey, Victor, it'd be good if you could come up with an idea."

He turned back towards them.

"We're going to carry on as if this were a normal day. Johanna and Ronan, go and search Azzedine Salah's office. Make sure you say hello to Vesperini and tell her I'm going to call her in soon. Sam, I'll meet you in my office. I need you to look up a few things online."

"And then?"

"I've got some calls to make."

"Oh no you don't," Ronan objected. "You tried that same trick last year with the Soultier family.* You're the first to insist we're a team, but as soon as things get hot, you plough ahead on your own."

They all knew it was to protect them, but Coste had made his mind up a long time ago, and assumed that they were all mature enough to do the same.

"Ronan, when do you think Groupe Stups will start staking out the flat?"

There was no need for him to say any more. The other three were smiling already. Ronan gave them the benefit of his experience.

"In the middle of the night. There are people about on the estates until two in the morning. Let's say three. The earliest workers leave around five, so the ideal time would be four in the morning."

"Are we going to do what I think we're going to do?" Sam said gleefully.

"Yes, we are, little man, we really are," Ronan replied, smiling broadly.

Before leaving the roof they allowed themselves a couple of minutes' more sunbathing on the odd assortment of chairs twenty metres up in the air, heads back, eyes closed. Johanna rested her hand on the nape of Coste's neck.

"Do you know something, Victor?"

"No."

* Lucas and Margaux Soultier: two of the main characters in the novel *The Lost and the Damned.*

"You bring something special to our lives. And I'm grateful to you for that."

"Well, kittens, I'm not sure a kidnapping is going to look that great on your C.V.s," he said.

Maybe what came next would be a catastrophe. Maybe a shitstorm was brewing on the horizon. But up there, just then, they shared a wonderful moment.

29

Jacques realised his mistake soon enough. By going to the police he'd put himself in much greater danger than if he'd simply gone on babysitting the stash. He blamed himself for making the wrong decision in choosing the honest path. Coste had explained Jevric's plan in great detail. And then his own, which was more "off piste".

"I came looking for your protection, and you're making a scapegoat out of me, is that it? Even if I do as you ask, that won't change a thing. You're not going to keep me hidden indefinitely. I was hoping to die in my sleep, not in a microwave."

"What's that?"

Jacques didn't have the stomach to explain.

"Oh, it's nothing, forget it."

Coste was holding the results of the searches he had asked Sam to make.

"You could go to your own place, far from Malceny."

"My own place? I don't have anywhere else."

"What about your house at Chanclair, in the Drôme?"

Jacques looked at Coste as though he had been going through his pockets.

"How do you know about that?"

"Tax returns on property," Sam piped up. "It's not very

complicated. What I'm wondering is why you've stayed so long in that death trap when you've got somewhere far more suitable for your retirement?"

This observation seemed to plunge the old man so deeply into his memories that he risked not surfacing at all.

"Monsieur?"

Ronan's interjection had no effect. Johanna sensed that something had been left unsaid, so she spoke softly to the old man, as if he were one of her children.

"What's the problem with that house?"

Taking a deep breath, Jacques explained.

"That was where my wife spent her final days. It's as simple as that. Since then, I haven't been able to face going back. Are you telling me it could save my life? I don't really appreciate the irony, but . . . perhaps it's time to confront my ghosts."

It took him a minute or two to finally accept their plan.

"So, if I've understood correctly, you'll spirit me away tonight before the other team arrives, then put me on the morning train?"

"It's not quite as easy as that. For the first few weeks, we'll have to follow the same rules as if you were going on the run. If it took us less than two minutes to find your shack in the Drôme on our databases, it won't take Jevric much longer to send a team there. You need a safe house, somewhere nobody would ever think of. I'll see to that. Tonight, though, you'll stay at Sam's flat."

"Going on the run . . ." Jacques muttered to himself. He would never have thought such a phrase could be part of his vocabulary. Especially not at his age.

"And until then?"

"I'll take you to the Groupe Stups office. You listen to them, say you agree to everything, and we'll take care of the rest."

Jacques looked calmly at each of them in turn, four officers he had met only a few hours earlier. Their actions since then had left him utterly bewildered.

"Why are you doing this for me? You're getting yourself into a difficult situation as well. You've nothing to gain from it. And all this for someone you don't know?"

"It's our great existential paradox," Johanna said drily. "We spend our days and nights helping complete strangers, but we're incapable of paying any attention to those close to us."

* * *

Coste had politely shooed everybody out of his office so that he could call Léa.

"How's it going?"

"It's getting nicer and nicer, which makes it harder and harder not to have someone to share it with."

"Even the birdies and the bell?"

"Stop, that's what's best about it. And I'm spending a lot of time with Maman. She made the mistake of falling in love with a man who thinks only of work. Do you reckon it runs in the family?"

Since she was leading him in the direction he wanted to go, Coste did not react to her dig.

"Speaking of family, I need your help. Well, your father's. Is he at his clinic?"

"He hardly ever leaves it. But really, I was expecting to be there in person the day you two met. What do you need from a private clinic in Paris?"

"A room to hide a victim in, for as long as my inquiry lasts."

"Don't you have a witness protection scheme?"
"That's weird. You believe in them too, do you?"
Léa Marquant let several seconds go by in silence.
"Promise me it's not dangerous."
"It's not dangerous."

* * *

To ensure complete secrecy, Jacques Landernes had been dropped by one of the Groupe Stups officers two bus stops before his home. He had walked the rest of the way and made use of those few moments of quiet to think things over.

When he opened the door to his flat, his living-room clock was showing 6 p.m. He kept his jacket on and did not switch on the light. He looked out of the window at the surroundings he was being asked to run away from. Clusters of kids outside the tower blocks, skulking in the shadows. Others gathered around a sports car that was way beyond their means, music blaring out of its open doors, competing with the constant drone of stolen mopeds. A giant playground with no school attached.

He remembered Coste's warning: "You'll only have a few hours to get ready."

Opening the wardrobe doors, he began to sort through his clothes and decide what to take and what to leave behind. Soon his few chosen items had been transferred into his small travel bag. He added a few towels and a toilet bag. Then he went to the glass cabinet in his living room, which held a lifetime's souvenirs.

"You need to travel light and only take one piece of luggage."

So the juggling began: a suit for three thick photograph

albums. The towels sacrificed in favour of the Made in U.S.A. trinkets sent by his daughter in recent years. Finally, he decided his dark blue alpaca overcoat wasn't worth taking at the expense of a selection of his favourite books, Salinger's *Catcher in the Rye* included. He made the switch and threw the rolled-up coat onto the bed.

"Of course, you'll take . . . everything else."

He retrieved the cardboard suitcase from behind the box of books and laid it on the bed as well. He inspected the contents yet again, possibly hoping that by coincidence those kids had been round during the day and taken everything. That would have relieved him of his responsibilities – but no, it was all there. The suitcase was full.

Then he glanced at the dark blue overcoat and felt bad about leaving it behind.

At ten-thirty that night, Sam put the two pieces of luggage in the boot of his car, then got behind the steering wheel. The old man was waiting silently for him, walking stick between his legs. Sam was amazed at what he was wearing.

"Aren't you dying of heat in that coat?"

"I didn't have room in my bag, and I couldn't bear to part with it. It was a present from my wife. Stupid sentimentality."

Before they got going, Sam reminded him of what he had to look forward to, once they had got past the risky first steps.

"In no time at all, you'll be in your country cottage and you'll see it was all worth it."

"I hope so, Sam. May I call you Sam?"

The officer smiled at him and started the car.

A few streets further on, he parked ten or so metres from the Malceny police station. Monsieur Jacques saw the funny side.

"So you've changed your mind? You're going to hand me over to the authorities?"

"Don't worry, it's not you I'm handing over. I'll be back in a minute."

The old man watched him get out, and followed his movements in the rear-view mirror until the opened car boot blocked his view. Sam tugged at the suitcase. As he was lifting it, the catch came undone and the contents spilled out: a few of the packets landed inside the boot, the rest on the ground. The gun bounced under the car. For a split second, it felt to Sam as if all the street lights were trained on him, and that all the car alarms were about to go off and give him away. But nothing happened. There was nobody about, no problematic witnesses to consider. He hastily picked up the packets of cannabis and cocaine, and recovered the gun. Carefully closing the suitcase, he shook it to make sure it was secure. If the same thing happened again inside the police station, the consequences would be decidedly more embarrassing.

He walked towards the entrance. From the street, he could see Emilie, the young policewoman, at the front desk. Exactly where she should be. It was nearly 11 p.m., and the only people in the waiting area were a man holding a bloody handkerchief to his nose and a woman glued to her mobile. No-one would pay him any heed. Sam felt for the rolled-up baseball cap in the back pocket of his jeans, and jammed it on his head. He went in, eyes lowered, dropped the suitcase by the front desk, and turned on his heel.

As agreed, Emilie made no attempt to stop him. If Jevric's team appeared later on and asked about it, she would tell them she remembered only a stooped old man using a stick. Jevric would conclude that Monsieur Jacques had panicked and fled his flat. Picking up her mobile, she sent Coste a brief text:

Package received.

Then she went to tell the duty officer a suspect package had been left in reception.

30

Arriving at his flat, Sam opened the car boot to take out Jacques's bag. He noticed a small dark packet at the back of the boot, and reached in to take it out.

He found he was holding a kilo block of cannabis that had fallen from the suitcase. He raised his eyes to the heavens.

"Seriously? You're really doing this to me?"

If it had been anyone else in the team, they would have passed this test without a problem. But since adolescence, Sam had nurtured a certain bad habit he still found difficult to shake off.

"Is everything alright?" his guest asked.

Sam quickly stuffed the packet into his backpack.

Jacques Landernes stood in the middle of Sam's living room feeling rather lost. He couldn't make sense of what he saw around him. In one corner, an old video game terminal like those in amusement arcades. A giant screen, connected to three consoles and a tangle of joysticks. The rest of the furniture consisted of an almost too inviting sofa and a coffee table barely visible under piles of computer magazines, electronic gear, a soldering kit and a computer. On the wall, a framed original poster of the first ever geek film: "Tron". The old man looked upset.

"Won't I be disturbing your children?"

Sam scanned the room and burst out laughing.

"Yes, I can see what you're thinking, but I'm the only kid here. Let's just say I never quite got round to growing up."

He tried to help Jacques relax by showing him his bedroom. Another television set on the wall, a king size bed that took up almost the whole room, and a big tennis ball alarm clock that Sam only had to throw angrily against the wall every morning to silence.

"Don't worry, I've changed the sheets. Tomorrow we'll take you to your safe house. Coste says it's a great place. I'll let you get settled. I imagine you could do with a rest."

Jacques did not reply, but sat on the corner of the bed with his hands on his knees. He turned his head towards the window, which gave directly on to another, much bigger building, with other windows, other bedrooms, other lives. He wondered whether he could change his own, and whether he would have the opportunity to do so.

"O.K., I can see your mind's elsewhere," his host conceded. "I'll be next door if you need me."

Sam sent Coste a text message to tell him everything was going to plan. Then he went into his study and switched on an anglepoise lamp. On his desk lay the kilo block of cannabis in its smell-proof bag. Like a kid with only one Christmas present, he opened it extremely carefully. As soon as the packet was open, the smell hit him. He couldn't suppress a smile of satisfaction. Uncut, flexible, good colour. Pure shit.

"I've never tried it."

Caught out, Sam gave a start.

"Fuck it, Jacques, you scared the life out of me . . ."

He recovered immediately.

"I mean, you really frightened me. Is everything alright?"

"Yes, everything's alright. I was just thinking that I would have appreciated this adventure more when I was twenty. It's very stressful."

He glanced down at what the lamp was lighting up on the table.

"Wasn't that meant to be in the suitcase?"

It took Sam a couple of seconds to think of a plausible explanation.

"Yes. I mean no. It's normal. In fact we always keep a sample for analysis. To work out where it came from and identify the . . . the networks, according to the . . . journey it's . . ."

"Do as you wish, it's nothing to me."

Not so plausible, perhaps.

Jacques turned on his heel and headed for the bedroom, dragging his feet. Sam thought of everything that the old man had been through.

"Wait a minute . . . did you say it's very stressful?"

* * *

Once they got started, they couldn't stop giggling for a good quarter of an hour. After carefully watching how it was done and taking a few puffs, Jacques had tried to make his first ever joint, but the resulting specimen was as disastrous as it was crooked. They smoked it all the same.

They opened up to one another. Sam told Jacques why he lived on his own. Jacques told him about Peter Pan syndrome; then about his wife and how they had met. Sam told him the reasons that had led him to become a cop. Jacques explained why he was called Landernes now, and not Leinberg as before.

It was rare for either of them to have the chance to speak so candidly. And neither of them had spent such a great evening since . . . for far too long.

Later, the T.V. was switched on, they got comfortable, and thanks to a third joint they laughed like little kids at a rerun of "The Fearless Vampire Killers" on cable. Especially the scene with the gay vampire. At the end of the film, it took Jacques two attempts to sit up straight on the sofa.

"I've got to hand it to you, Sam. The effect is pleasant."

He picked up the still sticky block of resin and turned it over in his fingers.

"It's just a shame it rots the estates."

"You could see it like that. But it's also what supports them. That's one of the reasons why the state won't legalise it. Selling cannabis brings dough to a section of the population the authorities have no idea what to do with. If they lose that way of earning money, they would have to find another source of income. Hold-ups, prostitution, kidnappings. It's the lesser of two evils in a hopeless situation."

"A lesser evil that killed Rose."

Sam had no answer to that.

"And which is forcing me to abandon everything and to be . . . what did you call it?"

"To be on the run, Jacques."

Jacques could tell that their conversation was troubling the young policeman, and he didn't want that.

"I'm aware of all that you're doing for me. You're a good person, Sam. I'm glad to have met you," he said before retiring to his room.

* * *

At four in the morning, Capitaine Vincent Sylvan entered the tower block, followed ten minutes later by his partner. Jevric and Chloe – the only woman in Groupe Stups, still hidden beneath her black baseball cap – had gone in via the underground car park. They reconvened in the stairwell, and began to climb the fourteen flights to Jacques's flat. By the sixth, Jevric was panting like a buffalo.

When they arrived, she knocked gently on the door with the Welcome mat. Then a second time. After a minute, she knocked loudly, for all the good it did her. The telephone rang inside an empty flat, and Jevric hung up in a fury. Sylvan's partner had a suggestion:

"Maybe we've been beaten to it. We should check, though, shouldn't we?"

The person who has the idea has to accept the consequences, and so he was stuck with going down to their car and back, and carrying the battering ram up fourteen flights. After two hefty blows, the door gave way. Jevric rushed into every room, swearing as she went. It didn't take her long to grasp what had happened.

"That cocksucker Coste! I'm not going to let him get away with this! I'll destroy him. Fuck it, I will *end* him. I don't give a shit if it's four in the morning, I'm calling the big chief."

Sylvan tried in vain to calm her down.

"Hang on, Lara, you can't be sure. The old guy could see we were putting him in danger. Maybe he got scared and ran off on his own initiative. Do you really think Coste would have kidnapped our key witness?"

Jevric gritted her teeth to hold back a flood of insults, then began snooping about in every corner. Finding a large stash of drugs would at least allow her to save face when she reported to the investigating magistrate. While she was on all fours looking under the bed, the two men from Groupe Stups approached their team leader. They spoke in lowered voices, avoiding each other's eyes.

"Do you think it's Coste?"

"Obviously it's Coste," Sylvan replied, a broad smile on his face.

"How can you be sure?"

"Coste follows his own code. The victim comes first and foremost! There's nothing easier to understand than someone who follows a code. I simply underestimated him."

"What about the gear then?"

"He's still a cop. We should hear about it in the next few hours. I'm not worried about that."

"You could say he's got balls," Chloe whispered.

"Yes, you could."

Lara Jevric reappeared from the bedroom, even more furious, if that were possible.

"What are you talking about?" she snarled.

Entirely unruffled, Sylvan took control.

"For a start, Lara, take it down a notch. We've all been had, not just you. The old guy was only half-convinced – we should have kept an eye on him. Secondly, we can't leave without being certain there aren't any drugs left here. So quit yapping and call the Dog Unit."

In order to call the Dog Unit, she had to go through Control. When she explained, the call handler found it a funny coincidence.

"You're looking for drugs? Your Malceny colleagues have had more luck than you. A suitcase full of the stuff was left at reception there."

Jevric almost dropped her mobile.

"What time was that?" she shrieked.

"Eleven last night. Why?"

"Cancel the dogs," she growled, before ending the call abruptly and turning towards Sylvan as though he was part of the conspiracy.

"The drugs are at Malceny. It's him! I'm sure it's him!"

31

Early the next morning, the mayor dived into the back seat of her official car. The driver knew the rules: don't speak unless spoken to. No polite chit-chat. Never get out of the vehicle to open the door for her. She was neither the president nor disabled, and in one of France's poorest towns, having a flunkey didn't go down too well. So the journey to her offices in the town hall was made in silence.

Vesperini had slept badly, in twenty-minute snatches. Her drawn features made her look ten years older, and the general lack of sleep since the start of this hellish week had left her irritable and short-tempered. Well . . . even more so than usual. Summoned first thing, Baptiste Cardel, her chief of staff, and Maud Jeansac only had time to exchange a few words before going in to see her.

"How is the Queen?"

"In a guillotine mood."

They took their seats, keeping a low profile. "In politics we allow ourselves twenty-four hours to grieve. After that, it's time to react," the mayor began.

Cardel laid in front of her a list of possible candidates for the post tragically left vacant by Azzedine Salah. He pointed to the first name.

"Bruno Chabert could be an excellent choice. He knows the

projects in the 'community life' sector. He has good contacts with the main social activists in the town. Sport, culture, extra-curricular activities – he could pick up all the dossiers and hit the ground running. He's often come to me with bright ideas, and he really supports the concept of politics as the thread that binds the social fabric. He's a true militant."

Vesperini stared at him in horror.

"What are you talking about, Baptiste? Are you off your head, or what? Politics as social fabric? Is this the crap they teach you at Public Administration College? You're not going to foist somebody on me who'll upset everything. The last thing we need is for this town to take an interest in politics! There are forty-three thousand inhabitants, the abstention rate is a record seventy-two per cent, and I want it to stay that way. The fewer voters there are, the easier it is to influence the course of an election; it's simple mathematics. Maths, not politics!"

"So what are the qualities you're looking for, madame?"

"I want somebody who knows people on the estates and can identify the no-go areas. Somebody who's respected there. I'm not going to send you round in your nice little suit, am I? How do you think the other town halls manage? Would you like me to give you a few examples? In Elisy, the new man in charge of neighbourhood centres has just come out of prison – why do you think they chose him? In Véry-sous-Bois, the director of school budgets can't read or write – where do you think they found him? Better still, in Courcel, the man in charge of subsidised employment calls prisoners coming to the end of their sentence into his office. He gives them reams of fake payslips so they can find a job more quickly and he can have them in his pocket. Every town hall does its best to have former criminals on their side, and 'former' isn't an essential condition.

That's the kind of profile I need. I don't want another politician. I only have to bang on my desk, and five crawl out from under it. I want a man on the ground. And by ground, I mean a minefield. Search our pool – it can't be too complicated. Look among the coordinators, the sports coaches, the highways department, parks and gardens. Everywhere we've stuffed people with no qualifications."

No qualifications! The illiterate, you mean, thought Cardel, who was proud of his impressive educational record and now felt as though he was being asked to put out the dustbins.

"I'll make another list for you, madame."

"Good. And what does the media situation look like?"

Maud Jeansac read through her notes, hoping not to meet the same fate.

"The inquiry into Salah's death is underway, so nobody wants to say too much or to link it with the other three murders this week."

"There is no link, but that doesn't mean they won't invent one. If it carries on like this, I'll be treated like some kind of mafia boss."

Given what he had just heard, Cardel thought this was an apt description. He blinked but made no comment. Maud went on:

"I wouldn't be surprised if you're soon contacted by the minister for the interior. He wants to intervene in the town. He put out a communiqué this morning."

"Read it to me."

Her press officer gave a little cough to clear her throat.

"I want to put a stop to criminality linked to drug trafficking. It is for all of us, collectively, to accept responsibility and take action. More than ever, it is necessary to concentrate our investigative efforts on the neighbourhoods and estates infested by the drugs trade. This for me is an essential priority for the criminal investigation forces, as is a fresh approach to combating criminal elements and targeting gang leaders."

"I don't come out of it too badly then," said a relieved Vesperini.

But Maud hadn't finished.

"Actually, you're mentioned later on in the statement. Shall I carry on?"

The black look she received, together with a lack of any verbal reply, prompted her to do so.

"However, the work of the police and justice system can only treat the symptoms of this criminal activity. We need to attack the problem at its roots. First and foremost, it is the responsibility of the municipalities and locally elected officials to promote policies of prevention and social integration within a framework based on mutual trust among all stakeholders. This cooperation is embodied by the Local Council for Security and Prevention of Crime, an agency whose efficacy I shall personally verify very soon with visits on the ground. Getting things done: that is our aim!"

As Maud read out the communiqué, Vesperini tore into tiny pieces the list of candidates Cardel had handed her only seconds before.

"Soon it's going to be my fault," Vesperini complained. "That guy would come out spotless using a dirty sponge. Just as well we're from the same party, otherwise he would have crucified me. Baptiste, contact the minister's chief of staff and ask him what this means. If he's planning a visit to Malceny, I need to know all the details. If he's hoping to make political capital out of it, I want to be in camera range."

She leaned back in her seat.

"O.K., if there's nothing else, I'd like a few minutes' peace and quiet."

Maud was about to stand up when she remembered a message her secretary had left on her desk that morning.

"This probably isn't the right moment, but the rabbi from the Heikhal Torah synagogue wants confirmation . . . for his son's bar mitzvah."

Vesperini frowned and blew out her cheeks.

"I'd forgotten about him."

"We could leave it till later, madame."

"Absolutely not. There are some things that can't be left to the next day. Jews and Muslims are two communities I don't want to have against me. How much is this bar mitzvah going to cost me?"

"Thirty-five thousand euros."

Cardel spread his arms wide in a hopeless gesture.

"All our accounts are in the red. Managing to finish your term without being hauled before the Regional Audit Office will be an achievement in itself."

"Stop trembling, Baptiste. You're like a teenage girl on her first date. Sometimes I feel sorry for you. Nobody wants to poke their nose into how town halls function. O.K., so the government has decided to control our budgets to look good in the public eye, but it's we mayors who appoint our finance officers. And my finance officer, Delsart, won't allow them to poke around. He's the son of my ex-brother-in-law, and family still counts for something, doesn't it?"

"So where do you think you can find the money?"

"Remind me: the National Agency for Urban Renovation gave us a grant for our Youth and Culture Centre, didn't it?"

"Yes, but it wasn't much. Forty thousand euros to rebuild the main hall after it was set on fire."

"That's perfect! We'll give it a lick of paint for five thousand euros, submit a bill for forty, and that's our thirty-five thousand right there. I don't have to explain to you how these things work, do I? And now, if you don't mind, I really need . . ."

The red button on her desk telephone began to blink. She could see her day was going to be interminable. Ready to snap, she pressed the appropriate button.

"What is it?"

"Sorry to bother you, madame, but there's a call you're going to want to take. Monsieur Salah . . . I mean, his father."

Vesperini's irritation evaporated as if by magic. Cardel and Maud took the hint and stood up as one. In her now empty office, the mayor took a moment to refocus. The day before, she had taken it upon herself to give the family the bad news.

"Put him on."

A click, and the call was transferred.

"Monsieur Salah, this is the mayor speaking. How are you coping?"

"Quite well. Thank you for your concern."

The voice on the far end of the line seemed astonishingly calm.

"If there's anything I can do for you or your family, don't hesitate to ask. I can only imagine your sorrow and how hard his loss must be for you."

"That's kind of you, but don't worry. Azzedine's death wasn't as complicated as all that. I wouldn't go so far as to say he didn't suffer, but according to my people it was all over in a few minutes."

Vesperini jerked the handset away from her ear as though it were red hot. A shiver ran down her spine, and the hairs on her forearms stood on end. Unusually for her, she was utterly lost for words.

"Be that as it may," the caller continued, "I'm glad to hear we're on the same wavelength, because in fact there is something I'd like to ask of you. To be honest, I put the same request to Monsieur Salah, but he didn't give us a satisfactory answer."

"Who are you?" Vesperini eventually managed to splutter.

"Wrong question. 'What do you want?' would be more appropriate."

Recovering from her initial stupor, Vesperini was determined not to lose face.

"You don't frighten me. As soon as I hang up, I'll call the police and they'll trace the call."

She could almost hear the smile at the other end of the line.

"Please do. But you won't, because we both know why your deputy is dead. You've recently lost three of your unofficial collaborators, the kind you don't acknowledge in public."

"I've no idea what you're talking about."

"I can understand your caution, especially on the telephone. Some of your colleagues in other municipalities have been the victims of unfortunate recordings. So I'll continue on my own. We've already taken over their turf and their trade, but that's only a means to an end – definitely not an end in itself."

"What more do you want then?"

"Nothing except a future."

A future founded on four murders, Vesperini thought.

"There are other ways."

"No, you're wrong. You only respect people who threaten your position. If we no longer frighten you, you'll crush us. As of now, with the trafficking under my control, I'm the biggest employer on the estates. I can keep them on a leash, or let them loose on you. But anyway, I don't think we should be fighting one another. It would be more productive to work together. If my civic sense is not mistaken, there's an election coming up. Your two first terms of office have been a success. I can help you secure a third. Guarantee votes from all the neighbourhoods, collect proxies, make sure all your opponents' campaign appearances end in disaster, ensure a friendly audience for yours, and take care of your security."

Vesperini rehearsed her reply before voicing it. Above all, it was crucial to avoid saying anything that could be used against her.

"I still don't understand what you want from me."

"And yet it's very simple. Selling drugs brings in a lot of money, but it's no different from Russian roulette. What we want is some stability. An afterwards. To be part of society. A life free from violence and danger, in a clean and pleasant environment. That might seem ridiculous to you, because you're accustomed to that kind of comfort, and you forget the luxury it represents. One only values oxygen when one is suffocating. All we want is a normal life like you see on T.V. Not just for me, but for my team. About a hundred people and their families. I'll send you the list at the appropriate time. But unfortunately that's not why I'm calling."

He paused, and when he spoke again it was in a very different tone.

"An important part of our merchandise was seized three days ago, and we need to replace it. You have a week to come up with the sum of two hundred thousand euros."

Vesperini found herself unable to reply. At least, not in any truthful way. She had just asked Cardel to choose a candidate from the estates, and here was heaven offering her one. Heaven or hell? Whichever it was, this one was not only too dangerous, he was far too expensive. With the best will in the world, at this point in her second term the amount he was demanding was impossible. She hid behind a fig leaf of bogus morality.

"You're out of your mind. Quite simply out of your mind! How could you imagine for a second I would collaborate with an assassin?"

"Nevertheless, you're going to have to get used to the idea."

"And if I don't? Will I be found dead as well? But then you wouldn't have anyone to threaten. After me, there's no-one. Or only people far too high up for you."

Suddenly she found she could breathe easily. In the safety of her office, nestling in her town hall, in the centre of her town, she found an ounce of courage. Or a lack of awareness.

"I'm not afraid of you."

Her hand was still shaking, minutes after she had hung up. The Queen had just refused an alliance in a context where it would have been useful to her.

Despite her answer, she began to think it over.

32

A little before ten in the morning, Coste entered the lobby of Dr Marquant's clinic. A two-storey building shaped like a doughnut, with an immense private garden in the centre. Given the price per square metre of property in Paris, and especially in the eighteenth arrondissement, so much green for a small number of well-off clients was nigh on indecent.

A secretary with a fixed smile, wearing a blue blouse with her first name embroidered on it, sat rigid behind a stainless-steel desktop. A metre to her right, her clone. Above their heads, a giant T.V. screen showed on a loop a film advertising the Alcedonia clinic and the services it offered. A few patients were strolling around, others stood chatting in dressing gowns. None of them looked seriously ill. All this, along with the soft background music, made the clinic seem like the latest fashionable spa.

One of the blue fixed-smile clones came to life and spread her hands wide, as if presenting the facilities.

"Welcome, sir. How may I help you?"

He thrust his blue, white and red police I.D. under her nose.

"Capitaine Coste, Police Judiciaire. I've come to see Dr Marquant."

Her look darkened immediately. With an urgent glance in her companion's direction, she sent her to find their boss. Coste took advantage of the wait to walk round the lobby. He went down the corridor and past the bay window with its view of the soothing interior garden. A dozen metres behind him, the lift doors opened and a man in a white coat came out accompanied by a nurse. They stood to one side to continue their conversation. The young woman responded to everything the doctor said with a giggle that was too innocent to be genuine. Head bowed, with a coy smile on her face, she took out a notebook and scribbled something in it. Tearing off the sheet of paper, she folded it in four and slipped it into the doctor's pocket. Doctor . . . There are some professions that are a big hit with the ladies. Like guys who play the guitar on the beach. They're always more successful. In Coste's line of work, women usually arrived battered, in tears, or dead. Which made things considerably more difficult.

The receptionist left her desk to interrupt the courtship ritual. She reached up to whisper in her boss's ear, and they both looked towards the police officer. Dr Marquant took a step backwards, a little too quickly, and the enterprising nurse put away her notebook and went on her way, head down. The two men advanced to greet each other.

"Dr Marquant?"

"Capitaine Coste?"

"I hope I'm not disturbing you?"

"Not in the least," the medic hastened to say, clearly ill at ease. "I was expecting you. Léa explained the situation."

Once installed in the doctor's office, Coste took his time to study his potential father-in-law. Perfectly groomed silver hair, manicured nails, Montblanc fountain pen in his breast pocket. A wall full of diplomas, and on the opaque glass desk the hypocritical family photo, with a blissfully happy Léa, barely eighteen by the looks of it, clinging to his arm. Coste felt a twinge of sadness.

"It's not often I'm in a position to help the forces of law and order."

"I don't doubt it, but this is quite an unusual request. We're trying to protect a witness. I have to bend the rules, and I'd like it to remain between the two of us. I'm sure you understand."

The message was clear enough.

"Can you guarantee we're not running any risk?"

"Provided you don't register this gentleman under his real name, I don't see what could go wrong."

"Fine. I've had a quiet room set aside for a whole week. Will that be sufficient?"

"Two weeks would be better, to give us time to complete our inquiry."

Faced with little choice, Marquant acquiesced, and the two men shook hands.

"If you don't mind, I'll ask one of our receptionists to show you the suite."

Back in the reception area, Coste caught sight of Sam and Jacques, momentarily dazzled by the luxury all around them.

"Make sure you don't lose Léa, Victor. With in-laws like that . . ."

He turned to the old man, whose doubts had been swept away by a smile from one of the nurses.

"Besides, the staff seem charming. You're going to be fine here, Monsieur Jacques. Farewell, Malceny. Look, there's even a private forest!"

"You'll come and see me, won't you, Sam?"

"Well, you know the main thing right now is discretion. It's a time to keep a low profile. On the other hand . . ."

He took an obviously brand-new mobile out of his backpack.

"I've got you a phone and a prepaid S.I.M. card. I've already punched in my number and the chief's, just in case. But don't worry. Take a look at this paradise – you'll have forgotten me in ten minutes."

Jacques fumbled in the inside pocket of his overcoat, and handed him a dog-eared book he had read a hundred times. *The Catcher in the Rye.*

"It's my favourite novel. I think you might see yourself in it."

As they walked back to their car, parked on the clinic forecourt, Coste couldn't help noticing his companion's worried expression.

"You're fond of him, aren't you?"

Sam was an orphan. No great drama there. Not these days, at least. Besides, everybody has their own quota of misfortune, and in their job they even assumed that of others, which helped keep everything in proportion.

"It's O.K. He's not a father figure for me. But thanks for your concern, all the same. Talking of families: how did you find your prospective father-in-law?"

"Accompanied."

"Oh, shit."

33

They came to a halt at a red light, and Sam turned on the radio news channel. The minister for the interior was finishing his speech. "Getting things done: that is our aim!" The presenter went on to mention the surprising discovery of a large amount of drugs left at the Malceny police station like so much lost property.

Sam puffed up with pride.

"Cool, they're talking about me! Holy shit, those journos are quick."

"It's not the hacks who are quick. It's our colleagues. At two hundred euros a scoop, every newsroom has a contact in the force. We're their first informers."

Sam thought this was as good a moment as any.

"Speaking of which . . . take a look in the glove compartment."

Knowing how it worked, Coste gave the compartment a kick. It opened at once, revealing a fat kilo of cannabis resin.

"And this is . . . ?"

"The suitcase broke open, and it fell into my car boot. I only saw it later on."

His boss seemed satisfied with the explanation, his only comment a laconic "O.K.".

"Is that all?"

"Whether you stole it or not, you've brought it back. So yes, that's all."

"Well, anyway, I've given it up."

"Since when?"

"Since last night, about two in the morning. And it really did spill out of the suitcase."

When they were only about ten kilometres from headquarters, Coste's mobile buzzed. A text from Ronan:

Jevric's looking for you. Just so you know, you're doing the door-to-door in Malceny.

* * *

The first thing Sam noticed when they reached the Groupe Crime 1 office was an empty white bakery bag on the table. He glanced accusingly at Johanna and Ronan, both busy on their computers.

"You could have saved us some."

"Breakfast. Courtesy of Groupe Stups."

"Always the same. Greedy pigs."

"You don't get it. A present from Groupe Stups. Empty."

Coste couldn't help laughing.

"Like how we left the flat for them yesterday. Not bad – they've got a sense of humour, at least."

Sam wasn't sure they should rejoice so soon.

"I'm not sure Jevric sees the funny side."

As though her name had been dog-whistled, Jevric herself burst into the room without knocking, foaming at the mouth.

"Where were you, Coste?"

"Morning, Lara. In Malceny, doing the door-to-door. Didn't Ronan tell you?"

"Yeah, don't worry. Your parrot learned his lines perfectly. So where is the old-timer?"

Sam did not appreciate this disrespectful way of referring to Jacques. At least, not coming from Lara Jevric's mouth.

"His name is Jacques Landernes, and the last I heard, you were the one responsible for him."

"You can shut your trap! Listen to me, Coste. If you think you're going to get away with this, you've got another think coming. Officers like you are a disgrace to the force. By the time I've finished with you . . ."

Before she could complete her threat, Johanna kicked back her chair and drew herself up to her full height.

"I advise you to cool it with the insults and threats. These gentlemen may be too polite, but as far as I'm concerned, you're this far away from getting a bunch of fives in your ugly mug."

Jevric looked daggers at Coste, as if expecting him to react. But his silence confirmed the team's unity, and she slunk back out of the office.

She was a wounded animal now. Which meant they had to be even more wary of her.

* * *

Sylvan studied the plastic bag Coste had just laid on his desk. Opening it, he discovered a brown slab of cannabis resin. The other packets of drugs, the gun and the ammunition were stacked on the low table in the centre of the room. He folded his arms and leaned back in his seat. It was up to Coste to break the ice.

"Did you put in your report how much the haul weighed?"

"This morning."

"Can you add a kilo of cannabis that fell out during the transfer?"

"It's doable."

These brief replies in a flat monotone made it hard for Coste to read Sylvan's intentions.

""All good between us?" he said.

The head of Groupe Stups hesitated a moment, his expression inscrutable. Then images from the previous night flashed through his brain.

"I ought to be mad at you, but I can't manage it. And my team wouldn't back me up anyway: I think they appreciate what you did. We don't always stop at red lights either. But above all, there was Jevric's face."

"I'd have paid to see it."

"When she grasped what was going on, I thought her head was going to explode."

He recreated the scene for Coste, in detail, lingering with pleasure on the nervous breakdown they had witnessed.

Now any tension in the room had been defused, Coste made to leave. But in spite of their friendly discussion, Sylvan gave him one last word of warning.

"Coste?"

The capitaine turned back towards him.

"Just once. Not twice."

34

Naturally, Commissaire Divisionnaire Stévenin had insisted on accompanying Madame Vesperini on her summons to the Groupes Crime office.

Obsequious. Coste hadn't used that word for years, but when he saw his divisional commander come in, bent almost double with respect, it immediately sprang to mind. So obsequious it was almost embarrassing.

"Capitaine. You could have gone to the town hall. Madame le maire must have more important things to do than come here."

Vesperini put a stop to any further polite exchanges.

"I imagine your officer's timetable is as crowded as mine, and in fact I'm indirectly responsible for that. I think my town is giving him a lot of work."

Reassured, Stévenin left the room, but not before giving his subordinate a meaningful look that appeared to be conveying simultaneously "Make a good job of this", "Be polite" and "Don't drop me in it".

Left on her own with Coste, Vesperini sat facing him, slightly uneasy at finding herself on the far side of the desk. She was more accustomed to taking charge than being led.

"How are you coping?"

The question knocked her off balance. She wasn't really

expecting to have to talk about herself. Then there was that look of his, slightly sad and very gentle, but at the same time stripped of all innocence. The look of those who know what people are capable of but keep the secret to themselves. Without being quite sure why, she felt she could trust him.

"As well as can be expected, I suppose. I often talk about violent crime in my speeches. It's very different when it affects you personally."

"I understand. How long had you known Monsieur Salah?"

"We worked together for eight years."

Coste opened the folder on the desk in front of him and took out a document. He handed it to her.

"How well did you know him?"

The sheet of paper was Azzedine Salah's police record, with a photograph of him taken years earlier, and the long list of his offences. She handed it back to Coste.

"None of this is news to me, capitaine. You think I don't check up on the people I have around me?"

"I'd be surprised if you hadn't. But maybe you could explain the reasons for your choice?"

She seemed to marshal her thoughts for a few seconds.

"First, you need to understand that I'm not the kind of elected official who prefers to pay a fine than to build social housing. In my town there are a number of difficult areas and estates that are gradually becoming isolated from the rest. I don't want them to become a town within a town. I want them to feel part of our shared future. But in order to do that, first of all I need to understand them. To understand what separates us in order to restore meaning to the idea of living in a community. How can one reduce social inequality if one doesn't know exactly what it consists of? Some of my associates have never set foot on an estate, and are far too scared to ever do so."

"Which explains why you took on somebody like Monsieur Salah."

"Although it wasn't exactly his criminal past that determined my choice, in a way it was just that. He knew about the many types of adversity that can lead to crime. He understood these people's aspirations, because they had been his once. He knew what made them riot, because he had done so himself. He represented a means of communication, a necessary link. The small-time crooks or dealers who poison those neighbourhoods are only a tiny part of it. I want to take an interest in all those who suffer in silence. I want to make them our number one priority once more, and to offer them the right to express themselves. I want them to be integrated into our town. The turnout for local elections on those estates is close to zero. So I'm a mayor for whom no-one has voted! That makes my mandate questionable. We have to regain popular sovereignty, so that the inhabitants of Malceny don't regard politics with suspicion, but with interest, trust and hope. Politics as the thread that binds the social fabric, isn't that the dream?"

Coste had not touched a single key on his keyboard.

"I applaud the sentiment. And your passion. Do you employ many men with Monsieur Salah's background?"

"Capitaine, towns like ours are the state's crutches. We have to make up for its indifference, its lack of interest. Every year in France a hundred and fifty thousand children leave the education system without a diploma or qualification. I don't blame the system – I'm the first to defend it. I have implicit trust in it, but it doesn't have the necessary means. Spending on students in the city of Paris is double that for a child in the surrounding towns. As a result, in Malceny only thirty per cent of children from disadvantaged backgrounds have a school leaving diploma, whereas the national average is eighty. Who do you think offers work to that other seventy per cent? Above all, the municipality. And the inequality is hardly confined to our schools! I have to provide what others take for granted. Housing, health, employment and, more tragically still, something to eat. Three-quarters can't even pay for their kids' school meals! Many people see that as the absolute minimum, but on those estates, it's a dream, a goal. We only value oxygen when we're suffocating. Furthermore . . ."

She broke off mid-sentence.

"You're not taking any of this down?"

Coste had long since understood he wasn't going to get much out of her rant.

"Yes, I was just about to do so. Shall we begin?"

Annoyed, she answered:

"Whenever you wish."

"Name?"

"Vesperini."

"First name?"

"Andrea."

35

Estelle Vesperini had skipped a class. She was twelve years old, in the second year, and her mother congratulated herself every day for having chosen a private school. "Like world peace, state schools are a noble ideal, but while we're waiting for these goals to be achieved, let's arm ourselves and protect our kids," she had said one day to the head of Collège Charles-Germain-de-Jouy. He had answered with a loud laugh and told her she was very droll.

It was the last week before the holidays, so there were no more checks and barely any homework. In this elite establishment reserved for the fair-skinned, an unusually relaxed atmosphere reigned. As the beach beckoned, the pressure eased off, allowing Estelle to spend the whole day showing off her birthday present: the latest smartphone complete with all the new apps she would never use, but which her friends were jealous of nonetheless. That was all that counted.

The moped drew up a few metres from the school exit. The driver wore a helmet, and Bibz, sitting behind him, had crammed a cap on his head that when lowered covered part of his face. Between his knees, a short-stock assault rifle, branded "SPYDER MR5". At half past five, the bell in the school's private chapel rang for the end of lessons. From the pocket of his tracksuit bottoms, Bibz took a printout of a Facebook page. It showed a smiling young adolescent, surrounded by her best friends. "Bring on the holidays!" followed by three smiley emojis.

A throng of young girls swept out of the school like a shoal of startled sardines. Bursts of childish voices, laughter, excited discussions. The impression that everything left unsaid during the school day had to be shared now, in the short walk from the school building to the world outside.

Bibz scanned their faces, searching for his target. He caught sight of Estelle behind the first group. Surrounded by her friends, just like on Facebook. The moped started up and they followed the group at a distance. When they were ten metres from the school, Bibz tapped the driver on the shoulder.

"O.K., get closer."

"Don't you want to wait until she's on her own?"

"Don't talk, just do as I say."

The moped lurched over and changed lane. When they were alongside the young girls, Bibz raised his weapon and fired gangster style: a burst from the hip without even aiming.

Estelle was hit in the neck. The collar of her blouse turned red. Another projectile hit her head; her hair was stained the same colour. Two others exploded against her backpack. Her companions weren't spared either; one of them was holding her head in her hands, scarlet liquid oozing through her fingers.

Recovering from their stupor, the girls stared at one another, daubed in paint.

* * *

Vesperini bounded two steps at a time up the school's main staircase. She strode along the corridor to the head's office and, without knocking, burst into a room decorated with a map of Gaul, another of France, and a third of the whole world. Estelle was sitting quietly, her red-stained backpack at her feet. Opposite her stood the headmaster, overcome with embarrassment. Why did it have to happen just a week before the summer holidays? Why did it have to happen to the Vesperini girl? He had dealt swiftly with the other children's parents, but thought it best to pay particular attention to Estelle.

Andrea seized her daughter and examined her from all sides.

"It's alright, maman. It's only paint."

The mayor turned and aimed the full force of her ire at the person she held responsible.

"What happened? Where are the little brats? And their parents?"

Estelle was afforded a rare chance to see the normally fearsome headmaster turn to jelly.

"Madame, it wasn't anybody from the school. It was probably thugs from outside."

Two years before, he had abolished obligatory school uniforms. The polished shoes, white knee-high socks, and identical grey and white tops immediately labelled the girls as well-off Catholics, and made them as much of a target for racists as a kippah or a veil. He went on:

"I'm sure it's only jealousy. It happens a lot. But I intend to inform the police."

Andrea Vesperini took her daughter by the hand, led her out of the office, sat her down on a chair against the wall in the corridor and went back inside, slamming the door after her. Normally, finding yourself seated on one of those chairs signified a black mark on your report and a difficult conversation at home. For once, though, the roles were reversed, and the thunder wasn't aimed at a student.

Estelle posted: *My mother is shouting at the head. She shouts at everyone anyway. School isn't prison. Its my home. Ive had enough.*

* * *

7.30 p.m., Vesperini family home

Andrea stuck her head round the door and saw Estelle hard at work. Just in time, the young girl had hidden her phone under a history book. Her bedroom seemed to have been taken by surprise at her brutal change from sensible little girl to rebellious pest, just as Andrea had been. Estelle had covered the blue and pink walls of her childhood with images of aggressive rap singers and Goth groups – for no other reason than to provoke her mother, who now came in and leaned against the wall.

"I don't feel like cooking."

"I can live with that."

"What would you like? Chinese, Indian, pizza, burgers, sushi?"

"You choose. I don't mind."

Vesperini went over and ran her fingers through her daughter's hair.

"I love you."

"You don't have a choice. It's an animal thing. For the protection of the species: we learned that in school."

At Estelle's age, every show of affection came back like a boomerang with a dose of cynicism and indifference thrown in.

"If you're intending to live here for a few more years, I'd advise you to watch your mouth, young lady."

"Don't worry, I plan to run away and become a prostitute in Qatar. That way you'll be left in peace."

Two seconds of silence. Estelle finally looked at her mother, and they both burst out laughing.

"I love you too. Sushi will be fine."

In her spotless kitchen, Vesperini was searching in the drawer for the restaurant menu when the landline rang. She had been waiting for this call for hours, and didn't let it ring a second time.

"Good evening, madame. I was in a training session, so I've only just received your message."

"Good evening, Monsieur Bastide. I need your services."

Estelle would not admit to her mother that, despite her apparent lack of concern, being shot at like a stupid pigeon as she was leaving school had in fact left her shaken. All of a sudden she felt trapped on her own in the bedroom. She went downstairs to look for company in the living room. At first she trudged down, like a moody adolescent. But then she heard some snatches of conversation from the kitchen, and continued on her way on tiptoe, to spy on her mother more easily.

"I don't give a damn about his training schedule, Bastide. Do you really think you're in a position to argue?"

Her mother was facing away from her, but it was clear from her voice she was very upset. Beyond her, the window looking out onto the garden was illuminated by a path of light that led down to the front gate.

"I'm not asking you if it's possible, I'm simply explaining

how it's going to be. If I don't get what I want, you can consider your club closed. Do I make myself clear?"

Vesperini hung up, leaving no time for a reply she had no interest in hearing. Still furious, she turned away from the window, but immediately changed her demeanour when she saw Estelle staring at her from the kitchen table.

"Do you have to terrorise everyone?"

Caught out, Andrea tried to justify herself.

"But I'm doing it for you, sweetheart."

"Don't bother," Estelle muttered, getting up and leaving the room.

Alone again in the kitchen, her mother turned off the light by the window and the garden disappeared in the night.

* * *

The next morning, Estelle stuffed her schoolbooks in her back-pack, together with her mobile, fully charged for another day. Breakfast wolfed down, she read the note left for her on the fridge door:

Call to tell me if everything goes alright – love, your mean mother.

She smiled, opened the fridge door, and took out two cartons of orange juice. Before leaving the house, she looked at herself in the hall mirror. Red trainers, skinny jeans, and a T-shirt with stripes in one colour too many. The pleasure of wearing whatever you like when you're twelve. She went down the steps into the front garden, opened the gate and looked around her. Leaning against the bonnet of a nearby car, she saw a black colossus in a tracksuit. He was about twenty years old, with a shaven head, broad shoulders, and arms that were too heavily muscled. Yet somehow she didn't feel intimidated.

The young man's voice corresponded to his physique: deep and slightly aggressive.

"Are you Estelle?"

"Yeah. And you are?"

"Markus."

"Really? Markus? Cool."

She searched in her backpack.

"Orange juice?"

"Yeah, alright."

She tore the straw from the carton, pierced the lid and handed the drink to her new bodyguard.

"Good. So where's your school?"

36

Vesperini had got the message. It wasn't hard: it had been written in paint all over her daughter. When she reached the town hall, she tried her best not to take out her murderous impulses on her staff. But the text she received on the dot of eight-thirty reassured her a little.

Safe and sound. The babysitters really cool!

Estelle hadn't taken much persuading to agree to a personal bodyguard. She even quite liked the idea. This sense of a star being harassed or a princess in danger really was something to boast about. Even better than a new phone.

Vesperini had spent a sleepless night, turning the unacceptable offer from a vulgar criminal over and over in her mind. Obviously, there was something dubious about it, even by the standards of the world of politics, but the more she thought about it, the more she saw that it suited her. Even better, everything came together more perfectly than she could have hoped. To such an extent that the collateral damage could be seen as acceptable.

In her office, she glanced at the framed portrait of her daughter on the desk. Taped to it was a straightened-out paper clip, with a cigarette stuck on the end like a worm on a hook. She had given up smoking when Estelle was born, and for twelve years now that cigarette had been defying her.

She pressed the SECRETARY button on her desk telephone.

"Do you still smoke?"

Standing at her window, she coughed at the first puff. Those that followed were easier, sweeping away twelve years of abstinence. When her telephone rang, she jumped like a guilty adolescent, and threw away her cigarette.

"Monsieur Azzedine Salah's father for you."

"Put him on."

A click, and the call was transferred. In the blink of an eye, a mother's rage won out over any professional calculation.

"You piece of shit!"

"Good morning to you as well, madame."

"How dare you?"

"You're not looking at things from the proper angle."

"The right angle! Are you messing with me?"

"Usually, any obstacles in my way are chopped down. Some are even tortured. All your daughter got was dirty clothes. Can you see the proper angle more clearly now?"

"That doesn't change a thing. You shouldn't have done it. All I needed was time to think it over."

"Think of it as me giving you a little push. A reason to think things over more rapidly."

"Promise me you'll never go near her again."

"As somebody who breaks so many of them, do you still believe in promises? Let's get back to what interests us . . ."

"Your money?"

"Your re-election."

"What I told you yesterday is the absolute truth. We don't have a spare cent in our accounts."

"Except that yesterday you ended it there, whereas today I get the impression there's something more."

"I think I've found a solution. But I'm going to need your help."

"How are you going to manage it?"

"That's easy. I'll provide the spark. I want you to take care of the fire."

PART THREE

THE CONFLAGRATION

37

Cries of joy. Vehicles strewn across the road, blocking the traffic. Dozens of roses on every windscreen. Some drivers joining in the celebrations with their horns, others showing exasperation at being held hostage by this frenzy of joy. And in the middle of this giant bouquet of flowers, a municipal police car, stuck like all the others, victims of a Seine-Saint-Denis wedding.

Two uniforms were desperately trying to get the traffic moving again, while the third member of their team was radioing in his report.

"Yeah, confirmed, chief. There's chaos at Tetris, it's going to take time. Can we have backup from the national police?"

Safely ensconced in the local Malceny police headquarters, Henri Gonthier, known as "Riri" or "Tintin" but also, though behind his back, as "that fat asshole", was polishing off his coffee, black boots up on the desk.

"Of course. Would you like the R.A.I.D. task force as well? All we need is for people to say the local cops can't even control a wedding. What make is it anyway?"

"What do you mean by that, chief?"

Wearily, Gonthier took his feet off the desk and prepared to give yet another lesson based on experience and infinite tolerance.

"To know what make it is, you only have to look at the

cars. If they're Porsche and Ferrari hire cars, that's Arab. If it's B.M.W. and Mercedes, it's African. And if it's those damn stretch limos, it's Asian."

"Ah, African, then," the officer replied frostily.

Gonthier had long ago created his own world atlas. There were the good, which meant most of Europe, although the Eastern part had some bad characters. After that came the neutral, those who only rocked the boat among themselves. This included the whole of Asia: Pakistanis, Chinese, Japanese and the like. And, finally, the bad, which meant Africa, with no distinction made between North and South. America, Oceania and the poles didn't figure in his atlas.

"Give the impression it's too much for you, so we won't be held responsible, and above all, don't attempt to intervene. If you stop your black from having his little dance, he gets bloodthirsty. When things have calmed down, you can leave."

"Fat asshole" suited him perfectly.

Gonthier headed for the breakroom, intending to steal a croissant. He was opening his mouth to stuff half of it in all at once when his mobile began to vibrate in his pocket. Nothing annoyed him more than being interrupted mid-snack. But nothing put him more on the alert than a call from Vesperini, top dog in Malceny's hierarchy. Finger on the seam of his trousers, he listened to her instructions, then dared suggest:

"It's going to be tricky, isn't it?"

The voice at the far end of the line became more heated. Gonthier crumbled under the weight of her authority.

"Far be it from me to argue, madame le maire. We'll do as you ask. I'm just saying it's going to be tricky."

38

During Ramadan, the Prophet advises breaking the fast shortly before the evening *Salat al Maghrib* prayer. A glass of water, a few dates, always an odd number of them. Just enough to help you forget your hunger and prevent you being distracted by the rumblings of an empty stomach. The real meal came later. So the men went to the mosque, and the women remained at home, because if the Book authorised their presence in the holy place, it was without any great conviction. "Don't forbid women going there. However, prayer at home is preferable."

The rite respected, it was time to return to the family, either in one's own home or at another's, to share a spicy, sweet meal. Neighbourhoods came alive as religion brought everyone together, whatever their faith.

In Malceny, this atmosphere was especially pronounced on the majority-Muslim Cosmonautes estate. At its centre was a circular area ringed with shops, in the shadow of four tower blocks so huge it looked as if they had descended from the sky. Armstrong Tower, Aldrin Tower, Gagarin Tower and Baudry Tower. The last of these space explorers was less well known than the rest, but at the town council meeting called to choose the names, that of the French astronaut Jean-Loup Chrétien had been rejected. Since some of the inhabitants would probably not have appreciated living in a Christian-sounding tower block, the choice of Baudry had been more diplomatic.

At dusk, the sun, though hidden from view, still offered half an hour of twilight. There were quite a few men in djellabas out in the square on their way back from the mosque, some veiled women, and a few who were defying the law by wearing niqabs that revealed nothing more than their eyes. All of them on their way to pick up a last bit of shopping or rejoin their families. A tranquil tableau, apart from the three municipal police vehicles and their nine uniformed passengers blocking the main exit from the estate.

The locals kept glancing in their direction. Intrigued, some wondered whether a crime had been committed. Others, more hostile, seemed offended by their mere presence. In the last vehicle, Gonthier was watching them in turn. He was already worried. Their chief's visible state of stress did nothing to reassure any of the other members of the team. After less than ten minutes in position, though nothing had happened, their nerves were ragged.

Three others were sitting in the lead vehicle, a small van with the national police insignia on the doors. Here too, courage was in short supply.

The driver sighed. "This is ridiculous."

"It's a huge risk for a simple misdemeanour," added one of the men in the back of the vehicle.

"It's twenty past ten. They haven't eaten all day, they're tired, they're on edge, it's still thirty-eight degrees, and we're going to offend their old ladies and their religion? Doesn't that sound like a stupid idea?"

"All we can do is pray we don't come across any burkas."

On the van radio, Gonthier's nasal twang announced the commencement of hostilities.

"To all vehicles, there's one for us. Batman at ten o'clock. Two men from each van follow me, head for our target. Drivers to remain in vehicles as backup."

There were about forty people in the square. The six uniforms got out of their vehicles, converged to form a single group, and strode towards a couple: a man in a djellaba accompanied by a fully veiled woman. The scene quickly attracted everybody's attention, and mobile phones were raised, ready to film. The police officers formed a triangle, two in front for the confrontation, two at the sides to protect them, and two in the rear to watch for any possible outflanking. The lawbreakers felt caught in a trap. Gonthier began to speak; just his tone of voice would have offended anybody's eardrums. Like a pet poodle, his fear was transformed into aggression. Puffing out his chest, he folded his arms across it.

"The niqab is prohibited, madame. Your identity papers."

The man at her side stepped forward and tried to calm the situation down in an admirably restrained fashion.

"We were simply out shopping, boss. We're going straight back home. You won't see us anymore."

"That's not on the menu. You don't get to choose what suits you."

To avoid any scandal and so as not to spoil this special day, the woman let go of her husband's hand, plunged it in her bag, and brought out a residence permit with a photograph showing her uncovered face. She handed it to the police officer.

"Yeah, well, that could be anyone. You need to lower your veil for me to check."

As Gonthier's men exchanged apprehensive looks, a moped appeared on the pedestrian street beyond the shops, roared into the square, and braked ten metres away from where they were standing. A second climbed the ramp up to the base of Aldrin Tower. One policeman noticed the crowd had doubled in size in less than a minute, and that a group of adolescents had gathered at the foot of Gagarin Tower. Impossible to say where they were coming from. Insults began to fly around; at first they were relatively measured.

"Racists!"

"Get out of here, you motherfuckers!"

Some of the police began to take preventive measures. A hand clutched a tear gas cylinder. Fingers closed round a baton. The man in the djellaba tried to reason with them.

"Please, don't do this. Not here."

The man's common sense had no effect on Gonthier, who, sweating with fear, ratcheted up the tension.

"You're the one making this difficult. If she won't lower the veil, we're obliged to take her in. Monsieur can come with her if that reassures him."

As he spoke, he reached out and grasped the young woman's arm, pulling her towards him. In turn, the husband placed a hand on Gonthier's arm.

That was all it took.

"I'll provide the spark," Vesperini had said.

Voices cursing in a range of accents bounced off the walls of the tower blocks.

"Sons of bitches!"

"Leave her alone, faggots!"

The mopeds revved up simultaneously and roared round the group. A grey breeze block exploded at the policemen's feet. Some of them instinctively reached for their batons, others for their guns, as they looked around them in panic. The man in the djellaba pleaded with them.

"Let us go . . . and go away yourselves, please."

But Gonthier would not back down. Not far away, the group of thirty who had gathered there earlier raised their hoods and wrapped scarves round their faces.

"You take care of the fire," the mayor had concluded.

The youngsters closed in on the police, surrounding them. One of them got behind a uniform and hit him on the nape of his neck, sending his blue helmet flying.

"Hey! You can't see our faces either. Why don't you take us in?"

Gonthier began to wave his gun around blindly, without aiming at anyone in particular. An adolescent a head shorter than him challenged him, pressing his chest against the gun barrel.

"What are you going to do? Shoot me? Give me your gun, you paedo. I'll show you how to use it."

While he was confronting Gonthier, another youngster slipped behind him and pulled the tear gas cylinder from the officer's belt. Whirling round, Gonthier tried to identify the thief, but he had already disappeared into the crowd. Overwhelmed, Gonthier found his brain was only processing half the information, and he realised too late that every member of his team had been isolated, trapped in the midst of ten or more assailants.

The other policemen fired their tear gas. It spread everywhere; a thick cloud enveloped the face of the woman in the burka. She cried out in pain and collapsed. High on righteous fury, the youngsters coughed and spluttered, but none withdrew.

Some way off there was an explosion, but everyone ignored it. Punches to the face, kicks at legs. A moped wove its way through to the police. The helmeted passenger raised his arm, hefting an iron bar. It crashed against a cop's shoulder. He fell howling to the ground, his collarbone smashed. Miraculously, the other five policemen managed to regroup around him. Whirling their batons, they succeeded in pulling back, dragging their injured colleague with them.

When they reached their vehicles, Gonthier understood why none of his colleagues in the rearguard had come to reinforce them. Two of them were struggling to get the third out of a burning vehicle. The windscreens of all three vans were splintered, their bodywork pitted by an ongoing hail of stones. One of them cut Gonthier's forehead, which began to bleed profusely.

There was so much stress and fear in the air that all rules of engagement were forgotten. Four policemen climbed into the rear vehicle, five others piled into the leading van, and Gonthier took the wheel. Without looking, he threw it into reverse, and in a crash of metal collided with the other vehicle, which hadn't yet set off, denting the wing and buckling the bonnet. Gonthier tried again to escape as the crowd surged around them. Turning the vehicle round, he slammed it into first gear and screeched away at nearly fifty kilometres per hour.

Emerging from the hornets' nest almost safe and sound, he changed into second gear and floored the accelerator. When he came to the junction where the road out of the estate met the main road, he looked neither left nor right. A moped appeared like a subliminal image and crashed into his side door. The two-wheeler turned a somersault: its driver slid across the bonnet and ended up two metres ahead of them. The passenger literally flew over the police van, landing twenty metres further on, only releasing his grip on the iron bar in his hand when he hit the tarmac. The force of the impact saw him bounce once, then his body slid along, all four limbs at impossible angles. Without pausing for thought, Gonthier roared off again.

"Fuck, what are you doing?" shouted one of the policemen. "We can't just leave!"

"Shut your mouth! If we stay, we're dead! Call the fire brigade: that's all we can do!"

The van sped off with a clanking sound, one of its tyres burst by the torn bodywork, the wheel rim scraping along the tarmac. The other vehicle must have beaten all speed records because it had already reached the safety of the municipal police compound.

The moped driver got to his feet, removed his helmet and peered all around him until he spotted the passenger's body. It had been thrown too far for there to be any life left in it. Limping over to the inert body sprawled on the tarmac, he knelt beside it. The inside of the helmet visor was covered in blood.

"Bibz . . . Oh shit, no!"

* * *

In the lift, two uniforms were continuing a conversation. The regular officer was explaining to the probationer the subtleties of their profession.

"Well, anyway, in situations like this, there's nothing you can do but be as brief as possible. Informing people of a death is the hardest thing we do, but in fact it's very simple. I've got my own personal technique."

One of them pressed the button for the ninth floor.

"First you ring the bell, and as soon as the door opens,

you enter. What's most important is to give the news without beating about the bush."

"What if there are kids present?"

"In that case, you ask them to go to their rooms. Then you separate one or two members of the family, and tell them that So-and-So has died in such and such circumstances. You don't go into details. You only say what's strictly necessary."

"Why don't you tell the whole family while you're at it?"

"Because all hell breaks loose! Everybody starts blubbing and hounding you with questions as if you were personally responsible. No, the best thing is to talk to a single person. If you see they're about to crack, you tell them they have to be strong for the rest of the family, then they have to tell the others, while you make a swift exit."

Reaching their floor, the two policemen headed for flat 921. The more experienced officer knocked several times, but nobody came to the door. At past one in the morning that didn't surprise him, so he continued until the person inside the flat woke up. The door opened to reveal an African woman in her fifties, tousled hair in thick strands, a loose T-shirt over a distended stomach. The acrid smell of alcohol, damp and sweat hit the police duo like a slap in the face. In spite of this, they maintained the stoicism appropriate for the kind of message they had to deliver.

"What do you want?"

"Good evening, madame. National police. May we come in?"

She screwed up her eyes to look at them, as though she found it hard to take in what she was seeing.

"No. If it's my kids you're after, they're not here and I couldn't give a damn."

Taken aback, the officer decided to proceed with his mission from out in the corridor. He stammered out the first words.

"I . . . Your . . . Your son Habibou was killed in a road accident this evening."

The silence that followed was unprecedented. No cries, no tears. No reaction at all. The policeman decided to repeat what he had said, thinking the information must have drowned in the alcohol the woman's brain seemed to be floating in.

"Madame, your son Habibou . . ."

"Yeah, I heard."

With that, she slammed the door in their faces.

FIRST NIGHT OF RIOTING

The Control Room had been alerted at five-thirty in the morning. Half an hour later, Commandant Auclair sent a detachment of riot police to block access to the gate in front of the municipal police headquarters. They now formed a compact line: three squads of soldiers in their black exoskeleton armour and impressive helmets, with the name of their group and section written in white on their backs, from 1A to 1C.

Behind them, a team of firemen were busy with a red Twingo that had been sent hurtling into the gate and had buckled it. Cables had been attached to its rear axle, and the breakdown truck was trying to free it, to the screams of shearing metal.

Only a few metres to the left of the main entrance, a raised bay window giving a view of the reception area had been smashed; shards of glass littered the ground. Inside, the blackened walls and ceiling were still smoking, while the floor had been flooded with water from the fire hoses that had arrived just in time to prevent the blaze spreading to the rest of the building. The smell of wet ashes and petrol hung in the air.

Early that morning, journalists had rushed to secure the first images of the Cosmonautes estate before it woke up and became aware they were there. Moving on a hundred metres, they snapped pictures of the scene of the accident, above all of the sand on the road surface that was intended to soak up the young victim's blood. Their tour had ended at the wall of black riot police silhouettes protecting the badly damaged police station.

A lightning attack that, to anyone able to read between the lines in Malceny, heralded what was to come.

39

The Boss tried to stay calm and prove to the person on the line that he knew how to control himself. And yet, if she'd been there with him . . .

"Is that what you call a spark?"

Vesperini was on her eighth cigarette by now, and her haze-filled office reflected her anxiety.

"The situation got out of hand. It's nobody's fault. And shit, don't play the big-hearted criminal with me. It was you who set things going."

She had hit home, and for the first time she sensed a certain unease on the other end of the line.

"That kid. I knew him."

"And I knew Monsieur Salah. You're leading your personal revolution: did you really think it would be the first one ever without a martyr?"

"He was the same age as Estelle."

She stubbed out her cigarette in the ashtray, fumbled for the empty packet, then crumpled it.

"Don't you dare mention her name. They have nothing to do with each other."

"Most of all, they didn't have the same opportunities."

"Well, anyway, it's too late to pull back now, so try to control your troops better. Go for the shops, public buildings – destroy whatever you like, create panic, but stop short of a direct confrontation. We can't have any more victims. Material damage, that's all."

"Starting a riot is easy. So is ending one. But nobody can tell what might happen in between."

Vesperini slumped back in her chair.

"Wait . . . you're telling me you don't know how all this is going to pan out?"

"I only control part of the estates, but with the kid's death you've given an open invitation to everyone to go out into the streets. An army with no commander."

"An army out of control?"

She recalled her favourite quotation. This time its meaning was more apt than ever:

"We have our hands covered in shit and blood. Right up to our elbows."

"Why? Do you imagine one can govern innocently?"

With that, he hung up. Andrea Vesperini was left speechless. This little thug knew his Sartre: that simple fact terrified her more than any other threat.

It's always more difficult to sell glass beads to educated natives.

Maud Jeansac knocked on the door and came in carrying four packets of cigarettes, wondering if it would be enough nicotine to calm the Queen's nerves. The news she was about to give her reminded her of those stories in which, for lack of any other target, it was the messenger who got shot.

"Have you heard of Copwatch, madame?"

"It sounds like the name of a film."

"No. It's an internet site. And the only film that matters

right now is of our municipal police in action on the Cosmonautes estate."

Vesperini tore open a packet of cigarettes, while Maud went to the computer to type in the Copwatch address. After a few clicks, the home page came up on the screen, showing an image of a film camera trained on police wielding batons, beneath it the self-explanatory caption: "The police are watching you. But who's watching the police?"

"It's an interactive site that sees itself as a citizens' observatory on police behaviour. As you can imagine, yesterday's drama did not go unnoticed."

She moved the cursor down until she came to an article entitled "State Assassins".

"During a violent and unjustified stop and search operation, Malceny municipal police deliberately manhandled a veiled woman. No matter how violent, is the response from the local community really to be condemned? After raising the temperature to boiling point, the police were forced to withdraw at almost seventy kilometres an hour, along a shopping street at one of the busiest times of day. Wearing the full-face veil can attract a fine of thirty thousand euros. But how much, you guardians of law and order, would you say the life of the child you killed was worth?"

At the end of the article was a link to another site showing a video of Gonthier, the head of the municipal police force, clearly in the process of tugging at the arm of a young woman in a burka, followed by his men spraying the crowd with tear gas. So it was official: the police had been the first to resort to violence.

"Can we block that site?" Vesperini asked anxiously.

"Technically yes, but that wouldn't solve anything. The video has spread everywhere. It's gone viral."

"What about the accident?"

"That took place just outside the estate, so nobody filmed it."

"Good. Bring all the staff together in fifteen minutes. I want a cast-iron media strategy in place around this crock of shit."

40

Everything was smaller. As with all self-evident truths, it was a stupid thing to think, and yet everything was . . . so small. Hands, brain, heart. Mentally, Coste went over what he always told new police officers in situations like these: "They're not your loved ones, it's not your grief." And yet he found it hard to cope with the sight of this child's body on the autopsy table, chest sliced open, vital organs laid to one side.

"He was brought to me with his helmet on. When I took it off, it was a real mess. If it's any consolation, to judge by the state of his skull, he died instantly."

"Has his family been to officially identify him?"

"Not yet. I don't know why, but that's been blocked by your colleagues."

Coste couldn't take his eyes off the table.

"Do you have children?" the forensic pathologist asked him.

"No."

"That should make it easier."

"That's not the word that springs to mind."

They continued their conversation in one of the I.M.L.'s offices, with its parquet floor and wood panelling. Coste found himself unable to refuse a glass of the strong spirits Dr Atlan retrieved from its hiding place behind a row of leather-bound volumes in a bookcase that reached up to the ceiling.

*

Back at Police Judiciaire headquarters, Coste met Ronan and Johanna, both carrying motorbike helmets. They took advantage of one of the endless corridors to report back on their morning's activities.

"We had the moped towed back to our car park."

"Were you able to go to the scene to take photographs?"

"Yes, with the forensics team. We should have them within an hour."

"Any witnesses?"

"No, it's a desert. If you want us to go door-to-door, you'll have to give us backup. It could just stir things up more."

"Meaning?"

"I can understand a country village being quiet. But for an estate like the Cosmonautes to be so calm after what's happened, that freaks me out."

Coste pushed open the door to Groupe Crime 1's office, and sat down at his desk, without any great enthusiasm. He opened a file, then closed it at once, and stared out of the window. It was one of those days that led you to check on the calendar the last time you had a holiday. He muttered to himself:

"Madame Rose, no leads. Azzedine Salah, all leads washed away in bleach. Habibou Doucouré, we had the name of the person responsible even before we knew the victim's. A series of investigations going nowhere."

Sam looked up from his computer.

"I may have something. Do you know Copwatch?"

"I've never been in their sights, but yes, I do."

Coste walked round his desk and leaned over his colleague's shoulder.

"You stink of alcohol, Victor."

"Leave him alone, will you?" Johanna cut him short, as

she joined them at the computer. "Or next time you'll have to attend the autopsy."

Mortified, Sam decided an apology would make things worse, so instead launched the video.

"O.K., three very short films in total. I've added a time code to give you a better idea. You can see six guys from the municipal police heading straight for that couple at top left. Apparently they're concerned about the niqab."

"That's not very clever during Ramadan," Ronan said.

"Now you can see how the trouble starts. The officer tugs at the woman's arm, the husband steps in, and in less than a minute they're surrounded by dozens of kids, faces all covered."

"That's quick."

"Yes, even for that neighbourhood. Afterwards comes a regulation stone throwing; the police respond with tear gas, then there's the blow from an iron bar, and our colleagues retreat."

"Wait, what's that?" Coste said, his finger on the screen.

"One of the police cars on fire. They left it where it was. The second video is more interesting."

Sam closed the open window and clicked on the second film.

"It's shot on a phone, so it's not top quality, but just look at the time code. At 23:06:30 you can see the three vehicles intact. The person filming turns to the arrest getting out of hand, the woman receives a stream of tear gas right in the face, then you can hear a strange noise, a sort of explosion at 23:06:55, and he turns back to the cars at 23:06:57, that is, two seconds later."

"The car is completely ablaze in two seconds?" asked an astonished Johanna.

"That's the problem. It has to be a Molotov cocktail. I don't see any other explanation."

Coste followed Sam's line of thought.

"You mean they were prepared for it?"

"I mean nothing makes sense here. An army of municipal police arresting someone for wearing a niqab on the worst possible day of the year. Kids who come swarming round by the dozen in less than two minutes with Molotov cocktails to hand. The only thing missing from this shoddy screenplay is the director."

Coste rubbed his face. Just like when you have a word on the tip of your tongue, he had a whole series of facts to piece together on the fringes of his synapses. He picked up a marker pen and went over to the whiteboard. On it he wrote everything rattling round in his brain.

"A take-over of dealers. Three dead. Two minders out of service, one of them on the canvas. So far, so good."

"Don't forget the mayor's deputy, who just so happens to be a former accomplice of one of the dealers," Ronan added, returning to sit on the sofa.

"Azzedine Salah. Crossed off the voters' ballots. And a risky arrest that's going to set the town on fire."

"Can you see any link between all that?" asked a bemused Sam.

"None, that's the trouble. An entire town is visibly about to boil over, and no-one knows where the heat is coming from."

Ronan gave him a friendly tap on the shoulder.

"And you were complaining we had nothing to do."

41

The sun was beating down on the blinds in Gonthier's apartment, striping the walls with shadow and light. Not a sound. No movement. He was sitting on a chair in the centre of the room, staring at nothing, his soul drifting through empty space. He had killed a child, and part of him had died at the same time. Whenever his eyelids drooped from exhaustion, the excruciating sound of crumpled metal woke him with a start. It was as though he could not allow himself the slightest respite.

Victims of a serious accident retain a sound or image, a memory that never fades. Gonthier discovered it was exactly the same when you were not the victim but the perpetrator. He was able to fast-forward, replay or pause this film, every second of which was engraved on his consciousness.

On the other side of the blinds, a calm, steady rumble roused him from his nightmare. On the other side was the world in which he had committed an unforgivable mistake, a world he felt excluded from forever. He stood up, and in three strides was by the window. Like a fugitive on the run, he pressed himself against the wall and half-opened the blinds.

Seven storeys below him, somewhere between three and six hundred people dressed in white were marching in silence, arms linked. Candles in their hands and tears in their eyes in memory of this child none of them had known. One banner proclaimed

AN ANGEL HAS LEFT US. A collective sense of empathy that delighted the media. Film cameras on their shoulders, microphone poles like so many pitchforks or scythes passing beneath the monster's windows. Gonthier strained to hear whether there were any insults, but there was nothing. Only an accusatory silence.

Occasionally, as a group of marchers went by, some faces turned towards his building. Nobody could see him, and yet he was sure their eyes were seeking him out. Gonthier moved away from the window and sank to the floor, head in hands.

The intercom buzzed with a loud, almost vulgar sound, invading his apartment and making him jump. Crossing his living room, he took the handset without saying anything.

"Monsieur Gonthier? Would you have a comment for the news at . . ."

He let the receiver fall from his hands. It began to swing from side to side at the end of its cable. Of course, now he was public enemy number one. He rushed over to his computer, typed "child", "death", "police" and "municipal" into his search engine. He was in every result: his surname and first name were everywhere. The assassin. The bastard.

The intercom buzzed aggressively a second time. Calmly gripping the box in both hands, he tore it off the wall. As if on cue, his mobile began to jig about. He was about to hurl it to the floor when he read the name on the screen: Vesperini. He went to sit in a corner and took the call. The voice was motherly, compassionate.

"The white march is being shown on television. How are you coping?"

"What about you?"

"Henri, this is nobody's fault. A dramatic accident, no more. You were attacked and tried to retreat. Who could hold that against you?"

"I don't think anybody gives a damn about what really happened. A kid is dead, that's all that matters to them."

"You need to get a grip. The Police Judiciaire is going to want to interview you."

"So that's what you're worried about, is it? That I'll tell them who ordered me to make the arrest? Because you're the one who created this mess . . ."

"Be careful what you insinuate, Gonthier. It was nothing more than an unforeseeable slip-up that nobody should be held responsible for. Remember the state you were in when I picked you up. And then there's everything else I've got on you."

The cop managed a smile.

"Do you really think you're in a position to threaten me?"

He was right: Vesperini had no hold over him. She tried to make him see reason.

"After the inquiry, the law will be on your side. You were in a difficult position, and you were responsible for your team. You simply need to let the storm pass."

"Of course, I've only got to wait six years for the law to take its course, the way it did for the police in Villiers-le-Bel,* or eight years, as it did for those in Clichy-sous-Bois, and then it will all be forgotten? What difference does it make if I'm found innocent or guilty?"

Vesperini had no answer to this. Exhausted, Gonthier reassured her about his intentions.

* On the night of 25 November 2007, gangs attacked a police station in Villiers-le-Bel, torched cars and vandalised shops. The violence was prompted by the deaths of two adolescents after a crash between their motorbike and a police patrol car at an intersection. The disturbances spread to neighbouring towns on the night of 26 November. 82 police officers were injured, four of them seriously.

"I'm already in hell, and I don't need anyone to keep me company. I chose to make that arrest, and I'll accept the consequences. Is that what you wanted to hear?"

"I . . . I simply wanted to make sure you were O.K."

"I'm fine, madame le maire. Perfectly fine."

SECOND NIGHT OF RIOTING

Rioters are divided into four categories: looters, arsonists, wreckers and hooligans. Whereas the first three only attack buildings, the last group target the forces of law and order. Out of vengeance, boredom, or following others. Often, out of pure pleasure.

And on this second night, all four groups were out in force.

At the entrance to the Cosmonautes estate, makeshift barricades had been thrown up. First there were supermarket trolleys weighed down with stones and bricks to serve as ammunition as the evening progressed. Then wooden pallets, waste bins, moped frames, and in the front line two freshly stolen cars, ready to be torched. If the police wanted to bring the estate back under control, they would have to do it by force.

Similar barricades had been built in ten or more strategic points throughout Malceny. The most impressive, almost twenty metres across, completely blocked the main access road to the shopping mall. With 150 stores spread over 2,500 square metres on two levels, it was likely to be the first target. And with its four public entrances and three exits via underground car parks, it was almost impossible to defend.

At 21.10, the police prefect authorised aerial backup, and one of the region's EC145 Civil Defence helicopters took off from its Paris base to fly over the danger spots.

At nine-thirty p.m., the barricades were set alight. Up in the sky, the helicopter crew could see the town going up in flames. The onboard cameras transmitted the images live to the Control Room.

The streets of Malceny appeared on their giant screen, one after the other, and when the video technician changed to thermal imaging, the town was lit up by all the fires. It was so striking that the room fell silent for a moment. Almost immediately, flashing lights went off at each of the operatives' desks, each of them an emergency call. Destruction, looting, violence: the town was erupting. And the answer to every call was the same: "Don't go out. Stay at home, don't open for anyone, and lock your doors."

The C.R.S.62 company had sent in two detachments: Alpha and Bravo. The Alpha men were lined up in tight formation in front of the barricade at the shopping centre. Flames more than three metres high shot up from the four burning cars lined up in front of it. Some of the new C.R.S. recruits witnessing their first riot looked to their more experienced colleagues for reassurance. During training, their instructors had prepared them for this kind of urban guerrilla warfare, but theory is never more than a pale imitation of reality. You have to add the noise, the smell of burnt plastic, insults screamed from all sides, stones, pétanque balls and metal bolts you spot at the very last moment when they crash at your feet or against an unfortunate colleague, and the fear that takes hold of you, a fear everyone deals with as best they can.

In the front line, less than thirty metres from the barricade, one of the new recruits, shield raised and visor lowered, jumped at a loud detonation. Then a second one. He took a step backwards.

"Are we being shot at?"

A powerful hand gripped his shoulder and pushed him back into line.

"Keep your position! Hold the line! Nobody is shooting at us, it's the windscreens exploding."

Reassured by authority, the young recruit stepped up again, but just then a fresh, even louder explosion robbed him of the last vestiges of courage. He crouched down as fear dug a hole in his stomach.

"Shit, now they really are shooting at us!"

"No, again. This time it's the tyres bursting. When they start using us as targets, I'll tell you."

Following instructions from the Control Room, the E.C.145 chopper flew over the main streets of Malceny. The thermal camera picked out scattered groups of silhouettes. Some of them spread out to cover as much territory as possible; others gathered to form small armies. As they advanced, vehicles were set on fire, shop windows smashed, bus shelters destroyed.

At 9.50 p.m., all the town buses received an urgent message and headed back as quickly as possible to the central bus depot, refusing to pick up any passengers. As he was following these instructions, the driver of the number 221 bus, which ran between the town hall and the town centre, was held up like a stage coach by thirty or so hooded youngsters and forced off his route.

Section Bravo had been given the task of protecting one of the most vulnerable targets: Malceny police headquarters. They were standing in closed ranks, waiting not exactly impatiently for an assault on the police station, when suddenly in the distance they saw a blazing number 221 bus heading straight for them. Halfway there, the intense heat made its tyres explode. The bus continued on its way in a shower of sparks from the wheel rims, then careered off course and slammed into a dozen or so parked cars, before toppling on its side and sliding for a few more metres. The flames were reflected in the C.R.S. shields and helmets.

It was pointless, but it made a wonderful display.

As for Section Alpha, they were ordered to reconnoitre the interior of the shopping mall, entering through one of the underground car parks. The thirty men in the squad broke into a trot and went round the building to reach the car park entrance. They crossed the vast stretch of grey concrete, slipping between parked cars in a cautious advance. Then they took the escalator up to the mall. On this level, thick smoke was pouring from some of the shops, while others were thoroughly on fire. At an intersection, they passed a children's roundabout. The little carriages had been ripped out and flung through shop windows. Smashed glass was strewn all over the floor, and there was that strange feeling of being in a looted and deserted mall. The officer in charge spoke into his radio.

"Negative. Nobody on the first floor. It's already been looted."

Section Alpha received fresh instructions from the Control Room.

"Remain on standby. Wait for info from the chopper for confirmation."

Reforming, the C.R.S. detachment waited, partly concealed by the quadruple escalator leading up to the second level. After a while, when he still hadn't received further instructions, the commander took a decision.

"Section Alpha, close formation. We're going up."

They formed a line, crouched down, and allowed themselves to be carried up slowly on the mechanical staircase. Each man had a hand on the shoulder of the one in front of him. At that moment, the helicopter began to hover above them, pointing its thermal camera at the shopping mall.

"E.C.145 to Control. How many of our lads are in there?"

"Control to E.C.145. About thirty."

"E.C.145 to control. Then they've got a problem."

The video image was retransmitted on their giant screens. Almost three hundred thermal outlines appeared. The Control Room commander seized hold of his microphone.

"Control to section. Get out of there! Do you read me? Section Alpha? Section Alpha, over!"

No-one had time to respond. A horde of two hundred and fifty hooded youths rushed at them, howling like banshees. They were wielding pickaxes, hammers and iron bars stolen from a looted D.I.Y. store. The C.R.S. men turned tail beneath a storm of projectiles and insults as cash registers and trolleys were dropped on them from the floor above. As he ran, their commander shouted into his radio.

"Section Alpha to Control! We're abandoning the shopping mall. Repeat, we're abandoning the shopping mall!"

After they were looted, the shops continued to smoulder until the first light of day.

42

Maud Jeansac had swapped her pumps for a pair of trainers. She crossed Malceny in the back of the car Vesperini had lent her, windows rolled all the way up in spite of the heat. A lingering smell of burning filled the streets, and on her way she passed scenes from the day after a battle. Boarded-up shop windows, waste containers strewn everywhere, still-smoking skeletons of burnt-out cars, and almost nobody about.

At 10 a.m. she was dropped off at the foot of Verlaine Tower in the Cité des Poètes. Grabbing her vanity case from the back shelf, she told the driver:

"I should be out in less than an hour."

Slightly uneasy, she pushed open the glass door to the lobby and rushed straight over to the lifts to avoid any awkward encounters. The lift groaned under her weight, the automatic door closed halfway, got stuck, and opened again. She decided it would be wiser to climb the nine floors on foot.

When she rang the bell at Flat 921, a door behind her opened an inch or two, revealing only the outline of a face keeping an eye on her. The badly lit corridor gave her goose bumps. She rang again, but this time left her finger on the button. After what seemed like an endless minute, the lock finally turned. Maud studied the person who answered, and realised she had underestimated the job she had on her hands.

"Madame Doucouré, you were supposed to be ready at ten o'clock!"

The woman shifted her feet so that she could scratch the inside of her buttocks more comfortably. It took her a good ten seconds to open her eyes fully, and a further twenty to understand what was going on. She ran her hand through her hair, revealing a cut coated in dried blood as she pushed back the thick matted clump on her forehead.

"What happened to your face?"

Bibz's mother managed only half the words, as though there was bad reception.

"I smashed . . . face . . . slipped . . . in toilet."

Maud entered the flat and closed the door behind her. It was all she could do to restrain herself from rushing to the windows to let in some fresh air. Grabbing a perfume bottle from her bag, she sprayed it on her jacket collar. A big mistake: the mixture of smells of sleep, food, stale farts and the expensive Guerlain perfume immediately made her want to throw up.

Bibz's mother collapsed on the living-room sofa, the cushions already hollowed out by her weight.

"Don't wanna go anymore."

Placing the vanity case by her feet on the floor, Maud opened it.

"You mean to your son's burial?"

"Don't try make me feel bad. You know nothing. He been dead to me a long time."

The mayor's press officer took a sealed envelope out of the case and laid it on the low table between them.

"Here are the two thousand euros, as agreed. And your benefits are being restored. We're also covering the funeral expenses. As you see, the town hall is not abandoning you.

But between you and me, nobody would understand it if you failed to put in an appearance today."

The mother struggled to open her eyes wide.

"Who is this 'nobody'? We've always been on our own."

The two women sat facing one another on the edge of the bathtub. Maud was using some wet wipes to clean the cut on Madame Doucouré's forehead, but Bibz's mother kept nodding off. Maud filled a glass with water and poured several sachets into it to make a reviving cocktail: double doses of Guronsan, Alka-Seltzer and citrate of betaine. The liquid began to fizz.

"Drink this. You ought to feel better in half an hour."

"Better?"

"Less bad. Come on, show me your wardrobe."

* * *

The car slowed at the entrance to Malceny cemetery, already blocked by a group of journalists kept at the gate by a last remaining shred of decency. The driver advanced a few more metres at snail's pace, then stopped. Maud glanced at her passenger, then peered out of the window to see how far they had to walk.

"Get as close as possible. I don't want anybody to see her staggering."

Above a hole in the ground, the metal struts of a cradle holding the coffin. The master of ceremonies was waiting for Madame Doucouré to arrive. Apart from a group of four strangers who were not content with the protest, the only mourners were Vesperini, Baptiste Cardel and a few other town hall employees press-ganged into attending. After looking at her watch for an eighth time, the mayor finally saw Maud approaching along a row of tombs, leading a woman dressed in black, with a veil the same colour covering her face. Almost identical to the veil that had caused all the drama, but the Catholic version. The two women stood either side of her. It took the master of ceremonies several seconds to realise there weren't going to be any speeches. No poem. No music. The small coffin was lowered gently into the hole, disappeared from view, and then the empty ropes resurfaced. The mourners were hesitant, unsure whether to leave or stay a while longer. Behind her veil, only Madame Doucouré seemed unmoved. Or maybe she had dozed off again. Vesperini took her arm, and they stood in silence, as though praying.

If there had been no good fairy hovering above Bibz's cradle, at least there were two witches perched over his coffin.

Cardel was outside the cemetery, propped against his car. He took the menthol cigarette Maud offered him, but at the first drag pulled a face and threw it on the ground. Ten metres away, the journalists had not budged, keen to snap a few images.

"Shall I take you back?" he offered.

"Not just yet. There's still the grand finale."

The chief of staff stared at her in disbelief.

"Maud, we're talking about the burial of a twelve-year-old kid here. I'm starting to think the Queen is seriously affecting your capacity for compassion. It seems to me that you're as bad as her."

But Maud's attention was fixed on Vesperini, who was coming out of the cemetery at that moment, and she did not respond to her colleague's jibe. Meanwhile, Cardel had quickly caught on to what was happening.

"Don't tell me she's going to do it!"

The mayor took hold of Madame Doucouré's hand and forced her to slow down. The invitation was obvious, and they were soon surrounded by T.V. cameras. Cardel couldn't believe his eyes.

"A statement to the press? Are you sure about this, Maud?"

"It's not about her, it's an appeal for calm. That's her role, isn't it?"

Vesperini waited for the microphones to be properly set up before she began.

"At the request of Madame Doucouré, I am taking it upon myself to speak today. Taking it upon myself, when grief stifles a mother's voice. I have no wish to make a political declaration, but out of respect for young Habibou, in memory of what he was and of everything he might have become, I am appealing for calm in our town. The incidents of the past two nights cannot be the response to this drama. Sorrow must not lead to blind violence. Madame Doucouré and I would like everyone to understand this. Thank you all, and I know that you will wish to respect the privacy necessary for mourning and reflection."

A few kilometres away, in his apartment, Gonthier pressed the mute button on his T.V. remote, and Vesperini continued talking without a sound issuing from her mouth. Peering out of the window, he was glad of this temporary respite. Drawn by the funeral, the journalists had abandoned his street.

43

Sam had swapped his tablet for a good old-fashioned paper book. Seeing him there, relaxed, with his feet up on his desk, nobody would have imagined that Groupe Crime 1's whiteboard was filled with three unsolved cases: Rose Carpentier, Azzedine Salah and Habibou Doucouré. Not counting the three executed dealers who were decorating the board in Groupe Crime 2. This was what was going through Ronan's mind when he returned from the gym and saw his colleague busy doing nothing.

"What on earth are you up to?"

"Reading a book."

"I can see that. What book?"

"*Catcher in the Rye* by Salinger. It belongs to old Jacques Landernes."

"Did he give it to you, or did you pinch it?"

"Dunno . . . It's got "For Sam" written inside it. Do you think that might be a clue?"

Ronan sat at his desk, visibly stressed.

"Having nothing to do drives me crazy," he said.

"Without any leads, there's no point rushing around like madmen."

"Uh-huh. Any idea where Coste has got to?"

* * *

After the burial, Vesperini left it to her press officer to see Madame Doucouré home. It wouldn't do for her to be seen hanging around in bars when the town was besieged by the press. The mayor had her driver drop her off at the town hall and strode resolutely across the lobby without deigning to glance at the receptionist. As soon as the Vesperini hurricane had passed, the girl picked up her telephone and dialled the chief of staff's internal number.

"The Queen has arrived at her castle, monsieur."

Cardel hurried to head the mayor off, taking up position at the entrance to the anteroom to her office.

"I've been trying to reach you for a quarter of an hour, madame."

Vesperini dug out her mobile and saw the five missed calls.

"Damn, I put it on vibrate in the cemetery. What's the problem?"

"Capitaine Coste is waiting for you."

She came to an abrupt halt.

"Unannounced?"

"So it seems."

"Who does he think he is? I'm his boss's boss after all. He needs to be reminded of his position in the food chain."

In spite of this, she put on her best smile and pushed open the door to the anteroom. Coste was buried in an armchair, but rose to his feet as soon as he saw her.

"Capitaine. I'm so sorry you had to wait. Next time, don't hesitate to make an appointment. That will allow me to free up some time, and above all save you from wasting yours."

"Thanks for your concern, but this won't take long."

Vesperini went into her office, threw her jacket across the back of the chair, and sat down.

"Please, take a seat, capitaine. How are your investigations progressing?"

"Not as rapidly as I would like, if I'm honest."

"So what can I do for you?"

"Absolutely nothing. I'm simply following the protocol. The municipal police are directly responsible to you, so I've come to inform you that we're opening an enquiry into the attempted arrest on the Cosmonautes estate. The one that led to the death of young Habibou Doucouré. If you have no objection, I should like to interview several of your officers."

"That's in everyone's interest. The more delicate the affair, the more necessary complete transparency becomes."

The conversation could have ended there, but Coste took advantage to embark on something the police term a "fishing expedition". He had nothing up his sleeve, no evidence, he simply wanted to see the reaction to his questions on the mayor's face. And so, carrying on in the same tone of voice, he cast his first line.

"I hope they'll be able to explain to me how they came up with the preposterous idea of doing a burka check at eleven at night during Ramadan, in the centre of a very difficult estate. Unless you yourself can explain it to me, that is?"

Vesperini raised an inquisitive eyebrow, but otherwise showed no emotion.

"I already have more than enough on my plate without attempting to coordinate what the municipal police get up to. I only see them at our tri-monthly meetings, where we set out the main priorities for law and order, security and public health. The decision to check identities on the Cosmonautes estate was never submitted for my approval, still less authorised by me."

"Obviously. I'll probably have more success if I put my questions to the chief of the municipal police, Monsieur . . ."

". . . Gonthier, Henri Gonthier. For the moment he has been suspended, but I hope to pay him a visit. To be frank with you, capitaine, I'm putting that off as long as I can, because I've no idea what attitude to adopt towards him. A child has been killed, so I am unable to publicly support him. On the other hand, he's done nothing illegal, even if the operation itself might seem ill judged."

"I understand. I imagine all these recent events must disturb you. First your deputy, whom you described as a friend when we first met – a former accomplice of the three murdered dealers – is himself killed. And then your police undertake an operation which leaves your town ablaze."

Vesperini frowned and, in a tone verging on condescension, emphasised every word of her reply.

"I am the mayor. And, as you say, Malceny is *my* town. You should expect to find me at the centre of lots of things, capitaine."

Coste understood that this marked the end of their conversation.

Once he had left, Vesperini realised she was out of breath. She still couldn't work out what the real purpose of his visit had been. Whatever it was, the capitaine wouldn't let go and, while it didn't seem as though he had made the connection between her and the hell Malceny had been plunged into, there was no question of giving him the time to find out.

She had to find a way to shake him off. Keep him at a distance. Offer him a shortcut that would bog him down. For the first time, she was impatient to receive the next call from her shameful associate.

44

At the first ring, Markus picked up his mobile. He read the name on the screen and at the second ring he answered it, trying to sound as natural as possible despite the circumstances.

"Am I disturbing you, Markus?"

"No, it's fine. I wasn't sure what to do, whether or not I should call you . . . well . . . I'm sorry about the boy."

"Thanks. I appreciate that. What are you doing at the moment?"

As if he could admit to the Boss he had a babysitting job that he'd been obliged to accept. What was he doing? Waiting for Estelle.

Markus looked around him. The clock on the front of the school showed twenty-eight minutes past five. In just under two minutes, the bell from the private chapel of Charles-Germain-de-Jouy was going to ring out, and place him in a part of town where he had no business being. Somewhere that the Boss knew well, since he had organised the mock attack on Vesperini's daughter.

"I'm playing a computer game," he lied.

"Are you free this evening? I'm getting all the teams together at the hub. We'll soon be back in business, and I'd like you to be there."

Markus looked up. Without warning, the big hand slipped to twenty-nine minutes past.

"Don't be offended, but . . . you know I don't get mixed up with drugs."

"No problem. I've always respected your choices. All I need is for you to lend me a spare set of keys for the boxing club. I'd like to store some merchandise there for a while."

Markus was in a tight spot. On one side he had the Boss, who controlled the neighbourhoods – not someone you wanted on your back. On the other, Vesperini and her threats to close the club. All of Markus's family lived on the estates, and he couldn't allow himself to put them in danger, or to become a pariah. But boxing was his future, his only way out, and the closure of the M.B.C. was unthinkable. It was an impossible choice, so he had to play both sides.

"Alright."

The big hand began to glide gently down to the half hour.

"Thanks. I need to know I can count on you."

Markus ended the call, and a fraction of a second later, the bell struck the half hour. He blew out his cheeks, put away the mobile, and allowed his blood pressure to subside.

A flock of sparrows, satchels on their backs, soon came hurtling out of the school gates. Estelle ran towards him, happy to leave behind her classmates, all of whom were staring at her, green with envy. Markus held out his hand, and she tapped twice on his palm with hers, then patted herself twice on the chest.

"I saw that on the internet," she said. "It's a hip-hop handshake."

The boxer couldn't help laughing.

"Whatever. You should try it on your mother. She'll freak out."

Estelle opened her backpack and rummaged through it.

"I've kept my snack."

"Yeah, share it out, I'm starving. And get a move on, I've got a training session."

"Can I come? Please, pretty please, please . . ." she begged him.

"No. Your mother was very clear. I have to take you straight home."

"She won't know, she never gets home before nine. Except when I get shot at."

"No."

"You've taken me home three times now, and come to fetch me three times as well. I thought we were friends. You can trust me, you know, I won't tell her."

"Seriously, what is it about the word 'no' you don't understand?"

* * *

Markus just managed to dodge Gordah's straight right, but his left hook was unstoppable and thudded into his cheek. Gordah went over to his opponent on the canvas, held out his glove, and helped him back to his feet.

"You're not in the ring, my friend."

"Sorry, I was thinking about your mother."

The Turkish boxer looked around the room, and in particular at the young girl installed on one of the front row seats. All smiles, she was using her phone to take photos of their sparring.

"So, you brought your fan club?"

"Forget her."

"You're the one who should forget her. You're hardly blocking any of my shots. She's distracting you."

Markus raised his guard and the two athletes began to

dance around the ring again. At the back of the hall, a group of kids from the educational boxing scheme, boys aged between eight and thirteen, came forward towards Estelle. Some sat in the row behind her, two others sat down on either side of her.

"You're not from here, are you? Do you want to join the club? You'd be the first chick – that'd be cool. If you like, we can train you."

"No thanks, I'm with a friend," she murmured, lowering her eyes.

Markus shot a quick glance from the ring as the kids swarmed round the young girl.

"That's a cool phone. Will you lend it to me?"

"I prefer not to."

"Don't worry, chill out, we're not going to steal it," said a voice behind her. "Trust us."

The boy on her left gave her a winning smile.

"You're pretty, you know. It'd be super cool if you were nice as well."

She handed him her phone. As soon as he was holding it, he took several steps back, asked all his friends to gather round Estelle, then snapped a series of photos. In the first one, she didn't look too happy, but by the time he took the last photo she was reassured enough to give a broad smile. The boy returned to his seat, and she held out her hand.

"Seriously? Did you really think I'd give it back? Do you know how much I can get for it?"

Estelle's smile faded. She was furious with herself for being so naive.

"It was a present . . ."

The young charmer held the screen up to his face and took a selfie.

"Here. It's a souvenir of me, in case you don't come back."

All the others laughed, making fun of her. Blushing, Estelle recovered her mobile, and Markus, his attention drawn to the laughter, turned towards the ringside. Gordah's uppercut slammed into his stomach; he doubled up in agony and crashed to the canvas.

"You see how she's distracting you?"

45

Leaving Vesperini's office, Coste went over in his mind everything they had said; this little exercise kept him busy all the way back to Groupe Crime 1. He found Sam at his computer, and Johanna glued to the telephone. His colleague's tone immediately told him what she was talking about.

"Stop, maman, we're not involved . . . No . . . I'm not saying I want to be there, just that I feel bad for the others. The Police Judiciaire never go to the front line during riots, it's our uniformed colleagues who run the risks. Listen, I had the same conversation with Karl until one this morning, so if you don't mind . . . Yes . . . Me too."

She hung up and asked her two colleagues:

"Do you get that as well?"

"My parents stopped watching the news when I joined the police," Coste said.

"As for me, family isn't a problem," Sam admitted, winking knowingly in Victor's direction.

Coste added:

"They're going to have to get used to it, because we're in real trouble. There are all the ingredients for several more nights of havoc. It's going to be a hot July. Kids who don't have enough money to go away on holiday flanked by journalists who have to find news even though nothing happens in summer. When you put two bored people in a room together, after a while they're bound to start playing games. Apart from that, any idea where Ronan is?"

"In the basement, at the gym. He's burning off energy."

"Johanna, go and get him. We're taking him for a walk."

Sam peeled off a Post-it from his desk and handed it to Coste.

"I reckon that will do him good. Here's Gonthier's address for you."

* * *

In the end, all they needed was the name of the street: there was quite a crowd outside the chief of the municipal police's apartment building. Two outside broadcast vans, several T.V. crews, freelance paparazzi and journalists from the print media. Bibz's burial might have afforded Gonthier a brief respite, but now he was the focus of attention again. The first to get a photograph or a quote would be that day's gold medallist.

Ronan parked some metres away.

"You have to be stupid to stir everyone up by carrying out a niqab check in the middle of an estate, but I still feel sorry for him. Can you imagine what must be going through the poor guy's mind?"

"Sam told me he lives alone," Johanna said. "Luckily for him. If your family had to put up with this as well . . ."

Coste got out of the unmarked car and warned the rest of his team.

"O.K., we'll push through the crowd. Don't answer any questions if you don't want your mugs to appear on television."

*

Gonthier had been stuck in his apartment for forty-eight hours, moving only between his computer and the window. Between insults and threats spreading like wildfire on the internet and the horde at the entrance to his apartment block. He knew that a new scoop drives out the old, and that one day soon he would be forgotten. But Malceny would never forget. And neither would he.

He went over to retrieve his mobile from the table, and sent a text message.

When the balcony windows on the seventh floor opened, all the T.V. and press cameras swung upwards. Coste followed them with his eyes. Gonthier appeared above the crowd. His stomach was aching, his head spinning. He looked up at the sun and allowed its warmth to settle on his face. That was something he wanted to remember. He clambered over the balcony rail, still holding on with one hand, then steadied himself.

At ground level, the journalists held their breath. Coste and Johanna realised at once there was nothing to be done, but Ronan shouldered his way through the onlookers and shouted up to Gonthier, almost cursing him.

"Gonthier! Look at me! Don't do it! You may think you'll never get over this, but I promise you . . ."

Gonthier took a step into the void. His body toppled from the seventh floor and an instant later slammed down onto a parked car. The vehicle's roof buckled, and its windows exploded. Ronan only just had time to turn away and protect himself with his arm. A shard of glass striped his cheek. The whole world stopped.

Silence filled his ears.

He froze.

No more sound. No more movement.

After a few seconds' delay, the alarm on the crushed car began to wail, startling everyone. Ronan went over to the inert body, the arms dangling over the sides of the car roof. He laid two fingers on the aorta. No sign of life.

Coste took out the car radio and reported back to the Control Room.

"Send a team from the Malceny station to the home address of the head of the municipal police. We have a suicide."

They had to prise Ronan away from the gaggle of journalists before he took his anger out on one of them. Luckily, Coste had a job for him. Johanna was posted at the entrance to the building while the two men rushed upstairs to the seventh floor. They found Gonthier's name on the bell button of the last apartment at the far end of the corridor.

"We don't know for sure he lived on his own," Coste said. "There could be somebody in danger inside. Will you take care of it?"

"With pleasure."

Ronan retreated to the wall opposite Gonthier's front door, then launched himself shoulder first. The door shook. Stepping back again, he flung his seventy-five kilos at it for a second time. It gave way, bursting open, taking part of the wooden frame with it. They entered the apartment.

"What are we looking for?"

"A farewell letter, a note . . . Actually, I've no idea, but we only have a few minutes before the Malceny police get here."

Gonthier's computer was still switched on. Coste asked Ronan to check the browser history. Then he saw the mobile phone and scrolled through the latest calls and text messages. His attention was drawn to one sent to Vesperini only a few minutes earlier:

As far as the kid goes, I hope to apologise to him in person. I'll leave you to deal with your guilt. I can't.

There is no police inquiry in a case of suicide, still less any possibility of removing evidence from the scene. So Coste slipped the mobile into his pocket. Ronan reported on what he had found:

"Nothing special. He spent the last forty-eight hours surfing news sites. That can't have done much for his state of mind."

Behind them, a squad of uniformed officers appeared in the doorway. Among them, a young policewoman they already knew.

"Capitaine, my respects. It seems you're never far from disaster."

"It goes with the job. Hello there, Emilie."

"Why did you break the door down?"

"To make sure the apartment was clear."

"Is that what I put in my report?"

"Yes, with an explanation. Write that the Police Judiciaire thought they heard noises inside – that should do it."

The young policewoman winked at him, and he responded with a smile.

Ronan and Coste went downstairs at a more leisurely pace. They found Johanna at the entrance.

"Find anything interesting?"

"Nothing special," Ronan said. "Unless the mobile Victor pinched has anything sensitive on it. Are you planning to share it with us?"

Coste took the mobile out of his pocket and handed it to them.

"See for yourselves."

Johanna took the phone. Just as she was doing so, it began to buzz. The word "maman" appeared on the screen.

"Shit! What do we do?"

"Nothing," Victor ordered. "Let it ring. It's none of our business, and besides, there's no reason for us to have the phone. She'll hear the news soon enough."

46

Night was falling, and before leaving headquarters Coste sat on the low wall surrounding the interior garden. He lit a cigarette, made a call on his mobile. Léa didn't even give him time to say hello.

"Can you tell me what's the point of going on holiday if I spend the whole time glued to the T.V. news? I hope at least they haven't got you mixed up in all this mess."

"You worry too much. The uniforms have to face all the stones and insults. The same goes for riots. Sometimes I wonder if we're doing the same job."

"What are you saying? You sound almost disappointed."

"No, but it's in situations like these I'm aware how cushy our job is in comparison. But with three cases on the go, we aren't short of work."

"Three cases? The last I heard there was a little old woman . . ."

"You can add a deputy mayor and a twelve-year-old kid."

"And you're going to manage to tie all of them up by the end of the week?"

Coste took a long drag on his cigarette.

"I'm not coming, Léa. I'm so sorry, I can't just drop everything and leave for a holiday. You understand that, don't you?"

There was a heavy silence on the other end of the line.

"I thought I was stronger."

"Stronger than who?"

"Than those police wives consumed with the fear of not seeing their man come home. Stronger than the images of violence on a screen. Stronger than being woken up in the middle of the night, or being stood up, stronger than cancelled holidays. But I'm no better than any of them. Just another woman in love. I feel guilty for having believed it. Guilty and stupid."

Coste didn't know what to say. Léa hung up on him.

47

In the Friends of Malceny-Haiti hall, the Boss was meeting with his six lieutenants, each of them responsible for a tower block. Driss was on his right, Colin on his left. To avoid any leaks, he hadn't invited the runners. The six stony faces of his audience, who were already whispering among themselves, were more than enough.

"This is only a hitch, you guys. You just have to be patient," he began.

"Patience is a sign of weakness," a lieutenant in a white tracksuit shot back. "That's what you told us, isn't it? It's been almost two weeks since you replaced the others, promising us more dough and more responsibility."

The other five nodded in agreement. He went on:

"All we've seen so far is two minders out of action, meaning we've nothing left to sell. When I worked for Dimov, we might have been screwed on the percentages, but at least we had money coming in."

Reassured that there appeared to be room for discussion, his neighbour added his two cents' worth:

"I know some guys in Saint-Ouen who can supply us with gear on credit. It's more expensive, but it'll help us keep control of the neighbourhood."

The Boss realised they were no longer so afraid of him.

"It's not even worth considering. We'd pay a third more for the stuff, and they'll send one of their gang to keep an eye on us. We may as well just bend over for them straightaway. If we let them get a foothold, they'll take us out one by one."

"Especially as you've already set an example."

They really weren't scared of him at all.

"Plus you promised us dough for the trouble we're causing every night."

"And what about housing? Cars? Paid holidays? The fake jobs from the town hall: are we supposed to be patient about all that as well?"

Caught out, the Boss changed his tone.

"You load of whiny bitches! What are you moaning about? I'm breaking my back trying to offer you something different to your crappy little lives, and just because I'm a few days late on my promises, you're all shitting yourselves?"

The youth in the white tracksuit tried to calm things down, but his sly smile and saccharine tone made the Boss want to pull out the gun he had under his T-shirt and put a bullet between his eyes.

"Stay cool, bro. If it's only a few days, that's fine. But you need to understand us: we've also got teams and people we need to keep patient. You know what it's like. They ask questions. They have doubts. The kids we take on are stupid, especially when they have time on their hands. Now you're telling us it will all be sorted out, and that'll reassure everybody. All that's good news . . ."

The Boss eyed his lieutenants. He understood he needed to regain control of the situation, and quickly. One day, when he had made good on his promises and was properly back in charge, he would have to decide what future lay in store for that loser in the white tracksuit.

"In precisely two days you'll have stuff to sell and the money I promised you. That's just for starters, but it'll stop you moaning. Warn your teams. I want everybody ready to go at ten o'clock, and all of you here an hour earlier."

His lieutenants stood up one after the other. They made sure to shake hands with the Boss before leaving, and the looks they gave him spoke volumes. Left on his own, the Boss told Driss to leave, and asked Colin to stay. Taking him by the scruff of his neck, his voice became more paternal.

"Do you trust me, Colin?"

THIRD NIGHT OF RIOTING

After midnight, one of the ten operatives in the Control Room received an emergency call. The 524th since he had come on duty. This one attracted his particular attention. From Malceny. The operator took down the info, then called the head of the Control Room, Commandant Auclair, on his direct line.

"I have a report of an assault taking place on rue du Général-Dorin in Malceny. A group of three people is harassing a young woman with an infant. The caller hung up, and I have no number for him."

From his office, Auclair had a clear view of the entire hive and its giant screens.

"Did you talk to the municipal police?"

"Yes. Général-Dorin is a one-way street ending in a fork. To the left it borders the Cité des Poètes, on the right it's a cul-de-sac."

"Anonymous caller, an estate, cul-de-sac, woman with a baby. It's too perfect not to be a trap. It stinks of an ambush."

"Should we ignore it?"

"That would be the most sensible thing to do, but unfortunately we're obliged to look into it. Does Malceny have a vehicle available?"

"No, they're all being used as backup for the riot police.

Even the defence dogs from the Dog Unit are on standby tonight."

"O.K., but get them to send someone to take a look. Be sure to tell them to take all necessary precautions. I want to know when they arrive and when they leave."

Auclair hung up, with the uneasy feeling he was sending lambs to the slaughter.

* * *

The commanding officer on board police car 816 Sierra received instructions from the Control Room, and then retransmitted them to his team.

"An assault on an estate. It has to be a trap. Général-Dorin is a den of thieves. Where's Emilie?"

"She's on the front line with the C.R.S. I asked her to run and check out what was going on."

Ten or so metres from where they were parked, the C.R.S. cordon was confronted by a line of six blazing cars effectively blocking the street, so that they had no way of knowing what was brewing on the other side. The flames cast giant shadows on the tower block facades. That morning, the newspapers decided it would be a good idea to print the total number of burnt-out vehicles: thirteen the first night, one hundred and thirty-six the second. So the rioters had their own record to beat, and it seemed they were up for the challenge. Beyond the crackle of the bonfires, there was a strange cacophony in the air. From all over the town, at different levels, came the sound of alarms from private houses, shops and public buildings, like so many cries for help that nobody could respond to.

Emilie rejoined her team, climbed into the front of the car, and adjusted her seat belt.

"Where are we going?"

"To an assault. Just hope we're not the victims."

The car set off, and the C.R.S. cordon parted to let them through.

* * *

Eighteen floors up on the Cité de Poètes estate, on the roof of Baudelaire Tower, a police officer wearing a black sweatshirt was busy setting up a video monitor attached to a computer keyboard. He switched it on, and a series of numbers flickered on the screen. Beside him, two other officers in identical black clothing opened a reinforced suitcase containing the U.A.V. Put more simply, the drone. About a metre long and sixty centimetres wide, it looked like a polystyrene glider, except for the built-in camera.

Several years earlier, the possible use of drones to monitor riots in towns had roused the indignation of many mayors in the region. Notions such as "privacy", "systematic aerial surveillance" and "individual liberties" were their rallying cries. Even though many witnesses swore they had seen drones in the sky during the 2005 skirmishes in Villiers-le-Bel, the government continued to deny they were being tested in urban areas. In other words, authorisation for a test in a real situation had been difficult to obtain, and the present deployment of three specialist agents had been carried out very discreetly.

One of them gently removed the drone from the box and laid it on the roof, wings unfolded. Standing next to the drone, the pilot synchronised his control box, hanging from a lanyard round his neck. Behind his screen, the technician checked he was connected to the gyroscope, altimeter and accelerometer, ready to enter the G.P.S. coordinates for a test flight.

"What shall we do then? Count the number of burnt-out vehicles?" the pilot said. "Compile a photo album of the wreckers?"

"Nothing like that," the technician corrected him. "We're here as phantoms. One fly-past at a hundred metres above the barricades, another at a hundred and fifty, a series of photos, a video with the two camera modes, and we'll have complied with the brief."

"That's not exactly 'Top Gun'."

The third member of the team had hung back a little, listening to his police radio. Now he came over to the others, increasing the volume. The voice of Commandant Auclair, the Control Room chief, was clearly audible.

"816 Sierra, let me remind you you're all alone in this, and that nobody here feels good about it. It's probably a trap, and it's going to be hard to supply you with any reinforcements, so go in on the tip of your tyres, over?"

"Roger from 816 Sierra. We'd figured that much," the officer said into the radio.

Then, adopting a vehicle commander's voice, he announced the mission.

"816 Sierra, zero plus three, objective Général-Dorin for an assault. Or not."

Up on the roof, the three men in black looked at one another. Since neither of his colleagues seemed willing to make a decision, the pilot decided for them.

"That's exactly what the drone was designed for. Surveillance of an area and backup for the police. We'll never have a better opportunity."

"Except that if we crash, the whole project is screwed."

"What if it really is an ambush?"

"To hell with it . . ." growled the flight technician.

*

The G.P.S. coordinates were entered, the propellers began to turn, then throb quietly, and the drone took off noiselessly into the night.

"Go on, my beauty, spread your wings."

The drone sped through the air above the tower blocks at seventy kilometres an hour. It flew undetected over Sierra 816, arrived at its destination more than two minutes before the police car, and went into geostationary mode.

"Nothing on my screen, and the light intensifier is on full. I'll switch to infrared."

The image changed from grey to green, and the scene appeared more clearly. The flight technician swivelled the video camera. He studied every detail, until suddenly he saw a mass of luminous dots appear. Zooming in, he called out:

"Shit! I've got a dozen thermal profiles at the end of the street. It doesn't look like an assault: they're all stationary. I'll zoom in."

* * *

816 Sierra rolled down almost the whole length of Général-Dorin without finding the slightest sign of a damsel in distress. At the far end, the road narrowed into such a tight funnel that parking was forbidden. The police car slowed, but didn't come to a halt. Back in the hive, everyone in the Control Room was listening closely to the radio. An unknown, slightly panicky voice took over the airwaves.

"Message for the crew of 816 Sierra. Make a U-turn. You're less than five metres from an ambush. There is no assault taking place. I repeat, there is no assault taking place."

Taken by surprise, Commandant Auclair pulled the desk microphone towards him.

"User . . . please identify yourself."

After three seconds' silence, he repeated his message.

"You are using a restricted police radio frequency. Kindly identify yourself."

In response, the giant screen in front of him quivered, and an infrared image appeared on it. Auclair studied it, and this time it was his voice that betrayed panic.

"816 Sierra, confirmed – you have a reception committee. Make a U-turn!"

As the driver was about to go into reverse, a group of ten hooded figures appeared out of nowhere and surrounded the police car. Despite their surprise at the vehicle's unexpected manoeuvre, they continued as planned. The first two smashed the windscreen with a baseball bat and an iron bar. Glass sprayed the inside of the car. 816 Sierra swerved, climbed the pavement, and crashed straight into an electricity post. Two more masked silhouettes came up alongside them. One was carrying a bottle; the other was trying to light it. When the rag jammed in the neck began to burn, he tapped his accomplice on the shoulder and threw the Molotov cocktail as hard as he could against the car bonnet. The bottle exploded, and Emilie and the driver were doused in petrol.

But nothing happened.

The burning rag had gone out as it was flying through the air.

The police and the arsonists stared at one another for an instant, unable to believe their eyes. Clinging to his wheel, soaked in petrol, the driver sat paralysed. Beside him, Emilie was apparently shouting something, but her lips seemed to be moving noiselessly. His brain had literally frozen. Then all at once sound was restored, and he heard his colleague's cries:

"Step on it, for Christ's sake!"

Seizing the gearstick, he slammed the car into reverse and, foot on the floor, extricated them from the trap without bothering about hitting anyone.

The drone hadn't missed a single frame of the action, and back in the Control Room, neither had Commandant Auclair. On screen he could see the car escaping to safety. He leaned over the microphone.

"816 Sierra. Everyone safe?"

Emilie pressed the button on her radio.

"Safe and sound. We're returning to base."

In the Control Room, some of the staff high-fived one another, while others applauded with relief, as if they had just carried out a successful rocket launch. Auclair wiped the sweat from his brow.

"Unknown user, you are on a private frequency. Identify yourself." Silence. The giant screen suddenly went blank. Auclair slumped into the nearest chair. It would have been unbearable to see three uniformed youngsters burned to a crisp.

The petrol-soaked car crawled slowly through the deserted streets of Malceny. Without a windscreen, its passengers felt the warm nocturnal breeze on their faces, and couldn't stop smiling idiotically. Emilie pressed the button on her radio once more.

"Hey, you guardian angels . . . Are you still there?"

The drone landed softly on the roof of Baudelaire Tower. The pilot folded its wings, and before storing it back in its case, spoke to it as though it were a brave young girl.

"Your first rescue, my beauty. Congratulations, now you're a real cop."

48

Coste held Gonthier's mobile, spinning it between his fingers. Across from him, his team was busy with croissants and theories.

"I don't see how it helps us," Johanna said. "Even if it was Vesperini who ordered the check on the Cosmonautes estate, there's nothing illegal about that. It's definitely stupid, but not illegal. Alright, so she lied to you, but if she had foreseen the consequences, I don't think she would have taken that decision."

"What gets me," Coste said, "is that now everything is tied in together. Vesperini with the municipal police. The municipal police with Bibz. Bibz with the drug minders. The minders with the dead dealers. And the dead dealers with the deputy mayor."

Ronan came in and put their coffees on the low table.

"So what are you thinking of doing? Going fishing again? If you're considering showing up at the town hall and shoving an ambiguous text message under the mayor's nose, on a mobile you nicked from a suicide's apartment, you're risking a roasting."

Something along those lines had occurred to Coste. Hearing it from another person was quite different, yet in the present situation he couldn't think what else to do.

Just as he was about to contact Vesperini's secretary to arrange a third meeting, his desk telephone rang. The conversation only lasted a few seconds; when he hung up, he responded to his team's inquisitive looks.

"Someone called Colin Faizon is down at the front desk with his lawyer. He's come to explain his part in the deaths of Rose Carpentier and Azzedine Salah. And he has a big sports bag with him."

Johanna, the newest member of the group, seemed not to understand, so Sam filled in the gaps.

"When you turn up with your lawyer, it's because things don't look good for you. And the sports bag is probably a change of clothes. In short, he's come to hand himself in, and thinks he might be jailed."

"This is a bit of a turn-up for the books, isn't it?" Johanna said. "One investigation cleared up by the suicide of the perpetrator, and now some guy appears out of nowhere offering to resolve the other two cases . . ."

"I don't much like ready meals," Ronan said, pulling a face. "I prefer to cook for myself."

Coste reassured him.

"Don't worry, we'll make sure he's served up properly."

* * *

Coste switched on his computer webcam to record the interview, and studied the two visitors. The lawyer, a man in his forties in a sober suit, with pen and notebook at the ready to make a note of any procedural irregularities. Then his client, who seemed somewhat distracted, as if he had been up all night, wearing clothes that were far too big for him, his hair tousled.

Informed of this unexpected turn of events, Stévenin, the Police Judiciaire's commissaire, had briefly appeared in Groupe Crime 1's office to check on things for himself, quietly shutting the door on which an INTERVIEW IN PROGRESS sign had been hung. Coste and his team were now on their own with Colin and his adviser. It was the latter who spoke first.

"My client wanted to come to see you today because—"

"Be quiet," Coste said very calmly.

"I beg your pardon?"

"Be quiet, please. The interview has begun, and I don't want to hear any more from you until it's over."

The lawyer knew the legal procedures as well as the capitaine, and shrank back in his chair, decidedly put out. Coste ignored him and turned to the young man.

"So, Colin . . . it is Colin, isn't it? You woke up this morning feeling the need to be at peace with yourself, is that right?"

For the first time, the youngster spoke.

"Yeah, that's right. I've come to talk to you about the old lady and . . ."

"Relax. You'll have all the time in the world to repeat the story you've been told to learn. What I want to know first of all is: how much did your trainers cost?"

"Two hundred euros. They're Yeezys," the kid replied proudly, though taken aback by the question.

"Yes, they're really cool. So how much does your lawyer cost?"

Colin appeared to be thinking this over, then turned to his counsel, but the man preferred to keep his head down.

"Don't worry," Coste helped him. "It's normal for you to know the price of your shoes, because you paid for them. The other thing was paid for you. And you, how much were you paid to come and turn yourself in on your own?"

"What the fuck are you talking about?"

Colin was at a loss, no longer sure of anything. His lawyer, perfectly aware of this, now spoke up.

"I think that's enough, capitaine. He's been grilled enough. You could let him speak a little, couldn't you?"

Coste agreed, but the scarecrow seemed to have forgotten his lines. Ronan bent down to whisper in his ear.

"You haven't rehearsed this properly, have you? Let me prompt you: 'I've come to talk to you about the old lady and . . .'"

"Yeah, that's right," Colin eventually managed to say. "I've come to talk to you about the old lady and Salah. I just take orders in all this. I work for some guys I don't know: they pay me to go and check that the stupid losers minding the gear are onside."

Coste's eyes narrowed. There are three kinds of French in common use. French among friends, where insults are used as punctuation. French within the family, which is slightly richer. And finally, French used in professional circles, more polished and codified. To be able to master all three of these in Seine-Saint-Denis made you a polyglot. But poor Colin seemed only to know the sort with insults. Even if the boy was making an effort today, Coste was expecting his ears to burn during the next few exchanges.

"But it's not just me. The boy who receives the orders is called Bibz. He was the one who gave the old woman a shake, but we didn't know she had heart problems. For fuck's sake, we didn't do anything: she was just old."

"Bibz. That sounds like a nickname. Do you know his real first name?"

"Habibou. He was the kid killed by those municipal police bastards."

Coste whistled with astonishment.

"Habibou Doucouré? I've underestimated you. I thought you'd come in to confess, but in fact you've just shifted all the responsibility onto a dead person. That's clever. Carry on."

"Shit, that's all there is. We did the same at the second minder's place, an old guy with a cat. But he didn't croak."

"So what's the connection with Azzedine Salah?"

"He hasn't always worked at the mayor's office. Before that he was like the rest of us, and he owed my boss a lot of dough. We were supposed to go and pay him a visit, but when he didn't have the cash, Bibz lost it. Just like with the old woman. I tried to calm him down, but he can't control himself."

"You're saying it was Habibou Doucouré, a twelve-year-old boy, who killed Salah? Is that what you want me to write down?"

"You know as well as I do: being twelve in Malceny isn't the same as in Paris. It's a different fuckin' world."

This observation brought a smile to Coste's face. He turned to Ronan.

"Call Malceny police and have them send us a copy of all the criminal records for Habibou Doucouré. I'd like to get to know him a little better, this twelve-year-old terror capable of making old ladies die of fright."

Then Coste turned his attention back to his guest.

"Just so we're clear about this: can you tell me exactly what the two minders were keeping for you?"

"I don't know. There was gear and dough."

"Both? How much? Be more precise."

"The drugs were some brown, some white, I'm sure of that. As for the dough, there must have been twenty-five thousand at the old woman's, and fifty thousand at the old man's. But he disappeared, leaving it all to the pigs. To you, that is. That meant there was nothing left at the minders', so we went to get the money Azzedine owed."

Coste shot a glance in Sam's direction before resuming his questioning, more pointedly this time.

"Stop. That doesn't fit. Now concentrate, and tell me exactly what there was."

"Fuck you! I know nothing about drugs, and the money is always in wads of twenty-five. One at the old woman's. Two at the old man's."

Fifty thousand euros in Jacques Landernes' flat? Coste remained impassive, but in his mind a storm was brewing. Sam left the office and the interview continued.

"Now then, your name doesn't appear in any of our records. You turn up out of nowhere and hand yourself in. What's the idea?"

"The old woman was the same age as my grandmother. And Salah – his mother looked after me a lot when I was little. So I feel bad. Real bad."

"I hope you've prepared another version with your lawyer."

"Yes, there's the version where I had no choice. The version where my boss uses a fuckin' drill when he gets angry. But deep down he's not really violent. He didn't want us to touch the old lady, or Azzedine. I've come to take the rap, so it doesn't affect his business."

Coste knew there was no point, but it was procedurally unthinkable not to ask anyway.

"Does your boss have a name, by any chance?"

"Go fuck yourself."

"You certainly have a way with words, kiddo . . ."

"If it puts my life in danger, I've got the right to zip it. It's the slob here who told me so."

Shifting uncomfortably, the lawyer tried to save face by scribbling something in his notebook.

"O.K., so in your exquisite French, have you got anything else to say to me?"

"Yeah, you can go take a running jump."

"We'll take that as a 'no' then."

49

Vesperini was rereading her notes in the back of her official car. Alongside her, Maud was awaiting the verdict like a pupil having her work marked, so much of the journey to Radio Monte Carlo passed in silence. When she had finished, the Queen turned to her press officer.

"Perfect. I think we've covered all the bases. That won't stop Bourdin yelling at me, but at least I'll know what to say. I would have preferred France Inter though."

"I know. They're supposed to get back to me, but I'm not worried, everyone wants you. Do you need the bullet points I've done for you?"

"No, I've got it all clear in my head. A call for calm. The town as victim. Appeal for the state to get involved to support deprived neighbourhoods. Curfew for minors, and the possible closure of schools while the riots are still ongoing."

Maud took back her notes and filed them in her briefcase.

"Given the circumstances, madame, I find you remarkably calm."

"That's simply because, in twenty-four hours from now, I won't have to deal with all this on my own."

"I'm sorry, but I don't think I follow."

Vesperini was amused by her lack of experience.

"Have you never wondered why for the past ten years or

so riots have never lasted more than four days? And why they never spread beyond the neighbourhoods where they started?"

"I've no idea."

"Remember Clichy-sous-Bois in 2005. Twenty-one nights of confrontation in towns across the whole of France. A state of emergency declared, and a bill for several hundred million euros. The government soon understood that to save money you have to nip these uprisings in the bud. Above all in places like Seine-Saint-Denis."

"What makes Seine-Saint-Denis so special?"

"Because we're the welcome doormat to Paris. All our political life is concentrated in the capital, and when the banlieues go up in flames, the stink reaches their windows. We're too close to the heart of the nation for them to allow the situation to become poisonous. Just look at how they leave Marseilles and Corsica to fend for themselves. Simply because they're so far from the centre that they're seen as little more than savages. And that's in mainland France. Throughout the French Antilles, social problems have been ignored and gone from bad to worse, but nothing has really changed. Did you know that this year there were twice the number of accounts settled in Guadeloupe than in Bouches-du-Rhône? And yet the media outcry only extends as far as Marseilles. I can assure you, the closer one gets to the Elysée Palace, the less chance one has of being forgotten. The government won't permit its next-door neighbours in Seine-Saint-Denis to go under."

"But what will they do?"

"Be patient. I'm hoping to find that out today."

50

After the interview, Colin Faizon had been put in a cell.

"Am I dreaming, or have we been robbed of fifty thousand euros by an eighty-year-old?" Coste asked his team.

"You don't know the half of it," Sam said.

"What else?"

"I've just been on the phone to Dr Marquant's clinic."

Coste understood at once.

"The old goat. When did he sneak out?"

"Most probably this morning. Nobody there was aware of it before I called."

"We gave him a mobile. Have you tried contacting him?"

"It just rings. No reply."

Coste rummaged through his memory.

"Wait – where was it he had a house?"

"At Chanclair, in the Drôme. I put Johanna onto it."

Ronan, Sam and Coste all turned expectantly towards Johanna De Ritter.

"O.K., I've spoken to the local police in Chanclair. They were a bit surprised, as I was the second person from the Police Judiciaire to ask the same question."

"Jevric?" Ronan said.

"Yeah. It was only to be expected. When Jacques 'disappeared', she searched everywhere and found the address."

"Did you ask them to send a car to have a discreet look around?"

"No point. They sent me an email with this attachment."

Johanna took a series of photographs out of a cardboard sleeve and spread them on her desk. They showed a stone house with no roof and one wall caved in, smothered in brambles.

"What is this ruin?"

"Let me present Château Landernes. Bought in 1980, and never inhabited. No danger of finding him there."

"He's been leading us by the nose from the start. Did the Chanclair police tell you anything more?" Coste insisted.

"Yes, but off the record. It appears the Landernes bought the plot from a developer. The land was supposed to be suitable for building on, and they poured all their savings into it. Except that the house sits on saturated ground, and after the first heavy rains the foundations sank by ten centimetres. Work was suspended, and never renewed. Jacques tried to take the case to court, but he didn't have the resources. The town hall sided with the developer, who, it just so happened, had another two building projects in the village. He was even backed up by the public notary who had certified the suitability of the plot. In other words, nothing was repaid, no damages, no interest payments. With a plot of land that was useless, bought at three times its value, and a house in ruins, the Landernes found themselves without a cent. All their hopes of escaping Malceny had flown out of the window."

It was Sam's turn to recall the conversation they had had with the old man.

"I thought his wife had died there, and that was why he couldn't face going back?"

"That's almost true. Six months later, his wife fell into a

deep depression and died soon afterwards. In a tower block flat they had no chance of ever escaping. Bad karma."

"It's enough to make you want to turn up at the town hall with a pump-action shotgun," Ronan exploded. "If you chuck in the dealers who exploited him, Rose's death, and Jevric's attempt to use him as bait when he came to us for help . . . it's a lot for one man to take."

Coste no longer knew what to think of their protégé.

"Except that apparently he's decided not to let himself be used anymore. Sam, track down his mobile. We have to find him."

The door to the office opened behind them. Their boss, Commissaire Stévenin, wanted to know what progress they were making.

"How are things going with that young lad Colin Faizon?"

Coste stood in front of Johanna to allow her to slip the photographs of the Chanclair ruin back in their sleeve.

"Actually, sir, I've got some news on that."

51

The privileges of rank: the commissaire's office was four times the size of anyone else's. But that wasn't the full story: he had to take responsibility for everything, far more than his subordinates. And so the events in Malceny and any crimes committed as a result were of great concern to him. His resolve and determination were simply a reflection of the pressure he was under.

"No, capitaine. You're to wind everything up and hand young Faizon over to the investigating magistrate this evening. My orders come from so high up I've got a stiff neck just from receiving them."

"Sir, let me at least ask for more time. Just twenty-four hours so I can get a clearer picture."

"Again: no. In case you don't have television, it's war every night in Malceny. For the moment, apart from Bibz's death, there's only material damage, but if this goes on, we risk having more dead bodies on our hands, and to my mind we already have enough. Shit, Victor, we're being offered someone who implicates Doucouré in two of your cases. Don't you see? To find somebody responsible in the middle of the riots is heaven sent. Do you remember Leonarda, the young girl who was arrested and sent back to Kosovo when she left school? That sparked a political crisis, but all we had to say was that the father was violent, that he sent his daughters out to beg, and that he had lied about where they came from, and she disappeared from the news in less than a week. The head of the Police Judiciaire would crucify me if we didn't seize this chance!"

Coste tried to restrain himself. He gritted his teeth.

"Sir, don't think for one minute I'm not aware of the repercussions of what I'm asking, or of the pressure you're under, but in this case we're clearly being blindsided. Who do you think is paying for his lawyer? He's a scapegoat, nothing more. He's a minor – the most we can pin on him is aiding and abetting. What is he risking? Two or three years at most. I'm not sure whether he's doing this for money or out of fear, but given time, I'd find out."

"Time I'm not going to give you, capitaine. You can have one more interview. Build a cast-iron case round this Habibou Doucouré, make sure you have enough evidence against Colin Faizon to nail him for aiding and abetting, and hand everything over to the investigating magistrate, Saint-Croix. Don't be so impatient. With a case as complex as this one, she's bound to open an inquiry, and then you'll be able to pursue your investigation."

"In a week at best. If he's arrested, you know very well that only the investigating magistrate is allowed to question him. Today is the only chance we have to put pressure on Colin; after that we won't even be able to go near him. Can't you see we're being manipulated?"

Stévenin had reached the limit of his patience.

"By whom? By the dealer above him? And when you've nabbed him, that won't be enough for you, you'll want the next one, and you'll end up with nobody! You really can't see beyond the walls of your office. There's no risk of you becoming a commissaire one day."

"God forbid."
Stévenin raised an eyebrow.
"Pardon?"
Coste left the room, slamming the door behind him.

52

The interview with the Radio Monte Carlo journalist had remained rather polite. Better still, Vesperini came out of it as a kind of heroine. And yet the return journey to the town hall brought her back to the reality of her situation, and tension gripped her stomach. She denied entry to her office to all but Delsart, her finance officer, whom she was anxious to see.

Nobody in central government wanted to get mixed up in what was going on in Malceny. The prime minister had passed it on to the Ministry for the Interior, who in turn had left it to the Secretariat for Cities . . . which reported to the prime minister. Even the discussion that should have taken place between the mayor and the minister had been downgraded to a meeting between her finance officer and a technical adviser. It was evident that nobody was willing to get their hands dirty, and that they all wanted as little as possible to do with her town.

A red light blinked on Vesperini's desk telephone, but Sébastien Delsart burst in without waiting to be announced. The elegant forty-something had held the municipal purse strings for almost ten years, and had a privileged relationship with Vesperini. While it was true that Sébastien was the son of her former brother-in-law, what she most appreciated about him was his creative accounting. Over-invoiced deals, bogus associations, secret financing of her political campaigns, buying votes, bullyboys, poster-stickers, caretakers and journalists, funding imaginary jobs and placing friends in good ones. Delsart had committed so many malpractices he could no longer see they were illegal. As they were not committed for personal gain, he almost enjoyed the game of cat and mouse with the government's regional prefecture, the public administration and the audit office. He saw everything simply as bank transfers. With an added pinch of malice a forethought.

Their mutual dependency even allowed him a certain familiarity.

"Hi there, Andrea."

"Please don't keep me on tenterhooks."

"Absolutely. It should happen this afternoon. They want you to splurge out as much as necessary on the estates. The tap is turned on full. Malceny spooks everyone, so we're being asked to sort it out as swiftly as possible."

"Have you worked out how it's to be done?"

"Yes. With the minister. I'm using one of our dormant associations; we can draw on it as necessary."

"Which one?"

"One of the very first I set up: the Association for the Rehabilitation of the Image of Neighbourhoods."

"How much are they advancing us?"

"Five hundred thousand euros from the prime minister's special fund. But they've already estimated the total cost. If the riots end within forty-eight hours, they're offering five million. You'll be able to afford a brand-new town, a nice re-election campaign, and loads of voters."

"Villiers-le-Bel got 4.6 million, so I wasn't expecting anything less. How do they intend to justify it?"

"We should receive some from the Ministry for the Interior.

They'll transfer funds via the National Agency for Urban Renewal. We can put the rest into another phantom association whose aim will be . . ."

He looked at the sheet of paper in his hand.

"Here it is: '. . . the construction of a new, healthier and safer environment'. I didn't have to think very long about that one: they pretty well dictated it to me. You know, I think they're getting used to this kind of thing."

Vesperini settled more comfortably in her chair.

"Good. In that case, get in touch with the bank straightaway. I need three hundred and fifty thousand in cash at once."

"As much as that?"

"They want me to sort this out in forty-eight hours? That's the price. Don't worry, they'll turn a blind eye."

"O.K., I'll see to it immediately," Delsart assured her, before turning on his heel and leaving the office.

Once she was alone, Vesperini lit a cigarette. It had been rather more complicated than expected, but she'd done it.

She had just got her hands on five million euros. By causing a riot in her own town, she'd achieved a historic first. Worse still, she had just held the state to ransom.

53

Johanna and Sam were processing all the legal documents required for handing the case over to the prosecution service at Bobigny regional court, where Colin was expected by the investigating magistrate. Saint-Croix's decision had come as no surprise: the youngster was to be transferred and detained in custody. Lost in thought, Coste was standing watching his two colleagues, when Ronan appeared with four chilled beers.

"All good?"

Victor nodded and reached out to take one of the bottles. He had come up with an idea, but didn't dare share it. He began by circling round and round it, like dogs do before they settle down.

"It would be good if the magistrate opened an inquiry into this case."

"How could she do otherwise?" Ronan said in astonishment. "We've only scratched the surface. There are still loads of facts to verify."

"Right. It would also be good to make sure we're in charge of that inquiry. Saint-Croix could very easily choose another department or Groupe Crime."

Sam, who hadn't grasped what his chief was getting at, looked up from the paperwork.

"And how do you propose to do that?"

"I'm not sure. We need to convince her somehow."

Johanna smiled. Sam stared at Ronan, who innocently slaked his thirst before realising everyone was looking at him, and finally cottoning on to what Coste had in mind.

"You lot cannot be serious. You want me to go and see Fleur Saint-Croix? May I remind you that the two of us are no longer on the best of terms."

"Wait, I'm not asking you to prostitute yourself. I'm just asking you to see if you can dig out any valuable information."

Ronan downed the rest of his beer.

"You're a bastard, chief. I came a real cropper with her, you know."

"Alright, forget it. I don't want to be responsible for a broken heart."

54

Some time after eight that evening, Coste decided to call it a day and leave his team to make sure Colin was escorted to court. He was about to go when his mobile started to dance on his desk.

It was Léa. He picked up.

"Are you messing with my head? I can't get over it. I've just had my father on the phone. Your witness has packed his bags. I thought he was in danger."

"He still is, I promise you."

"And do you promise me he was nothing more than a witness? Because protected witnesses who do a runner aren't very common, are they? Victor, lying to my father is one thing, but you really don't want to lie to me!"

Coste put down his jacket and sat on the office sofa.

"Jacques Landernes was a minder for some drug dealers. Jevric wanted to use him as bait, and she wasn't bothered what happened to him after that. We had to get him out and find him a safe place to hide."

Léa had finished boiling over. Now she literally exploded.

"You hid a drug dealers' accomplice in my father's clinic? What's wrong with you? You lie to me, compromise my father's career, and all for some guy you'll never see again?"

"I'm not doing it to make a friend of him, but because it's fair."

"Shit, how you love that word! And do you think you're being fair with me?"

Coste did not reply.

"You lied to me, Victor. You really are a prick."

55

Vesperini was the last official left in the town hall offices. The cleaning ladies were already pushing their trolleys along the deserted corridors. She was anxiously awaiting the call that came in on her desk telephone, and she picked up immediately.

"Madame le maire: my people are getting dangerously impatient. We're at the start of the fourth night. You told me the government would be quick to react."

"Don't worry, they have been. The money will be there tomorrow. Just tell me how you want to do this, but please let's not have the old chestnut of a basement car park at two in the morning."

"I was planning something far simpler. I consider that you've shown good faith and I can trust you, so I'm going to give you my telephone number. Get into your limo, call me, and I'll tell you the address for our meeting. Does that suit you?"

"What would suit me would never to have crossed paths with you."

"If playing the victim allows you to sleep better, I advise you to do so with people who don't know you as well as I do. I heard your radio interview this morning: you were very convincing. Your approval ratings are climbing all the time. If you keep to the script we've written together, you're more than likely to win a third term. And I imagine that the amount you're handing over to me is only a fraction of what you're going to receive. How much: a million, a million and a half?"

By not divulging the size of her pay-off, Vesperini hoped to prevent the Boss's demands escalating dangerously. She ignored his question, waving a red rag under his nose.

"There'll also be the fifty thousand euros you demanded for the family of the young man who turned himself in. All told, I think I'll have kept my side of the bargain. Now you keep yours. I'll give you a hundred thousand to calm your troops. It's time to put a stop to it before there's any more drama."

"Agreed. They'll be as good as gold."

"Don't be stupid. Just get them to calm it down a little: I don't want to lose my status as an Urban Priority Zone. That would be like losing a Michelin star."

"I don't know which of the two of us is more dangerous, madame."

"You kill people. Does that answer your question?"

FOURTH NIGHT OF RIOTING

9 p.m., Barricade 16, C.R.S. 62nd Company, Charlie Section

For simplicity's sake, the barricades thrown up in Malceny had been numbered from one to twenty-three. Although municipal workmen tried to dismantle as many as possible during the day, at nightfall they sprang up again, higher and more solid than ever.

Facing his troops, Commandant Charles Barion, barrel-chested and hands clasped behind his back, was halfway through his pep talk.

"Well, my little ballerinas, as you may have noticed, this isn't the 'March For All' you get in the smart areas of Paris. It won't be Versailles Catholics on the menu tonight. We're not going to get babies and buggies chucked at us, but machetes and bombs. Not the same thing at all. So keep your eyes peeled and look out for your little colleagues."

Then he shouted in a voice worthy of a warm-up act:

"Who protects the C.R.S.?"

The reply from fifty men rang out as one:

"The C.R.S.!"

"Correct!" the commandant acknowledged.

Then he turned towards two police officers, a man and a woman, who had two Belgian Malinois dogs sitting at their feet.

"As a special treat tonight, we're being backed up by the Dog Unit. Watch out for your fingers! I warn you, they're not the sort of dogs who like to be stroked. You're to consider them as part of our squad. And believe you me, they smell better than you and can read better."

In the third row, right in the middle of the squad, one of the C.R.S. expressed his doubts.

"Dogs? Seriously? Why not cats as well while we're at it?"

A few mocking laughs could be heard, then everyone focused on Commandant Barion again.

"I don't want you to act on your own initiative. I decide what we do, and what weapons to use. Just because you hear shooting doesn't mean it's a firearm; if it's only fireworks we stay calm. And a tiny reminder: in order for it to be self-defence, the attack has to be present, unjustified and real, and our response must be necessary and proportionate. In short, wait till you get a bullet up the arse before you're certain you can hit back."

The comedian in the middle of the squad was no longer so keen on laughing. He turned to his neighbour, as inexperienced as he was.

"Do you think they're going to use real guns?"

"They're not completely stupid. They know that if they attack us with stones or fireworks, we can only respond with batons, Flash-Balls, and tear gas. If they turn to guns, so do we, and then it becomes a shoot-out."

A police major, who up until then had been listening devotedly to the commandant, swivelled round towards the two young recruits. His bull neck and rugby-prop build made them pay attention to what he had to say.

"Point one, shut your mouths. Point two, in Villiers-le-Bel we were shot at eighty-one times, without ever receiving the go-ahead to reply in kind. And point three, shut your mouths."

* * *

11.30 p.m., Barricade 16, C.R.S. 62nd Company, Charlie Section

Seeing the C.R.S. remain motionless, the masked rioters had grown in confidence and were now positioned in front of their own barricade, only a few metres from the police. Wild, provocative gestures, tentative advances towards the shields, and the usual deluge of insults. In the midst of all the flames and smoke, the latent tension and violence, the slightest misstep would lead to an immediate escalation.

Held tight by their handlers, the defence dogs were also experiencing an adrenalin rush, as if by a process of osmosis. A little further away, behind the wall of supermarket trolleys, pallets and burnt-out vehicles, a bright light turned the whole of one side of the street an incandescent red: two distress flares had been set off. The two hooded youngsters holding them knelt down beside three 50-centimetre-long toughened plastic tubes. Using the flame from one of their flares, they lit the fuses on three powder balls and rammed them into the barrels of the tubes. Wrapping T-shirts round their hands, they picked up their improvised mortars, held them at arm's length, and aimed for the C.R.S. lines. Two balls of fire flew through the sky and landed three metres to the rear of the squad, exploding at their backs with a deafening roar and giving off more than two thousand degrees of heat. The third projectile missed its target, climbed higher, and ended up on the balcony of a sixth-floor flat. A second later it exploded, blowing in the windows, setting fire first to the curtains and then to the entire room.

Commandant Barion immediately called the fire brigade. The fireballs had only just missed his men, and the mortar launchers would adjust their aim. It was no longer possible to stay still. They had to disperse the twenty or so rioters armed with baseball bats, iron bars and golf clubs who were preventing them from seeing what the rest of their adversaries were up to beyond the barricade. As he was about to give the order to charge, one of the dog handlers came up to him.

"If you let us try, we can clear a way for you with just a few muzzled attacks."

The C.R.S. commandant looked at him sceptically.

"There's only two of you, and twenty of them."

The female handler came up, her Malinois with a white patch on its chest close by her side.

"That'll be just about enough for Djinko."

"Show us what you can do, then."

The dogs were let off the leash. They had identified their targets a long while since, but even though they were now free, they didn't move forward a centimetre.

"Djinko! Attack!"

"Baïka! Attack!"

The muscles on their hindquarters quivered, and then the two Malinois hurtled towards the rioters. The first one in Baïka's way took its muzzled mouth right in the chest and was sent three metres through the air before crashing to the ground. His neighbour didn't even have time to see him disappear before he felt Djinko's thirty kilos smash into his chin. A canine knockout.

"Djinko! Baïka! Heel!"

The two police dogs trotted back to their handlers. Thirty seconds later, they had been unleashed twice more. With each new attack, their victims were either tossed aside or knocked to the ground. But some of the braver rioters stood their ground, either unaware of the danger, or too high on the violence to care. Among them, far too close, was one of the mortar carriers. He had forced his way through, and now he was about to aim his weapon at the front line of the C.R.S. Exchanging glances, the two handlers agreed wordlessly to remove one of the muzzles. Djinko's. Unfortunately, in all the confusion, the dog had picked out another target, easily identifiable by the red scarf over his mouth. In a split second, Djinko rushed at him, jumped up, and knocked him over. Spared this attack, the mortar carrier ran off without any attempt to go to his companion's aid. Before Red Scarf could get back on his feet, Djinko had time to land, spin round, and stand, jaws gaping, above the boy's face, bared teeth almost brushing his skin. The dog stared the young rioter in the face. The youngster almost wet his trousers.

"Djinko! Come to heel!"

The dog ran back, leaving his terrified quarry. But the animal, the only police weapon that had a mind of its own, was hungry for more. Just as his handler was trying to slip his leash back on, Red Scarf stood up. Escaping his master, Djinko leaped straight at him. In the same instant, protected once more by the barricade, the youth with the mortar fired straight at the C.R.S. The fireball shot across the battlefield and landed a metre from the dog, before exploding and setting his hindquarters alight. Djinko collapsed, fur ablaze. He howled pitifully, and the cry of pain brought everyone to a standstill. The dog tried to stand, fell back, and began to wheel round on his front feet. A smell of burnt fur and flesh added to the horror of the howling. Against all expectation, Red Scarf took off his jacket and threw it over the dog, beating out the flames, as Djinko's handler left the ranks and ran towards the rioters, with no thought for her own safety.

"Christ, Laure, what are you doing?" her colleague shouted.

She didn't even turn round.

"I'm going to get my dog."

56

In the morning, it took Ronan several minutes to find his things. Boxers in the folds of the sheets. Trousers in a ball at the foot of the bed. Gun on the bedside table. Bare-chested, gun in his waistband, he followed the parquet floor along the corridor to the living room, and then the kitchen. He found Fleur sitting there with a cup of coffee, wearing the T-shirt he was looking for.

"You haven't seen my T-shirt by any chance, have you?" he said with a smile.

She studied him for a few seconds.

"I prefer you like that."

She got up to pour him a coffee, then, setting the steaming cup in front of him, gave him a kiss on the back of his neck.

"I thought the first night was a fluke, but you're actually very talented. Sugar?"

"Yes, please. We didn't really get the chance to talk last night. Or rather, you didn't give me time."

Fleur sat down opposite him and proffered a smile that invited him to continue.

"You're going to take me for a real bastard, but I swear it wasn't my only reason for coming."

"That's so sweet of you. Did you think I hadn't realised? Look, I'd love to give you another twenty-four hours for your investigation, but I have my orders as well. Everyone's happy for Habibou Doucouré to go from innocent victim to the devil incarnate. And as for the second question, the inquiry is likely to be given to the head of Groupe Crime 2, Lara Jevric. It's a delicate matter, and the prosecutor's office thinks she's more docile, whereas that Coste of yours is harder to control. All you had to do was ask."

Feeling wretched, Ronan didn't raise his eyes from the coffee he was stirring mechanically.

"Stop doing that with the spoon." She laughed. "I haven't passed you the sugar yet. You're not angry with me, are you? After all, it was you who came to screw the young magistrate in order to keep your case. A noble sacrifice, but now you know there's no point, apart from offering ourselves pleasure. A great deal of pleasure, right?"

She stood up in front of Ronan, took off the T-shirt, then left the kitchen and headed down the corridor.

"I'm going to take a shower. Put your cup in the sink before you leave . . ."

* * *

Johanna sometimes told herself she left two children at home only to find two more at police headquarters. This morning she was amused by the way Sam and Ronan were gently teasing one another. When Coste came in, Ronan piped up before he could pose the question.

"Sorry. Fleur . . . I mean Saint-Croix, is under the same pressure as us. The inquiry will probably go to Jevric's group. It seems she's more docile while you . . . well, you're less malleable."

"That doesn't surprise me."

"Surprise!" Sam said ironically. "Ronan's tool can't open every lock!"

Disgusted, Johanna decided they were all as bad as each other.

"You guys make me laugh. You all think you have a magic wand between your legs."

"Remind me to put that on the front of a T-shirt," Coste said. "Well, anyway, given the smile on your face, Ronan, it doesn't seem you're too cut up about it."

"Because I can differentiate between work and the rest of my life. I'll teach you if you like."

Considering the conversation Coste had had with Léa the previous evening, the remark hit home. And since they'd now fully explored their colleague's sporting exploits, he changed the subject.

"Any news from Jacques? What's with his mobile?"

"He's invisible," Sam replied. "He must have removed the S.I.M. card."

"Up to date with all the new technologies, our eighty-year-old."

"Maybe his employers gave him a crash course."

Coste did not seem amused, but then it was easy to understand why he was short on enthusiasm that morning.

"Right. If I'm not mistaken, we don't have any more cases on the go, do we?"

"A blank sheet," Sam confirmed, pulling the computer keyboard towards him. "Shall I book you a ticket to Provence?"

"It could be a bit more complicated than that, I'm afraid. Léa found out what our 'witness' was really up to. It didn't go down too well . . ."

None of them dared make a joke of it. Coste went and sat behind his desk, almost invisible behind a stack of files.

"What's all this bumf?"

"It's what you asked me for yesterday. Copies of all the legal documents held by the Malceny police concerning Habibou Doucouré. And as it's no use to us now, at least we'll have scrap paper until the end of the year."

"No, send it all over to the magistrate. Our successors will be able to make use of it."

57

Maud Jeansac left the town hall, crossed the street, and entered the Malpoli café-brasserie with the morning paper under her arm. Vesperini had her own private table up on the first floor. The room wasn't open until midday, so she could make full use of it. Maud greeted the manager, climbed the stairs, and found the Queen in semi-darkness, staring at a cup of tea. Her face betrayed no emotion. Maud laid the paper in front of her.

"Did you know about this?"

The Queen unfolded the newspaper and read the main headline: FIVE MILLION EUROS UP IN SMOKE – WHAT THE MALCENY RIOTS WILL COST FRANCE. She read the article in silence; as she did so, the furrows on her brow gradually deepened. Impatient and excited, Maud did not let her finish it.

"To be honest with you, I can't work out where the leak came from – the opposition or the majority party – or whether or not it's good for our image. On the one hand, the state is showing it's engaged, but on the other, since we're on the same side as the government, we're going to seem like their privileged pets. There are lots of towns in France that could do with similar investment, and here we are, multimillionaires in only four days. The town hall is going to come under close scrutiny. We really have to watch how we use this manna from heaven."

Vesperini looked up from the newspaper.

"What are you saying? Did you think I was going to build myself a swimming pool?"

"I'm sorry, I didn't mean that at all. I completely trust Delsart."

"Get in touch with the chief of staff at the Ministry for Urban Affairs. If by any chance this came from them, tell them they're not doing us any favours."

Once Maud had left the café, Vesperini shoved the newspaper away from her. Changing her mind, she seized it furiously, crumpled it into a ball, and threw it on the floor.

* * *

On the way back from his regular morning meeting at the bank, Sébastien Delsart entered Vesperini's office as he always did, without knocking. In each hand, he was carrying a black metal attaché case. He put them down on the first armchair opposite the mayor's desk and sat in the second.

"Hi there, Andrea."

"I'm always surprised by how little space a huge sum of money takes up," the Queen said.

"Normally we begin handouts two months before an election. I get the impression that Father Christmas has come early this year."

"And normally, it would be Azzedine Salah who dressed up with a fake beard and a red hat. I never thought I'd miss him so much."

Then she turned to consider the two attaché cases.

"Is it all there?"

"I still don't understand why you made me split it in two, but yes, it's all there. One case with two hundred thousand, the other a hundred and fifty. Are you really sure you want to do this on your own?"

"Why? Do you want to go and negotiate on my behalf?"

Delsart burst out laughing.

"You're joking! Me? On those estates? I'd have the life expectancy of a baby in the middle of a motorway. But I don't reckon you'll do much better."

Despite their close relationship, Vesperini had not taken her finance officer into her complete confidence. She preferred to keep some of her projects to herself.

"Don't worry, I've got a new go-between."

"Your boxer?"

"He'll be perfect for it," she lied.

Dismissing him, she lit a cigarette. Within a few hours, or perhaps even minutes, she was finally going to meet a man she was still unable to classify. Expert blackmailer or collaborator? Murderer or electoral ally? She took two long puffs on her cigarette, then began to follow the agreed plan.

Once she was installed between the two cases in the rear of her official car, she took out her mobile, but somehow didn't dare punch in the number she knew by heart.

* * *

Sam had been told to take all the records kept by the Malceny police on the young Habibou Doucouré to the prosecutor's office, for the attention of Fleur Saint-Croix. But since he'd been involved in the case only to see it stolen from him, his curiosity got the better of him, and he leafed through the top file. A robbery with violence from January of that year. An unusual comment on the final page of the charge sheet attracted his attention, and he decided to check a few more. Use of prohibited drugs in February. Assault on a police officer a month later. The kid kept up a regular rhythm. And at the end of each charge sheet, the same oddity. With a flick of the mouse, Sam booted up his computer.

In the next office, Ronan had taken over Johanna's place opposite Coste. Stretching out his legs on the desk, he looked for something to occupy his time. Today's newspaper would do fine. He opened it and turned the pages until he came to the sport section.

Sprawled on the sofa, Johanna had considered taking Ronan to task for putting his dirty shoes up on her desk, but was overcome by the general sense of lethargy in the room. Even Coste was affected. He studied his two colleagues until his gaze fell on the front-page headline: FIVE MILLION EUROS UP IN SMOKE.

Something stirred deep in his brain.

At first it was almost nothing. Then it was positively leaping up and down in front of him.

He jumped to his feet and leaned over his desk to snatch the newspaper from Ronan, leaving him with a torn corner between his fingers.

"Hey! You're the boss! You only have to ask."

Coste read the headline, and then a bit further, before picking up a marker pen and going over to the whiteboard.

"Can we know what's got into you?" Johanna said, sitting up. "What have you found?"

Coste handed her the newspaper without looking in her direction.

"The thing I've been searching for all week. The motive."

He waved his hand for them to be quiet, as if what had just gone through his mind might fly away at the slightest sound.

"Shhh! Above all, shhh! Give me just a minute to concentrate."

He held the point of the pen over the centre of the board, then wrote in capitals: MALCENY.

Sam burst into the room. He was expecting to find the rest of the team dozing off from either heat or boredom, and was slightly surprised to find them all on their feet: Coste at a whiteboard filled with notes, arrows and question marks surrounding the word "Malceny"; Ronan and Johanna standing behind him, looking somewhat anxious.

"His brains are scrambled," Ronan warned him. "We're waiting for it to pass."

Sam waved the twenty or more sheets of paper he was holding proudly.

"You can wait a long time, but you'll always be missing the little whatsit."

Coste turned towards him.

"That's exactly it! I just need a little whatsit. A tiny arrow to join it all up."

"Well then, take a look at this," Sam said.

Ronan went up to him, smiling.

"I don't know why I'm all excited when I don't understand a thing, but I reckon this is going to be good."

Sam swept all the magazines and loose sheets of paper off Johanna's desk. He spread out eight charge sheets written up when Habibou was released from custody.

"O.K., listen up. I've been looking at the latest charges against Habibou Doucouré. We all agree that he's a minor, so at the end of his stay in custody, who is supposed to come and collect him?"

"An adult. A legally responsible member of his family," Coste quoted from the regulations.

"Correct. And yet it's always the same person who comes to fetch him, and his name isn't Doucouré, it's Novak. Tony Novak. I've done some digging into the guy, and you won't believe what I found. Guess what he does for a living?"

* * *

Vesperini's car was stationary, engine running, just beneath the town hall windows. She glanced again at the two attaché cases, took a deep breath, and finally plucked up the courage to dial the Boss's number. The first ring sounded in her ear. Then a tune suddenly resonated through the vehicle. At first, she didn't understand what was going on. The second call was accompanied by another tune inside the car. She shuddered. Her driver took his mobile out of his pocket and cut the connection.

"We'll drive on a little, if you've no objection."

Their eyes met in the rear-view mirror. He engaged first gear and set off.

* * *

In the Groupe Crime 1 office, the news exploded like a firecracker.

"Christ almighty! So he's Vesperini's driver?" Coste cried.

"That's why they let him pick up the kid. Seeing that he's in custody at least once a month and nobody in his family wanted to come and get him, the arrangement suited the juvenile police. The mayor's driver: that's reassuring. The magistrate gave permission the first time, and after that it became a habit. Between ourselves, Vesperini is no idiot: Tony Novak really is a driver."

"Yeah, we'd understood that," Johanna cut in.

"No, not just any kind of driver . . . the sort we talk about in serious crimes. He drives getaway cars for hold-ups. He's only been caught once, and that was because he was shopped. Six years for a bank heist in Seine-Saint-Denis. I've talked to the guys in the Organised Crime Unit: he's a legend there. He knows the region like the back of his hand. He could lose us on a tricycle if he wanted to."

"He's at the centre of everything," Coste agreed. "And right from the start. He wasn't just protecting Habibou Doucouré, he was giving him orders. He's the new boss Groupe Stups are looking for."

* * *

The car was travelling through Malceny in no particular direction. Vesperini had always appreciated the way the man drove: no jolts, smoothly, almost sensually. He was so discreet that over the years she had forgotten he was there. She tried to recall all the sensitive conversations she had held in what she had thought of as being one of her most private retreats. Delsart, Cardel, Salah, Jeansac . . . He had been witness to so many indiscretions, plans, strategies and secrets. He must have been spying on her all that time. Black hair plastered back, chiselled features. She stared at him in the rear-view mirror. It was perhaps the first time she had looked at him so closely. But she was being indiscreet.

"I bet you can't remember either my surname or my first name," he said gruffly.

"Antoine . . . ?" Vesperini flailed.

"Almost. Tony. Tony Novak. I was taken on by Salah when I came out of prison because of . . . let's say because of my talents as a driver."

The Queen struggled to regain her composure.

"If he'd been aware of your sense of gratitude, he'd no doubt have chosen somebody else."

"I can see you don't allow yourself to be thrown for very long. And now we've been introduced, I believe you have something for me. I need to get business on the estates going again before our neighbours muscle in on my turf."

She picked up the cases one after the other and laid them on the front passenger seat.

"And you're forcing me to be part of it."

She saw him smile as he observed her in the rear-view mirror.

"Your sudden fits of indignation amuse me. It must reassure you to think you're different from me. But it's you who created me. Me and this perfect ecosystem that nobody can escape from."

"'Ecosystem'. Did you learn that word in the prison library?"

"No, in prison I learned how to make a knife out of paper and how to check there was no crushed glass in my food. I learned the rest at the faculty. Besides, 'ecosystem' isn't quite the right word. 'Vicious circle' would be more appropriate."

"Alright then, tell me your story," Vesperini said with a sigh, a prisoner in her own car.

"You don't know how to deal with the thousands of kids who have no qualifications or jobs, but I do. I give them work and they provide their families with a living. As a result, drug trafficking keeps your deprived neighbourhoods calm, and like the hypocrite you are, you let us get on with it, as though you weren't perfectly well aware of the reasons behind it. Better than that, you use us. You pay us to guarantee your safety during your election campaigns; you pay us to bring in votes and proxies. You make use of us to cement your power, and, to be sure we remain loyal, you even hire some of us to be part of your team. You collude in the evil that is undermining your town so as to keep control of it. You're even ready to set it ablaze. The serpent bites its own tail. A vicious circle, then."

Vesperini had sunk back into her seat as if wanting to put as much distance as possible between her and the man she was now dependent on.

"It seems there are always good reasons for our poor choices," she admitted finally. "But now, a period of relative calm would suit both of us."

"Obviously. I'm not likely to sell much on the streets if people are too scared to go out. And you have to prove you have a firm grip on your town if you don't want the army to intervene. Our interests align. I'm getting my people together this evening to tell them to calm things down, but my orders will only be followed if they're offered some motivation. They need to know I have the money."

"You have all you need in one of those attaché cases."

"In a situation like this, it would be a huge mistake to pay for a service before seeing the results. First they have to spread the word, then I'll pay them. I'll only take the case I need. I'd like you to keep the rest for me."

"Do you trust me that much?"

"I don't even trust my little sister. But I know that the money will be safer in your home than on my estate."

Novak turned his head, still keeping his attention on the road. He handed his passenger a newspaper.

"Something to read while I take you back?"

Splashed across the whole of the front page, the five million euros Malceny would receive.

"By the way, we have to discuss how we're going to

redistribute the money we've earned together. I'm counting on a raise. And I want Azzedine Salah's post."

* * *

After dropping Vesperini off at the town hall, Novak drove a few kilometres to the outskirts of Malceny. His destination was only ever passed on by word of mouth. Taking an unmarked turning, he left the road and followed a bumpy, tree-lined dirt track. At the end of it, he swerved between stacks of rusty car bodies and piles of tyres until he came to a shelter made of wood and corrugated iron. The place looked like a car scrapyard, or a supermarket selling second-hand parts whose provenance didn't overly concern the customers. As the gleaming black official car drew up, a stocky, dirty man, with a rag over his shoulder and hands filthy with grease, came over and opened Tony's car door.

"Hey. You come to see the baby?"

The two men walked round to the back of the shelter where, under a grey tarpaulin, stood a car the artist-mechanic had lavished attention on. He flung back the tarp. As he opened the bonnet, the two men's eyes gleamed like pirates discovering buried treasure.

"A Citroën C5 with a V6 engine. From the outside she looks tame, but I can tell you she's a really hot bitch. I've lightened the bodywork, improved the air intake, modified the exhaust, and souped up the engine. I couldn't boost her anymore or she'd explode when you turned on the ignition. It's not a car anymore, it's a jet plane. But it doesn't come cheap."

"Nothing ever does, believe me."

Novak went to get the attaché case and handed it to the mechanic.

"Put that in the boot of the jet."

"Is it for this afternoon?"

"Yes, and I'll be back tonight to park it when it's all over. You'll have to stay and wait for me here. That's not a problem, is it?"

"No, Tony, of course not. You know I'm at your service."

58

Coste pushed open the door to Le Malpoli and, paying no attention to the staff busy preparing things for the midday kick-off, went straight up to the first floor. He approached Vesperini's table, pulled back a chair, and sat opposite her.

"Who gave the game away?" she wanted to know.

"Maud Jeansac. Your headquarters here aren't bad. But don't blame her: I had to threaten her with my gun," Coste said, exaggerating somewhat.

"Your blue eyes and a smile would have done the trick."

Coste looked at the table, strewn with newspapers, an open diary and a glass half filled with an amber liquid.

"Isn't it a bit early for that?"

"My town is the scene of urban guerrilla warfare. You ought to be surprised to find me even vaguely sober. What can I do for you?"

Coste felt inside his jacket pocket, pulled out a mobile phone, and placed it on the table.

"It belongs to Gonthier, the former head of your municipal police."

Vesperini took the blow on the chin. She responded innocently:

"Shouldn't that be with his personal effects, for his family to collect?"

"Yes, but luckily I stole it in time. The final messages are very interesting. Especially the one he sent just before his suicide. Shall I read it to you?"

Vesperini's shoulders slumped. She pushed a curl behind her ear.

"No thanks, I know it by heart."

Then she recited:

"As far as the kid goes, I hope to apologise to him in person. I'll leave you to deal with your guilt. I can't. It's been the soundtrack to all my sleepless nights recently. So what?"

"At the very least, this message proves you were the one who ordered your people to carry out the niqab checks."

"Yes, and that's perfectly legal."

"It doesn't explain why you denied it at our last meeting."

"Because a child was killed and, however bad I might feel about that, it's publicity I can do without."

Coste rewarded her with an unconvinced twist of the mouth.

"Unless these riots are exactly what you've always wanted?"

"That doesn't make sense. Where is this leading?"

"To the five million."

"That's ridiculous. I've never done anything for personal gain. Everything I do is for Malceny."

"Or for Tony Novak."

Barely concealing her amazement, Vesperini seized her glass, and downed half its contents at a gulp. She took a deep breath to refocus.

"Would you be a darling, capitaine?"

"If I can," he said.

"Say what you've come to say, so we don't waste any more time."

Coste settled back, picked up the glass, and took a swig as well.

"Fine. A deputy who was a former dealer, a former hold-up merchant for a driver, and a jackpot riot that enables you to do a historic deal. All this against a background of multiple homicides, with you always at the centre of things."

"I agree I haven't chosen wisely, but as for the murders . . . unless incompetence is a crime these days, I don't see anything that could land me in prison."

"That's the magic of politics. Even with all the necessary evidence against a head of state, a minister or a member of parliament, it's impossible to send them to jail. And yet a simple rumour can end a career. You're in all the newspapers and on every airwave. The media would lap up this kind of scandal."

Vesperini looked at him, intrigued.

"I don't understand you, Coste, Do you want to destroy me?"

"You deserve it for putting the lives of hundreds of officers at risk every night, but the fact is, I need you. I know Novak is the new boss in the neighbourhoods. And I suspect he was the one who had the previous three main dealers executed, but since he always uses others to do the job, it'll be almost impossible to pin that on him. I also know that as a result of our two raids he no longer has any money or drugs to sell. Hence the riots: too intelligent an idea to have come from you. But considering the farewell message Gonthier sent you, I think you were ultimately responsible. What I can't understand is your deputy's murder."

Vesperini was exhausted. Unmasked, yes, but above all exhausted.

"So this is what it's like when you come to the end of a case? This little moment when you hold all the cards? It must be very rewarding."

Coste did not react.

"Salah served as an example. A warning. There were others,

but he was the first. I was threatened, my daughter attacked. Novak simply wanted to show me what I was risking if I didn't collaborate."

"I'm happy to pretend to believe that things didn't go your way, despite everything. But I imagine that with so much money and what you can do for your town with it, you're bound to be re-elected. You know, I've always thought there were two basic motives for a crime: money and sex. You've narrowed my horizons. There's only one: power."

"What do I need to do for you to see me as a victim?"

"First of all, put a stop to these riots. You seem to be the only one capable of that. And following that, I want you to give us a heads-up on Novak."

Vesperini did not hesitate to seize this unexpected opportunity.

"Nothing more than a heads-up?"

59

The atmosphere in Sylvan's office was electric. What Coste was proposing was audacious, crazy even. Before he committed his team, the leader of Groupe Stups wanted to know every detail of the planned operation.

"So he has two hundred thousand euros to go shopping with, does he? And what do we know about him?"

"A name and an address. Tony Novak, Verlaine Tower, in the Cité des Poètes in Malceny."

"That's not enough, Victor. We have to prepare in advance for a high-speed chase. Things have changed since police college, you know. We have no idea how they'll play it with the convoy. If he's concerned about security, there'll be three vehicles. A car in front to check out the roads, about thirty kilometres ahead of the others. A common make so as not to attract attention. Then a high-powered car with the stuff in it. And finally another powerful one in the rear to make sure they're not being tailed and to create a diversion if we try to intervene. Normally, the first car is sent ahead to the rendezvous to check the quality of the drugs. Dealers are well organised, but we're doing everything on the hoof."

"Listen, Sylvan, I've been taken off the case and you're getting nowhere investigating the deaths of those other dealers. And this guy is about to slip through our fingers. We've no other way of getting to him. We've seized his merchandise and his money, so he can't wait any longer."

"Without tapping their phones? Or putting a tracking device on their vehicles? Blind man's bluff, in other words? My team's going to love the shot of adrenalin, but I can't promise anything."

An apologetic voice inserted itself into their conversation.

"As for the phone, perhaps I can help."

Sylvan leaned over to Coste to avoid being heard.

"It's weird having her there, like some kind of stool pigeon. Couldn't we do without her?" he whispered.

"I don't trust her, so I prefer to keep her close. Besides, I've given her no choice."

"Does Stévenin know she's with us?"

"Of course not, as you can imagine. Otherwise he'd already be serving her coffee and his apologies."

Sylvan turned towards Vesperini, who was sitting in a corner of the room.

"For a high-speed exchange like this, madame le maire, they don't use their usual mobiles. They only have burner phones they throw away once the deal is done."

"Sorry," she apologised.

"No, in fact your info could be very useful to us. If there's nothing happening on his official number, it will be because something is going on."

Then Sylvan spoke to Chloe, his right-hand woman:

"O.K. Get Novak's number from the mayor. Get a G.P.S. on it, and prepare a discreet vehicle. We're going to test the temperature at Verlaine Tower, to see if there's any unusual activity."

* * *

Chloe put on her blue and strident yellow jacket and climbed into the driver's seat of a postal van, the Trojan horse for many of their operations. Once she reached the estate, she clasped the mobile between her hand and the steering wheel to film through the window and drove past the Verlaine tower block without slowing down. Parked cars. A few kids. To the untrained eye, nothing out of the ordinary. She drove on for a few streets before parking and contacting her team.

"First signs are that, it's very calm. Second, there's a beautiful C5 with a white shirt on a hanger behind the headrest, and two kids sitting on the bonnet. I'll be on channel 3 on my radio awaiting instructions."

Sylvan hung up and repeated the information to Coste and his team.

"The C5 must be the car with the stuff. It's one of the few models that has hydraulic suspension to correct the balance, which means you can't tell if it's heavily loaded. The clean shirt is for a sales rep and the two kids on the bonnet are there to stop anyone putting a bug underneath. Normally, their vehicles are in lock-ups or an underground car park. It looks as if you're right, and he's in a hurry. The problem is, we don't know where he's heading: Spain, Belgium, Amsterdam? We're going to have to take a chance."

"What kind of chance?" Ronan said anxiously.

"We'll try a reverse tail."

Sylvan turned the dial on his radio and pressed some buttons to find channel 3.

"Sylvan to Chloe."

"Receiving."

"Keep Général-Dorin under surveillance. It borders the Cité des Poètes estate, and it's the only exit they have."

"But we don't even know whether they're heading north or

south. Whichever it is, it's bound to be a motorway, and I'll be spotted in my yellow van."

"I know. Stay where you are, and I'll have you replaced by the family car."

* * *

Ten minutes later, a Seat Ibiza with a BABY ON BOARD sticker on the back window and a Dora the Explorer sunshield pulled up behind the van. Chloe seemed better suited to such a vehicle than her sinister-looking, unshaven colleague, so they swapped places.

She had not been behind the wheel for long when she saw in her rear-view mirror that the C5 was pulling out. She could follow it for long enough to get an idea of which direction it was heading. Radio propped between her thighs, she announced:

"Chloe to Sylvan. I've just been passed by Target. I can tail him for five minutes before I'm discovered. I hope that's enough."

After several streets, still some way ahead, the C5 left Malceny and turned on to the slip road for the motorway.

"Chloe to Sylvan. Target heading for the A86, northbound. I'll overtake him."

In Sylvan's office, Coste's team and Vesperini held their breath, as if they could endanger the operation merely by breathing. The head of Groupe Stups explained to Vesperini:

"If your guy wanted to drive to Spain, he would have had to enter Paris, take the périphérique and join the A10. But instead he's going towards the A1, then the A2 towards Belgium or Amsterdam. That's his only option, and we know the route, so Chloe can get in front of him to make sure. That's why we call it a 'reverse tail'. For the moment, everything's O.K."

As predicted, the target left the A86 for the A1. Chloe

drove on a further seven kilometres, eyes glued to her rear-view mirror. All of a sudden, the C5 deviated from the expected route.

"Chloe to Sylvan, they're signalling to go off. They're leaving the A1 and taking the N2. I'll have to come off the motorway as well. Are you sure the exchange is today?"

"Either you've been spotted, or they're taking precautions to make sure they're not being followed," Sylvan said.

Chloe's voice came through with more urgency:

"No, wait! They're taking the N104 . . . Shit, you know what that means? They're going to stay off motorways. I'll have to pull out or they'll see me. Returning to base."

Naturally, no-one in the Groupe Stups office apart from Sylvan had understood what the change of route implied.

"It's unusual," he said. "Novak is going to avoid all the toll booths and big interchanges by taking trunk roads and national ones. It's longer, but much safer for him. I wasn't expecting that."

"So it's no longer a high-speed chase?" Johanna said.

"No, it's the opposite. We're seeing it more and more often. It's a slow-speed shuffle."

"So we're screwed?"

"Let's just say it's more complicated. We're going to need backup."

* * *

Sylvan had pinned a road map of France to the wall above his hunting trophies and souvenir photographs. His office had never been so full, and he cleared his voice before starting to speak.

"O.K. It's now fourteen hundred hours. The target took the N104, and at the speed he's travelling, he should already be back on the N2. E.T.A. to Belgium: four and a half hours. For Amsterdam, he'll need seven hours. Let's calculate he needs a good hour for the meeting, the exchange, and to load up. That means he'll be heading back at either eighteen-thirty, or at twenty-one hundred hours. We can't intercept him on a national road. Even if he's playing the quiet family man and respecting speed limits, he's bound to have souped up his car engine. And we don't know if he's going to fill the car up, still less where."

"Are you telling us he's invisible for a journey of several hundred kilometres?" Coste said uneasily.

"Not entirely. We know at least one place he has to pass through. Whether he goes to Belgium or Amsterdam, the first town in France he comes to on his return route is Maubeuge. I've just spoken to the Police Judiciaire in Lille, and they've agreed to provide backup. We've told them the car's make and licence number, so they're going to mount covert surveillance at every entrance to the town. It'll be easier to intercept him at a red light than when he's doing 110 kilometres an hour on a national road."

His presentation finished, he turned away from the map.

"Ladies and gentlemen, this is going to be an all-nighter. So you'd better phone home and say you'll miss the start of the film."

The office emptied little by little. A nervous Vesperini went over to Coste.

"Is smoking permitted in your offices?"

He put an ashtray on the table.

"Help yourself. Smoking and drinking coffee is all we're going to be doing until this evening."

* * *

As the hours went by, the tension increased. The police knew how to cope with it, but, given the stakes, Vesperini was less successful. With five empty cups and an overflowing ashtray in front of her, she had sent a whole series of text messages, most of them to her daughter.

On the stroke of midnight, Sylvan's mobile began to ring and vibrate. He recognised the tone of the voice at the far end of the line. Loud, excited, that of police officers a few seconds away from action:

"Lille to base. Your C5 has just entered Maubeuge. We're calling in all our teams and preparing to intercept them inside the town walls. I'll stay in touch."

Sylvan pressed the speaker icon and laid the mobile on his desk. After an interminable moment's silence, they heard the roar of car engines, tyres squealing, doors slamming.

Two hundred and twenty-two kilometres from Seine-Saint-Denis, the Lille Police Judiciaire, flashlights levelled and weapons pointed at the windshield, were surrounding the C5. Police cars in front and behind it prevented any possibility of escape. The driver was hauled out, pinned on the bonnet, and handcuffed. One of the police opened the car boot, and his face lit up. The voice on the line to Sylvan had regained some of its calm:

"Positive news for you. Interception made and boot full. Pleasure to work with you."

In the Groupe Stups office, everyone was on their feet, as much relieved as excited. Some of them shook hands, others slapped each other on the back. Despite its chaotic and ill-prepared start, the operation had been a success. Coste went over to Vesperini, who had refrained from joining in the celebrations.

"That's all for tonight. I'll have you taken home, madame."

"You've all been incredible," she admitted. "What is he likely to get?"

"On his own and with a boot full of drugs? Between eight and ten years. Considering the number of enemies he's made to climb to the top, he'll have other things to think about in prison than you. You're safe."

"Where does this leave us?"

Coste burst out laughing.

"You mean there's an 'us'?"

"You know very well what I mean."

"As Gonthier said, I'll leave your guilt to you. And anyway, who knows, I might need you in the future."

Vesperini offered him an embarrassed smile.

"You see how easy it is to make bad choices."

She extended her hand. Coste hesitated before taking it. Long enough for Sylvan's telephone to interrupt them.

"Seine-Saint-Denis? You still there?"

"Yes, still here," Sylvan replied. "Just about to pop the champagne."

"Don't do that yet. We have a small problem. The guy in the photograph you sent us is not the one in the car. We don't have Novak. Do you read me? We do not have Novak."

It came as a rude shock to all of them.

"But we did find a mobile on him. He had enough time to send a text, probably one already prepared."

Vesperini's extended hand dropped back to her side. A leaden weight descended on everyone's shoulders. They thought they had reached rock bottom, until Chloe's voice submerged them still further:

"Sylvan! Coste! The telephone you asked me to track . . . it's moving!"

"Novak's official one?"

"Yeah. I'm sorry, I wasn't paying attention."

Coste rushed over to look at the map on the computer screen where a red dot was moving.

"He's not at the Cité des Poètes any longer. What street is he in now?"

"Wait, I'll zoom in . . . Rue Nicolas-Lebel."

Vesperini turned white. Spots began to dance in front of her eyes, and she almost fainted. Johanna just managed to catch her and help her sit down.

"Hey, madame, are you alright?"

"He's going to my house," she scarcely managed to get out.

"And who's at home?"

60

Tony received a message that put an end to the furrow he was ploughing as he paced up and down his living room. He read it, cursed wildly and punched the plasterboard wall so hard it caved in. Twice. The police had intercepted his driver.

"Son of a bitch!" he screamed.

He thought about the precarious situation he was in. His impatient lieutenants. He'd promised them both money and merchandise to sell. Within forty-eight hours. And the two days were up at precisely nine o'clock the next morning. To turn up at the Friends of Malceny-Haiti centre with his hands in his pockets and only excuses and a fresh delay was unthinkable. If he wasn't big enough to keep their respect, and he couldn't at least pay them, his head was on the block. Literally. Pocketing the apartment keys, he went down to the car park and climbed into Vesperini's official car. There was still the hundred and fifty thousand euros. Enough to buy him time.

On the way, he dialled his associate's number.

* * *

"Who's at home?" Johanna repeated.

"Estelle, my daughter."

"Alone?"

"No, she's with her . . . babysitter."

Coste turned to Ronan.

"Bulletproof vests for everyone. Get two cars ready. The lead vehicle heads as fast as it can to the address, one minute ahead of the second one. Madame Vesperini, you go in that one."

"Chloe. Prepare a third car!" Sylvan insisted. "There's no way we're going to let you go on your own," he told Coste.

Vesperini was shaking so badly she could hardly stand. When her mobile rang and she saw the number, she almost collapsed again. Her voice was barely audible.

"It's him . . . it's Novak."

Coste snatched it from her and gathered his thoughts.

"Put all your mobiles on silent. Shut the windows so he won't be able to hear any police sirens. One cop in each corridor to stop anyone coming in. Take all the landlines off the hook and keep your traps shut!"

The phone rang a second time. Coste stood opposite Vesperini and looked her in the eye.

"Take a deep breath. You had nothing to do with what happened tonight. Whatever he asks of you, tell him it can wait until tomorrow. We need to get him away from your place. Try to sound upset on his behalf, but not responsible. That should do it . . ."

When the mobile rang a third time, Coste handed it to her. Vesperini's first "Hello" got stuck in her throat. All the police in the room grimaced.

"Hello," she tried again.

"It's Tony, I'm just arriving at your place," he growled, leaving her no choice.

"At this time of night? Why? What's wrong?"

"The load was intercepted. I need the other case."

A detail Vesperini had not mentioned to Coste.

"Listen, my daughter's fast asleep. Can't we do it later? I'll give it to you tomorrow, when you come to pick me up."

Novak responded even more curtly and ended the call. When Vesperini finally managed to take the mobile away from her ear, she looked completely crushed.

"Well?" Coste pressed her.

"We can't meet tomorrow," she said, almost in tears.

"That's ridiculous. What does he want?"

"The money that was supposed to calm the riots. A hundred and fifty thousand euros."

Coste bit his tongue: this wasn't the moment to ruffle her feathers.

"It would have been easier to give it to him tomorrow at work."

"Except that he needs it right now, and we won't see each other tomorrow. Tomorrow . . . is Sunday."

Coste punched his temples with both hands.

"Damn stupid Sundays! I never see them coming! Shit! Warn your babysitter. And tell them to lock all the doors and not to open for anyone!"

61

Markus was feeling relaxed, sprawled on the long living-room sofa in Vesperini's house. Estelle, delighted by this evening with her babysitter, had even offered to make sandwiches. For her, this was almost a date. After they'd eaten, he'd asked her to put on his favourite film: "Rocky". She'd spent the whole time staring at Markus, giggling at the way he dodged the punches in sync with his idol. When he was about to play the second film, she made her doe eyes at him and persuaded him to watch "Love Actually" instead. She knew all the dialogue by heart. In the first few minutes, he'd rolled his eyes once or twice, but then, against all expectation, he had been caught up in this story of broken and mended hearts. At ten past midnight, Estelle received the order to go to bed.

"If your mother sees you're still up at this time of night, she's going to give me a hiding."

"Aw, the tough guy's scared of maman," she mocked him.

"Everybody's scared of your maman."

Though used to getting her own way, Estelle had resisted without too much trouble, and at twenty past twelve she was dozing on Markus's shoulder. He turned down the volume on the television, listening to her steady breathing, then closed his eyes as well.

*

The sound of the doorbell snapped them both out of their slumbers. Still groggy, Estelle rubbed her cheeks.

"It's my mother. I'll go and open the door. I'll tell her you forced me to stay up late," she said with a smile.

Markus seized a cushion and threw it at her. She stood up and trudged wearily across the room. He looked at the time on his mobile. Fifteen minutes had flown by. While he was still holding it, the mobile began to vibrate, and Vesperini's face appeared on the screen.

That should have been enough of a warning for Markus.

He answered the call. Desperate and at the same time hysterical, the voice shrieked:

"Don't open the door to any . . ."

When he realised that the person on the phone couldn't possibly also be at the door, the mobile fell from his grasp. And why would she have rung the bell so late at night anyway? He leaped off the sofa. If he'd been in his studio flat, he would have reached the front door in two strides, but this stupid bourgeois villa had a whole labyrinth of corridors. When he was only a few metres from the entrance, he recognised the voice.

"Good evening. I'm a friend of your mother's. Could you get her for me, please?"

"She's not at home this evening," Estelle said, taking a step backwards, suspicious of the man standing there. "What do you want?"

But the intruder was no longer listening to her. Instead he was looking over her shoulder.

Novak and Markus confronted one another, the girl in between them.

"What the fuck are you doing here, boxer boy?" Tony hissed, his face twisted with disgust.

Estelle slipped behind her protector, out of sight. Markus could feel her face pressing into his back.

"Stay calm, Tony. This isn't what you think."

Novak took a step forward, slammed the door behind him, and began to shout.

"She told me she was at home! What is this crap?"

Vesperini's lie. Markus being here. The loss of his merchandise. At first, all this information telescoped in Tony's mind, then it slipped into place. He was alone. He had been betrayed. The police would soon be there. He stepped to one side to face the first window, lifted the lace curtain and looked outside. A calm night, deserted streets.

It was no longer a question of the estates, or drug dealing. Now he had to escape, quickly, and get as far away as possible. But he knew that to run without money always landed you behind bars. And he still had money. A hundred and fifty thousand euros were stashed somewhere in this house. He needed them. He pointed his gun straight at Markus.

"Where's the other case?"

Markus gently pushed Estelle back along the corridor. She was unable to stop tears rolling down her cheeks as she saw him advance towards the intruder, palms spread wide in an attempt to pacify him.

"Tony, I swear to you I don't know what you're talking about."

Sickened, Novak looked him in the face, but this wasn't the moment for lengthy discussions. The boxer was a threat, and Novak was well aware he could be laid flat by a single punch.

"You disappoint me," was all he said. "A lot."

He raised his arm, aimed his gun, and fired. Blood splattered the wall and a red stain appeared where the bullet had entered. Markus stared down at the hole in his chest, then the world shook and he fell flat on his back.

"A betrayal, a bullet. Sonofabitch!"

Distraught, Estelle ignored the stranger and his gun and flew to Markus, her heart about to explode, repeating a sad litany of short, breathy "no"s. She touched his face, the eyes closed, felt the bleeding wound, then looked up. Her features were contorted with rage.

"You . . ."

Novak seized her by the hair, and she yelped in pain.

"Shut your mouth!"

Putting away his gun, Novak dragged the girl into the living room, and threw her on the floor. Engulfing Estelle's hand in his own, he pulled up her index finger. Without hesitating, he snapped it with a dry click, and her cries echoed through the house once more.

"Listen to me, you little whore. You've got a minute to tell me where the attaché case is before I break another one."

Estelle's screams drowned out his words. Her lips were trembling with pain.

"I don't know . . . I'm sorry, I don't know."

"Show me your mother's study. Do it!"

Grabbing her arm, he followed her directions and dragged her upstairs so violently her feet hardly touched the steps. He kicked open the study door. Elegant, but above all spotlessly tidy. So much so that a rapid glance told him that what he was looking for wasn't visible. He pushed Estelle into her mother's armchair and began to ransack the place, opening drawers and searching the cupboards. He swept everything off the desk, knocking over the lamp. Its cone of light swung in all directions, as if it too was hysterical. At the end of his tether, Novak shouted at the young girl:

"A fuckin' black metal case! It's here! It's got to be here, dammit!"

Estelle didn't reply. Instead, she smiled at him.

A shadow appeared on the wall behind Tony, the silhouette multiplied by the lamp rolling on the floor.

"Good luck," she whispered.

Novak turned round. His hand reached for his weapon, but he didn't even have time to touch it. Markus was waiting for him. Jaw clenched and muscles straining, he launched the most powerful blow of his entire life. It smashed directly into Novak's windpipe, crushing it like a biscuit. The cartilage crumbled, he gasped for air, but there was nothing more than a whistling sound in his throat. He fell to his knees and raised his hands to his neck. The veins on his forehead began to bulge. Despite the agony and the burning in his lungs, his face was a mask of hatred. Then he collapsed onto his stomach, one arm folded beneath him, the other one still extended. A prolonged jolt, then nothing. His body slumped.

As he went down the stairs, Markus forced himself to ignore the butterflies dancing in front of his eyes. There was no guarantee that Tony had come alone, and he had made Estelle swear she wouldn't leave her mother's study. Blood was seeping from his wound onto his left hand, and red drops began to fall from his fingertips. He went down the front steps and crossed the garden, making for the street, still clutching Tony's gun, ready for anything. In a deafening roar of sirens, he was soon surrounded by police cars, hastily drawn up in a semi-circle around him, their flashing lights bathing everything in blue. Confronted by twenty or more officers training their weapons on him and shouting words he couldn't hear, Markus knelt down and dropped the weapon on the lawn.

Estelle appeared in her bloodstained T-shirt, barefoot, tears streaming down her cheeks. Panting, she ran to Markus and threw herself in his arms, almost knocking him over. Then she turned towards the policemen and disarmed them with a single look.

"Lower your weapons," Coste ordered.

62

Perched on a chair in the corridor of the emergency department at Jean-Verdier hospital, Vesperini was studying her daughter closely. Still wearing her bloodstained T-shirt, Estelle was too nervous to sit still for more than five minutes at a time, pacing between the waiting room and the door with the porthole they had been prohibited from entering. She even seemed to have forgotten the splint round her hand and fingers.

"Darling, please come and sit down."

Estelle turned round and walked back to her mother. She had grown up a lot in a few hours. Even her voice sounded more assured.

"Are they going to take care of him?"

"Of course, the doctors are with him. He'll be fine."

"What about his family? And his boxing club?"

"We'll have time to talk about all that."

"No. Tell me right now, and I'll never ask why a man came to shoot us because of a black briefcase."

Vesperini stared down at the floor.

"Whatever you like. But please sit down."

At four in the morning, the surgeon came out of the operating theatre and joined them. The bullet had entered between shoulder and heart, then passed under the collarbone before exiting. Minimal flesh wounds. No vital organs hit. Only a mild anaesthetic needed as there was no repair work to be done. They should be able to see him in an hour.

* * *

Vesperini had to fight with her daughter to make sure she got in first to talk to Markus. She pushed open the door and found him propped up, shoulder and chest swathed in bandages. She sat in the armchair next to his bed, and said:

"I owe you a lot, Markus. So much I don't even know where to begin."

The young man replied in a slurred voice.

"It's the kind of thing that happens when you play both sides."

"I know, it's my fault. For a while I thought Novak could be my link between the town hall and the neighbourhoods. To be frank, I didn't have much choice."

"I was talking about myself."

Vesperini seemed surprised.

"I don't understand. Did you work for Novak as well?"

"Not really. Like everybody else, I did things for him from time to time. I was there the evening Azzedine was killed. I tried to stop it, but, as you say, Tony never really gave anybody a choice."

And yet the danger Markus should have been most afraid of was sitting right there. Vesperini was already weaving her web around him.

"With Azzedine Salah I had a connection to the estates. A way of understanding them, getting closer, helping them. That was all I ever wanted. Now I have no-one. And my town is still under siege."

Markus turned towards her, grimacing with pain.

"Malceny is my town too. And I know the estates. I grew up there. Maybe I could help you?"

All the Queen had to do now was to close the trap. Markus had promised himself he would escape his background using his fists. She was about to lead him down a much less honest path.

"Are you sure? You know, if that's what you choose, I can offer you a new life. Stable employment, housing for you and your family. Do you know The Citadel? The apartments there are magnificent. And, of course, I'll arrange it so that you can continue your boxing training. In fact, I've always thought that club was too small."

These few sentences left Markus feeling his future was far clearer. For him and his family. Naively, he imagined he owed her something.

"How are you thinking of calming things down?"

"Forget it. I refuse to involve you in all that yet. I've made mistakes, and put my daughter in danger. I'll find a solution by myself. For now, you need rest, rest and more rest. I just hope there won't be too much damage or too many people injured tonight."

Markus used the remote control to raise the headboard on his bed.

"Listen. Those people behind the barricades – I know them all. They're not doing this in memory of Bibz or for the woman in the veil. They're doing it because Tony said he'd pay them. It must work both ways."

In her mind's eye. Vesperini saw the black attaché case that had never left the locked desk drawer in her office. She played the innocent.

"You mean . . . pay them to stop?"

"If the other side can do it . . ."
Vesperini stifled a smile. Got him!

* * *

Their conversation at an end, the Queen left Markus's room. Maud and Estelle were deep in conversation out in the corridor. When she saw her boss, the press officer asked how she was feeling.

"Later, Maud. Drop me at the town hall. There's something I need to pick up from my office. First, we'll go and see the medical secretary. I want Markus out of here this afternoon. If he needs a home nurse, I'll pay for one."

Despite everything she had just been through, it hadn't taken her long to resume her old bad habits.

"Isn't that a bit soon?" Maud said anxiously.

"Are you a doctor?" Vesperini snapped.

She was about to tell her daughter to go in and see Markus, when she realised the chair was empty, the door to the room open, and that from now on, Estelle would not wait for her permission.

Estelle immediately sat on the bed, unable to wipe the silly smile from her lips.

"Does it hurt?"

"What about you?"

The two of them burst out laughing, and she stretched out alongside him, nestling her head on his uninjured shoulder.

63

7.50 a.m. Roissy-Charles de Gaulle airport

From his position, Sam had a clear view of the row of walk-through metal detectors and the police security check. He had his copy of *The Catcher in the Rye* in the back pocket of his jeans. After their busy night, Coste had given the team two days off, but first he wanted to tie up a loose end.

"Going somewhere?"

Sam smiled, then turned round calmly.

"Hi there, Victor. How did you know?"

"Stop, before I get annoyed. Jacques taking the S.I.M. card out of his mobile to avoid being tracked? Did you expect me to believe that?"

"Yeah, I was afraid you weren't going to swallow that one."

"Don't get too carried away. Nothing's settled yet. Have you checked everything? His name on the wanted list? His photograph sent everywhere? Border controls?"

"I cancelled it all more than forty-eight hours ago. I used Jevric's pin number and password. She put Jacques's life at risk to help solve a case, so it seemed to me she deserved a taste of her own medicine."

"How did you get them?"

"From the Post-it taped under her computer keyboard."

"What a joke! You can put the most sophisticated technical

measures in place, but human error always leaves room to dream. You have to be pretty stupid to leave them there."

Sam laughed. "Ronan does exactly the same."

"There's still the X-ray check," Coste worried.

"Fifty thousand euros is only a hundred notes of five hundred. All he needs to do is hide them intelligently and smile like a harmless old fellow. We of all people know how well he does that."

"I imagine you explained everything to him properly."

Neither of them had got any sleep the previous night, so for a while they let themselves be lulled by wave after wave of travellers.

"Do you think we're going out on a limb?" Sam said.

In recent days, this was a question Coste had often asked himself.

"It's easy to see the world split into Good and Evil. Black and white. In fact, everything happens in the grey area in between."

"Do you mean Vesperini?"

"Among others. But as for Jacques . . . I think it'll be the only justice that comes out of this whole investigation."

Sam took the book out of his pocket and handed it to Coste.

"Besides, we can't really say he lied to us all the time. He was always honest with me."

Coste stroked the book cover then flicked through a few pages.

"*The Catcher in the Rye*? I read it when I was fourteen. You'll have to refresh my memory."

"It's the story of a young kid who leaves for New York to give his life a new direction."

* * *

Jacques Landernes passed through the police identity check without a problem. After that he was ushered to the queue for the metal detector. It was July, and there were thousands of travellers in the airport, so he hoped he could take advantage of the crowds and the harassed staff: the holiday mayhem. He took off his shoes, put his coat, wallet and belt on the conveyor belt. Then, without knowing why, as though somebody had tapped him on the shoulder, he turned round. His heart started pounding in his chest, but neither of the policemen standing beyond the glass wall twenty metres away moved.

Coste greeted him with a nod, then the old man exchanged a long look with Sam, who held up *The Catcher in the Rye.* Surrounded by the crowd, Jacques discreetly showed him the new copy he had just bought. A very special copy containing, on every third page, a five-hundred-euro banknote. He placed it in the bottom of his cabin bag and let it be carried towards the X-ray machine. Then he walked through the metal detector and recovered his belongings on the far side.

Without a hitch.

Within a few hours, he would be telling the whole story to his daughter.

And of course, he would make sure to include the two policemen and the fresh start they had given him.

64

Victor Coste enjoyed the sense of lethargy produced by a lack of sleep. A sort of gentle exhaustion he could put an end to whenever he wished, simply by stretching out. And yet he was a long way from his apartment, sitting at a table on a Paris café terrace, watching the world go by, his brain registering absolutely nothing. The wall clock showed ten; she must be awake by now. And anyway, he loved her voice when she was half-asleep.

"I never meant to hurt you," he began.

"Well, you could have fooled me."

"I've just seen our witness again. We're sending him out of France. There'll be no problems for the clinic."

"Did you do it for him or for my father?"

"Do I have to choose?"

Always avoiding her questions. Léa had had enough of it.

"This relationship of ours is going to be the death of me. There's no way I can tie you down. I'm not even sure you really want me to."

Coste did not know what to say, and she profited from his moment of doubt.

"I'd prefer to end it here, Victor."

It was exactly what he had feared hearing. But was he sure

he wouldn't be making her false promises? That he'd really be able to change?

"Perhaps it's for the best," he conceded.

And that was that. Him on the café terrace. Her in an empty house.

Coste stood up and paid for his coffee with a few coins.

It had been a long two weeks, and he wanted to go for a walk before returning home.

As he left, he dropped the train ticket he had bought on the table.

Provence was beautiful at that time of year. Someone would make use of it.

TRANSLATOR'S NOTE

Administratively, France is divided into 96 *départements*, where the central government is represented by the *préfet* or prefect. The *départements* are numbered alphabetically: Ain is No. 1, Paris No. 75. In the 1960s, as Paris spread outwards into the *banlieues* (suburbs or outskirts), separated from the inner city by the *Périphérique* or ring road, three new départements were created: 92 Hauts-de-Seine, 93 Seine-Saint-Denis, 94 Val de Marne. The action of the novel takes place in Seine-Saint-Denis, formerly an area of heavy industry, but more recently one with a high proportion of tower blocks and a substantial immigrant population.

NOTE ON POLICE FORCES

S.D.P.J. 93 – Saint-Denis Police Judiciaire 93: the police force responsible for France's Département 93, led by **Commissaire Stévenin** and incorporating:

> Groupes Crime – the crime squads. Led by **Commandant Marie-Charlotte Damiani**. This unit breaks down into Groupe Crime 1, led by **Capitaine Coste**, and Groupe Crime 2, led by **Capitaine Lara Jevric**.

Groupe Stups – the drug squad, led by **Capitaine Sylvan**
Brigade Criminelle – central crime squad operating out of 36 Quai des Orfèvres
Brigade de protection des mineurs – child protection department operating from 2 quai de Gesvres
Brigade de répression du banditisme – organised crime squad
Brigade des moeurs – vice squad
Brigade de répression du proxénétisme de Paris – anti-prostitution squad
Inspection Général des Services (I.G.S.) – police inspectorate, led by **Commissaire Dariush Abassian**

NOTE ON POLICE FORCES

S.D.P.J. 93 – Saint-Denis Police Judiciaire 93: the police force responsible for France's Département 93, led by **Commissaire Stévenin** and incorporating:

Groupes Crime – the crime squads. Led by **Commandant Marie-Charlotte Damiani**. This unit breaks down into Groupe Crime 1, led by **Capitaine Coste**, and Groupe Crime 2, led by **Capitaine Lara Jevric**.

Groupe Stups – the drug squad, led by **Capitaine Sylvan**
Brigade Criminelle – central crime squad operating out of 36 Quai des Orfèvres
Brigade de protection des mineurs – child protection department operating from 2 quai de Gesvres
Brigade de répression du banditisme – organised crime squad
Brigade des moeurs – vice squad
Brigade de répression du proxénétisme de Paris – anti-prostitution squad
Inspection Général des Services (I.G.S.) – police inspectorate, led by **Commissaire Dariush Abassian**

OLIVIER NOREK served as a humanitarian aid worker in the former Yugoslavia before embarking on an eighteen-year career in the French police, rising to the rank of capitaine in the Seine-Saint-Denis Police Judiciaire. He has written six crime novels, which have sold a million copies in France and won a dozen literary prizes.

NICK CAISTOR is a British translator from French, Spanish and Portuguese. He has won the Valle-Inclán Prize for translation from the Spanish three times, most recently for *An Englishman in Madrid* by Eduardo Mendoza, published by MacLehose Press.